BRIDE OF MONTROSE

A GOTHIC ROMANCE

CYNTHIA KEYES

Printed in North America
First edition, 2023

Created with Vellum

To KG, the newest and sweetest member of our household, who spent hours snuggled up around my feet as I wrote. Thank you for your patience and tolerance.

OTHER BOOKS BY CYNTHIA KEYES

The Smuggler

The Spy

The Meadows

The Heiress

PROLOGUE

LORD MONTROSE SELECTS HIS BRIDE

Lord Montrose stood in the shadows, gripping the balcony rail. His perfectly tailored black attire emphasized his massive shoulders, and extraordinary height. He towered over his estate manager and friend, Hamish. "She is the one. I will make the offer tomorrow," he said, his eyes not straying from the scene below. His darkly handsome face held in profile. It was comfortable for him to present such a stance, even with Hamish, who certainly was familiar with his disfigurement.

The musicians began to play a country dance. He watched as the young woman maneuvered through the dance steps, smiling each time she came together with her partner, and exchanged a brief word. She wasn't too young, nor was she too beautiful. She had acceptable looks. Her auburn hair was done up in braids around her head and garnished with small buds of flowers. They were her only accessory. Her pale-yellow gown was not the latest fashion and looked as though it had been recycled many times. She was exactly what one would expect from a woman who was impoverished, yet genteel.

"You're sure?" his man asked, shaking his head. "I can't say I like this scheme, Jules. Why not meet her, let her get to know you before you decide? She might just choose you as her husband on her own…without all the bribery."

"Do you honestly think that would work Hamish?" He turned to his man, exposing the ravaged left side of his face. A wide scar ran from his chin to the corner of his left eye. Stark and almost white against his swarthy complexion, it pulled his skin into puckered ridges across his cheek. When he grinned as he did now, the left side of his face only twitched in response. It left him with a permanent half smile, a sort of sarcastic grimace, which he thought suited him well enough.

"Well, it might…if you at least tried to be a little charming," Hamish answered.

Julian laughed, a dry joyless sound. "Hamish, you overestimate my charms. No. I have what the woman needs. I don't think she will have much choice, given her family's financial situation—a turn of events which suits my plans perfectly. My money will make the decision—a bargain benefiting the both of us. I save her family from ruin, and she provides me with the heir I need. She will swallow her revulsion and do her duty."

"I think you are misjudging this woman. From all

our reports, she appears to be a sensible and intelligent person. You might be surprised by her reaction to you."

"The only reaction I need from her, is her agreement," he said, his gaze back on the dancers below. Lady Madelyn Guilford, his quarry, threw back her head and laughed at something her partner said. From this distance he could not hear the sound, but her merriment was obvious. For a moment, his heart yearned for a scenario where that joy would be directed his way.

He quickly squashed the thought. He knew well the expression of repugnance in the eyes of anyone he met, especially the fairer sex, though most were quick to hide it behind polite exchanges. The love of a woman could not ever be for him. If she agreed to be his wife and produced an heir, that alone would be enough.

CHAPTER 1

A BARGAIN IS STRUCK

"You must get up my girl. Your mother wishes to speak to you. Come on, up, up."

Madelyn groaned. "Heavens. What time is it? Why would Mama want to see me so early this morning? She knows the ball went until almost dawn last night. Surely, whatever it is can wait a few hours?" Madelyn pulled the pillow from beneath her head and flopped it over her face. "Tell her no," she muttered.

"She insists," said Milly. When this pronouncement had no effect on her charge, she added slyly, "There are men here. I think you may have an offer."

Madelyn peeked out from under the pillow. "Men?"

"Men. Two of them; I let them in myself. They arrived early this morning and have been with your mother for two hours now."

"Oh goodness." Madelyn tossed the pillow aside and sat up. "I doubt it's an offer, Milly. I am guessing they are here to evict us." She sighed. Life was about to take a bitter turn for her family. There would be no stopping the misery that would befall them now. She stood, straightening her heavy cotton nightgown, and trudged across the room, where Milly waited by the washstand, facecloth in hand.

Last night, she'd known the ball was likely to be her last. She had been determined to enjoy it. And indeed, this morning the time for reckoning had come. There was no help for it but to dress and face the day.

Her father, may he rest in peace, had always managed to find the worst possible investments. His last venture had left them with no money, and a mortgaged home. When he died two years ago, the family was left destitute. There was only a small allowance, provided when her grandmother passed. It was barely enough to support her mother, Lady Guilford, and four daughters: Madelyn, Beth, MaryAnn, and Clarice. They were forced to apply to their father's brother, Uncle William, for help to cover the mortgage. He had reluctantly agreed.

But just last week they received word from Uncle William that he was no longer able to carry the cost of maintaining their household. In fact, he had quit paying the mortgage some time ago and their house was about to be foreclosed. Mother had been frantically arranging to move in with her estranged sister, Margaret. Only yesterday the woman had begrudgingly accepted, welcoming the destitute family into her home, but with the condition the girls work for their board. Not the best of prospects for all concerned.

Mother was convinced the proposed arrangement was an act of brutal vengeance on her sister's part and had been distressed since receiving the letter.

For the past two years, her mama, and no doubt her Uncle William, had hoped Madelyn would alleviate some of the financial pressure by making a decent match. She was the only daughter of marriageable age, being six years older than her next sibling, Beth, who had only just turned sixteen.

But those efforts had failed. No one had been interested enough, or wealthy enough to take on the burden of supporting a household with four unmarried girls. To make matters worse, Madelyn herself was not the ideal young woman most men of her class desired. She was too intelligent and too brash to hide that quality, forever putting forth her opinion when it was least wanted or appreciated. Despite her best efforts to be the gracious young woman most men expected, she was unable to curb her tongue and portray the model of decorum her mother so hoped her eldest daughter would be. Madelyn knew she was a bitter disappointment to her family.

Milly fastened the bow on her charge's best dress. Madelyn went through the motions, too tired to wonder about the choice of gowns.

"Your mother asked that you meet her in the library." She handed her a cup of lukewarm tea, laced with cream and sugar as was her preference. "Drink this. It will wake you up." Milly looked at her charge and scowled. "There is no time to do up your hair.

We'll leave it down. After all it is your best quality." She pulled a piece of hair from each side of the girl's head and secured it with a clip at the back, letting it fall in waves past her shoulders, then looked at her critically. "It will have to do." She reached over and pinched Madelyn's cheeks for color before taking the cup from her hands and pushing her to the door. "Off you go."

On the landing of the stairs, her eight-year-old sister Clarice met her with teary eyes. The child grasped her arm and walked down with her a few steps, patting her reassuringly as they progressed. Madelyn paused, tugging her arm away. "Whatever is wrong with you Clarice? Have you lost the blasted puppy again?"

Clarice shook her head no, while biting her bottom lip. Staring at Madelyn with mournful eyes, her little sister pushed past her and scurried back up the stairs.

At the bottom of the staircase her other two sisters stood and waited. They too behaved as though doom and gloom had descended. Maryann's face was red and puffy as it always looked after she had shed tears. The eviction process must have begun, she thought grimly.

Beth stepped forward and squeezed her hand. "You don't have to say yes," she whispered.

Madelyn only had time to glance at her with confusion before the library door opened. Her mother gestured for her to enter and then turned to her sisters. "Go to your room girls," she said with a stern look, "and stay there until I send for you."

Mother stepped back to let her pass, closing the

door briskly behind them. She paused for a moment to scrutinize her appearance, nodding with approval at the choice of her best day dress. "Sit down Madelyn. You and I must have a chat," she said, pulling back a chair in front of her father's massive desk before taking a seat in his leather chair behind it. Her mother was always a model of decorum and grace. She was a handsome woman, with thick auburn hair, much like Madelyn's, and even features under her black lace cap. Though she had set aside her black gowns a year after father died, she had been unable to completely abandon the dark tones of mourning and restricted her wardrobe to somber colors in conservative styles. However, her severe choice of clothing had always been tempered with a cheerful and gentle disposition; especially when interacting with her children. Today, her formality was disconcerting.

Never in all the years she had known her mother had she seen this side of her. She sat across from her now with a face so serious Madelyn shivered with dread. Something terrible must have happened. Perhaps her Aunt Margaret had turned them down and they faced the poor house, or life on the streets. She braced herself for what was to come.

Mama took a breath and began in a business-like tone. "I have had an offer for your hand in marriage from Julian Stallridge, Lord of Montrose..." she announced, pausing to allow this information to sink in. Madelyn felt her jaw drop. Her mind refused to process the news.

Her mother ignored her dumbfounded expression and continued, "It is a substantial offer; one we cannot afford to ignore. He has agreed to purchase our home in your name. The money from the sale would cover the mortgage with enough remaining to provide a proper dowry for each of your sisters, and a little to spare. Without the burden of a mortgage and with my meagre income, it would allow us to live decently... well, at least until all the girls are married."

In a moment of silence, her mother rested her hands before her on the desk. When Madelyn did not respond she pressed on. "This offer is more generous than anything we could have hoped for...It is the answer to our prayers."

Madelyn was speechless, but her heart was beating wildly. She forced herself to take a calming breath. A proposal? The house purchased in her name? Dowries! It was all too much to take in.

She looked at her mother's face. The older woman's mouth was set in a firm line. Surprisingly, the jubilation she would have expected from her under these circumstances was not evident. "Do I know Lord Montrose? Why are you so glum?" she asked.

Her mother colored slightly. "No. I do not believe you have met. He, however, has seen you. He finds you acceptable both in appearance and social standing."

She waited for her to continue. Something was odd about this proposal. She wondered just what her mother was so hesitant to share with her. "Again Mother, why are you so glum? I should think you would celebrate this event. It is exactly what you hoped for, is it not?" When Lady Guilford still did not reply she asked, "Is he ancient? I suppose he is sixty or some such thing?"

Lady Guilford cleared her throat. "No, he is not ancient. His Lordship is thirty. But there are some... difficulties." She raised her eyes to gaze directly into her daughter's face. "I will not deny I want this marriage. It solves all our financial problems, and it gives your sisters their only chance at a respectable future. As for you, a life of comfort, beyond anything we could have hoped for..." She paused, giving Madelyn a stern look before adding, "I trust you will do what is best for the family."

Madelyn swallowed. "What are the difficulties?" Her imagination went wild. Whatever the so-called 'difficulty' was, the longer her mother delayed, the more nervous she became. She had every intention of accepting this offer. There was no choice. Nothing could be worse than the future Aunt Margaret had proposed, relegating her and her sisters to the life of indentured servants.

Her mother answered bluntly. "First, he intends to take you North, to Yorkshire, far away from the family. He warned it would be unlikely you would spend much time in London in the future..." Her mother looked at her and hesitated, a hint of sadness in her eyes. But then she straightened her shoulders and continued in her no-nonsense voice. "Lord Montrose is a widower. His wife died at least ten years ago. There were no children. After her death he enlisted in the British army for a time. He was injured while in service in the Americas. The left side of his face is badly scarred. He also told me he has an injury to his left hip. However, it is not noticeable, or at least I was unable to discern it. Though he does carry a walking stick as many fashionable gentlemen do."

"Oh." Madelyn could think of no response. For the man to have made such a settlement there must be some gross impairment. So, she was to marry a scarred and crippled man, and be secluded in the wilds of Yorkshire, she thought numbly. Well, it could have been worse. She grimaced. Her suitor could have been over sixty years of age and a bloody tyrant. Or he could have come with a pack of unruly children.

"I have every confidence you will do your duty and accept the man. You more than anyone know the position we've found ourselves in." Lady Guilford set her hands on the table in front of her once more and waited for her daughter's reply.

Madelyn's stomach churned. In her girlish dreams she had always imagined a marriage with a man she loved, who loved her in return. Her father had not been a successful man. Yet he and her mother had always had their love for each other. But love had not saved their family from ruin after the death of her father, and it would not save her and her sisters now.

She cleared her throat, forcing out her words, "I will do what I must. May I meet this Lord Montrose before I make my final decision?"

Her mother smiled for the first time in the interview. "Of course. He and his man are waiting in the parlor. I will introduce you."

The house was oddly silent as they left the library and crossed the hall to the parlor. Madelyn glanced to the balcony above and was not surprised to see three dark heads at floor level, peering through the banister rails. She smiled.

When she walked into the parlor, two men rose to greet them. The taller of the two stepped forward.

Her mother announced, "Lord Montrose, let me present my daughter, Lady Madelyn Guilford."

She had time to register only that he was large, impeccably dressed, with broad shoulders and a tanned rugged face before she lowered her head to do a graceful curtsy. When she rose, she vaguely heard her mother introduce the second man, a Mr. Hamish McGowan. Her gaze was fixed on the gentleman who would likely be her future husband. He faced her, raising his chin slightly and turning to display the ravaged left side of his face with its puckered slash, as though insisting she examine it.

Careful to keep her expression impassive, she studied this man who would be her husband. The left side of his face had indeed suffered a grave injury with a wide scar dominating the length of his cheek. His profile held a shock of white scar tissue with raised ridges, swollen a painful pink, contorting the skin into a grimace against an otherwise swarthy complexion. The disfigurement was somehow made worse when set against the perfectly sculpted features on the right side of his face. He had long dark hair pulled back and secured with a leather thong, and blue-gray eyes. The scarring was a grievous sight, but not horrific. She dismissed it as irrelevant to her circumstances. In truth the man was handsome.

She let her gaze wander to his board shoulders, then down his body to his fashionable trousers, stretched tight across thick thighs and long legs tucked into riding boots. He was tall and strong. She was reminded of the mythical warriors of old; heroic figures she had read about in the ancient tales of battles fought long ago in the highlands of the North.

Yes, she thought to herself, this man's a warrior. Even the ghastly scar fit her definition. She smiled, thinking the blue war paint worn by the fierce tribesmen of the past would have suited him well. She could picture him riding on a massive steed, and brandishing a mighty sword, as he charged the enemy. Her whimsy made her smile wider.

After slowly surveying his body, she looked again to his eyes and realized with a start that he was aware of her scrutiny. His eyes sparkled with what she thought might be curiosity or amusement, or something else. Her cheeks began to burn.

Her mother was speaking, but Madelyn had missed what was said entirely. All eyes turned to her as though awaiting a response. "I—I am pleased to make your acquaintance sir," she stuttered, hoping it was an appropriate reply. When Mr. McGowan chuckled, she could only blush at her mistake.

Her mother quickly intervened. "As I was saying it is such a lovely day, I thought the two of you might take a stroll in the garden. It will give you a chance to talk." She walked to the double doors, which opened to the back patio and flung them wide.

"An excellent idea," Lord Montrose said holding out his arm. "Shall we?"

She took his arm. An immediate feeling of well-being enveloped her. It was as though a warm strength emanated from him. Her body began to relax as he wordlessly led her from the room. Once outside she took a deep breath and straightened her shoulders. She glanced at him from beneath her lashes. She faced his right side. He looked outrageously handsome.

He led her to the garden bench, where the two of them sat down with their arms still entwined. It was a short bench, forcing them to sit closely together, her shoulders and hips touching his intimately. Again, there was a sense of comfort and safety in his nearness. Wondering if it was her imagination, she purposely let her body relax against him. The sensation remained.

His right side faced her, its classic features looking for all the world like drawings she had seen of Roman statues. He did not turn to her, but instead held his head stiffly forward. She was unsure if it was from shyness, distaste for her, or an attempt to hide his ravaged cheek.

When he spoke, his deep timbre sent a shiver down her spine. "I know this proposal is a surprise for you. I must first apologize for the lack of courtship. Under the circumstances, I thought it best to keep our negotiations strictly on a business level." His voice was steady and quiet, but forceful. She ruled shyness out as a possibility.

"A business level?" She looked up at him, surprised. She had not expected romantic words—or perhaps she had, at least a few. "Do you not want children then?" She realized the improper nature of her question and cringed. It was exactly this bluntness which had turned away potential suitors in the past.

"I do want children. It is the very reason I hope to marry," he answered. She looked at him and noted that this time it was he who colored ever so slightly.

There was a minute of awkward silence. He still refused to look in her direction. "I see no point in drawing out the whole endeavor," he said, "I am sure your mother laid out the bargain clearly for you. Will you accept me as your husband, or no?"

She stared at him, willing him to face her. He did not. Instead, his arm held hers gently, his body against hers still felt safe and comfortable, and his words were spoken softly. She took a calming breath.

"If you wish to refuse me, I would that you said so now."

"I would be honored and pleased to be your wife," she blurted, surprising herself with the quick admission. The words had just spilled out, without her having analyzed for even a moment the ramifications of them. She felt her cheeks redden again and wondered if she would forever be blushing like a girl fresh out of short dresses in his presence.

He smiled for the first time.

"But only if you look at me," she added recklessly.

The smile died on his lips. He turned ever so slowly toward her, his face serious, and his eyes unreadable. She looked directly into their depths, noting they were more gray than blue. He leaned forward. She could feel his warm breath on her cheeks. For a moment she thought he would kiss her and found herself involuntarily raising her chin and leaning in toward him.

But he did not. Instead, he shifted back abruptly. She sighed, unconsciously expressing her disappointment. His brows rose with a curious glance before he turned away once more.

He cleared his throat, not acknowledging the moment they had just shared. "I have acquired a special license. If you have no objection, I wish to be married the day after tomorrow. There are papers to be signed, and titles to be transferred, but all should be accomplished by then."

A ripple of panic flipped her belly. She stood and twisted her hands nervously. "So soon?"

Without the titillating distraction of his nearness, the reality of the situation threatened to overwhelm her. In just two days she would leave everything she had ever known. She wanted to object, then run to the safety of her room. There she could bury herself in the covers and will this scenario and her uncertain future away.

He too rose to his feet and must have sensed her rising hysteria, because he took her small hands in his and squeezed them gently. He turned toward her. Again, she found herself gazing into the clear depths of his eyes. "It will be all right." he said, his voice a soothing balm. "Whatever the future is between us, you will always have my protection and loyalty."

His declaration had the ring of a vow to it. His words calmed her. She wanted to give him something in return. "And for your generosity to me and my family, I will give you my respect and loyalty."

He laughed. It was a joyful sound, with more than a hint of relief. For the first time she realized he too must have found the situation difficult. Looking at her with a satisfied expression he said, "I believe I have chosen well. You will make a fine mistress of Montrose Manor." Together they walked back to the house and the open doors to the parlor.

The phrase 'mistress of the manor' set off another wave of panic. "Oh dear. I just realized I am quite possibly the worst choice you could have made for household management. I know nothing about it, I fear…I tend to become lost in my books, and I...I—"

He laughed again, taking her hand as they entered the parlor. "You are all I require in a wife," he said.

Mr. McGowan looked at them quizzically, his head tilted to the side, as they entered the room. "Is it settled then?"

"It is. We wed the day after tomorrow." Lord Montrose answered.

Her mother could not be happier. "How wonderful!" Lady Guilford clapped her hands together. "I know it is morning, but I think a toast may be in order." She turned to Milly who stood quietly by the door. "We have one bottle of champagne hidden in the cellar for just such an occasion. Please fetch it for us."

Madelyn was feeling as though she had been taken up in a whirlwind and was being spun about. In two days, everything in her world would change. All her life she had dreamed of finding her one true love—of recreating the happy days she had witnessed between her mama and papa before their world had come crashing down. Now there was only a quickly arranged marriage to this stiff and distant man. She wondered if she would forever regret this day. But there was little choice.

Taking a calming breath, she reminded herself that she, her sisters, and her mother would face dire consequences if she refused. And she ruefully admitted there was something appealing about Lord Montrose. Despite his massive size and ravaged face, he emitted a gentle manliness. Perhaps with him, she could build the loving home of her dreams.

She realized she was still gripping his hand. It took an effort to loosen her hold. For better or worse, she had made her choice. It was the right decision for her sisters and her mother. But would it be the right choice for her?

CHAPTER 2

LADY MONTROSE HEARS THREE TALL TALES

Leaving London was a relief after a wedding breakfast punctuated with tears and the occasional wail from her younger sisters. Outside of Hamish McGowan, the guests had been restricted to family; the only notices sent beyond the household were to Uncle William, and Aunt Margaret. The latter invitation was sent purely out of a need to gloat, with a note attached, thanking Aunt Margaret for her generous hospitality. Albeit now no longer needed.

It took three exhausting days to reach York. The weather, a miserable combination of intermittent showers and howling wind, made the roads a slippery mess. Her husband and Mr. McGowan had purchased a score of horses and two carts full of goods in London. Thus, their party made a lengthy train as it crawled northward.

For the most part she had been left to herself; the gentlemen riding their horses and only joining her inside the coach to escape the worst of the rain. It gave her plenty of time to contemplate her future. Julian Stallridge, Lord Montrose, was now her husband, which made her Madelyn Stallridge, Lady Montrose. She'd spent the first part of her journey practicing this new name and title.

The hours of jostling about in the coach, and trying to sort out her future, had begun to wear. She tried to avoid thinking about the challenges she would face as Lady Montrose—managing a household or building a relationship with her husband who had ignored her the past few days. Instead, she spent the time reviewing her history of Yorkshire, using the battles of Marston Moor, during the republican years and the Battle of Towton in the War of the Roses as benchmarks to guide her. Somehow, she managed in this way to keep her growing apprehension at bay.

Upon their arrival in York, Lord Montrose announced he had business to conduct, and thus they would spend two nights at a coaching inn. She was allotted a room of her own, a generous purse, and a lad named Jimmy, who would accompany her on any shopping excursion she might take. It was a welcome relief to escape the jarring coach, and even enjoy a proper bath.

She had hoped her husband would at least take her to dinner in the public dining room that evening, but it was not to be. The first night in the inn, she saw nothing of the man, and ate a lonely supper in the sitting room of her suite.

Part curiosity and part petty retribution for the lack of interest shown to her by her new husband drove her onto Coney Street the next day for a whirlwind of shopping. The streets were wider in the market district, and to her delight, paved and tidy—a recent change much bragged about by the various shopkeepers.

A variety of shops lined each side of the street, with broad windows displaying their many wares. The walkway along the stretch of business fronts was more of a promenade than purely a shopping experience. It was populated by the upper classes in their afternoon finery; a kaleidoscope of colored parasols punctuating the brick sidewalks. But loitering was not for her today. She was bullishly determined to spend every penny allotted to her.

She managed to find a pair of ready-made sturdy boots, and three books—a massive tome on British architecture of the sixteenth century, and for light reading, two penny dreadfuls. She also splurged on several bolts of cloth, two bonnets, and various fripperies for her own selfish adornment. Poor Jimmy was quite loaded down by mid-afternoon. In the end, they had to have some of the purchases delivered.

Once back in her room she decided to take matters into her own hands, sending Jimmy with an invitation for her husband to dine with her. It was her honeymoon trip after all. She received an immediate reply: Lord Montrose regretted he would be otherwise engaged for the evening.

His response left her pacing her rooms in frustration. It was clear their marriage would be a difficult one. Her first reaction was to plan a subtle revenge and return his indifference with her own. It took a good part of the evening before a more practical approach prevailed. Her life would be a lonely one if she alienated her partner and husband. She had certainly had a taste of that loneliness the last few days.

With three sisters, moments of quiet and privacy in her home had been rare. She had treasured any time spent alone. However tonight, she would gladly have accepted intervening in a battle between Clarice and Maryann or chasing a mischievous Beth to retrieve her private journals.

She sighed. There was little she could do at the moment to improve relations with her new husband. She could hardly force him to spend time with her. But once in her new home, she decided she would embark on a campaign to get to know the man. Surely there would be a way to bridge the gap between them.

She dug through her things to find the penny dreadful she had purchased. The story she had chosen involved a young woman sent as punishment to the wilds of Yorkshire, where she ultimately took bloody vengeance on her brutal keepers. A perfect novel for this night's reading.

THEY BEGAN their trek North again early the next day. During this final leg of their journey Madelyn was to hear three legends.

She kept her coach window open, despite the gathering clouds, relishing the rough Dale country with its views of rocky cliffs and moors covered with purple heather. She began to realize the sheltered existence she had lived, never leaving the well-known streets of her neighborhood in London. To her Yorkshire was a foreign land, unpopulated and mysterious—the land of myths and fairy creatures.

Lost in her daydreams, she failed to notice that the sky had become an ominous dark blue, shrouding the wild landscape in shadows. A sudden burst of lightning and a rumble of thunder rocked the carriage, shaking her from her reverie. It was immediately followed by a gusting downpour, forcing her to tug the window closed before she got drenched. The coach came to a stop and moments later the carriage door swung open. Both Lord Montrose and Mr. McGowan climbed in, shaking off their brimmed hats and cloaks as they settled.

Her husband lit the coach lamp, basking the dark interior in a soft copper light. It felt safe and comfortable in the carriage, with the rain pouring down outside. Madelyn felt sorry for the poor coachman still out in the storm, and hoped the fellow had something to protect him from the driving rain, as the coach lurched forward once again.

"Oh. It's a bitter brawl this one. Sorry to invade

your space ma'am, but it's not to be endured out there," Mr. McGowan said with an apologetic smile.

"No apologies necessary, Mr. McGowan." She gave him her best smile. "I am pleased with the company. There has been naught to do but enjoy the sights. And have I enjoyed them—it is a strange and beautiful land."

"You must call me Hamish, ma'am. Mr. McGowan is too formal now that we are so close to home."

She glanced at her husband. "Are we nearing your home now?"

Julian pulled his hat down and turned in her direction. "Our home," he said with a quirk of his lips. "And it is not far now. We should reach Montrose Manor just after dark if we aren't laid up by the storm."

"I'll be glad when we get there," Hamish growled. A flash of lightning lit up the skies, followed instantly by a crash of thunder. "It's a powerful storm, that is for certain. We will want to be out of it before nightfall."

Madelyn wiped the moisture from the coach window with a gloved hand and peered out at the rocky windswept hills. The rain partially obscured the view, yet even in the downpour the moors were darkly romantic. "It is awe inspiring, this land," she said.

"You like it, do you? It's rough country, but it gets in your blood." He too looked out the window. "Do you see those two boulders just there?"

Madelyn again peered through the glass, seeing two huge boulders in the distance. They were just off the road and scarcely visible in the rain. She nodded.

"Well, there is a legend about those stones, and

some of the wild country you have seen today. It is said they're the grave markers for the giant Wade. One's his head stone, and the other's the marker for his feet."

Madelyn estimated the stones to be at least forty yards apart. She looked at Julian who raised his eyebrows and smiled. She knew she was about to hear a tall tale.

"See Wade the giant lived in these hills with his wife, the giantess Bess. They each built a castle: Old Mulgrave and Pickering. But they only had one hammer, and so they tossed it back and forth, giving a holler to warn of its approach. And the thunder you are hearing now is the echo of those very shouts…" He paused. As if on cue a clap of thunder sounded.

Madelyn laughed. "Is that so?"

"Oh aye, it 'tis." Hamish grinned. "I am sure you noticed the piles of rocks we've passed along the way. Well, the story goes that the giants liked to live quietly. They raised cattle. Every night Wade had to bring in the cows for milking. He noticed they had a little trouble coming across the bramble, so he decided to clear a path for them. Bess helped, carrying the stones in her apron. But stones in these parts can get mighty heavy and each time her apron strings broke, she dropped a pile of boulders. They are still visible today, as is the causeway old Wade built for his cows."

Madelyn laughed. "I have seen piles of rocks, and the causeway, too, I think. But it sounds like a tall tale to me."

She looked at Julian who gave her his crooked smile. "All true," he said.

Hamish smiled, his eyes twinkling with mischief. “And finally, did you notice the gouged amphitheater of a valley a while back.”

“I did.” Madelyn answered, eager to hear his explanation.

“It seems the lovebirds did not always get along. Once, in a raging argument, Wade became so angry with Bess that he gouged out a handful of the land and hurled the mud at his wife. And that is how the valley came to be.” Hamish grinned. “Of course, you’re wondering if he hit her. Well fortune was on his side, and he missed. But the pile of dirt landed, creating Blakey Topping, still seen today.”

Madelyn laughed, waiting to hear more tales. Hamish nodded and winked at Julian. “The land here is rife with legends of every sort. It was once the home of King Arthur and his worthy knights.”

“I didn’t know that. Here on the moors?”

“Oh yes. In fact, very near here is Richmond Castle, said to be the final resting place of King Arthur himself. There is a wild tale about that. But this one I will let Jules tell.”

Julian leaned back in his seat, tipped his hat even further onto his face and chuckled. “Thank you for that Hamish,” he said with a wry grin.

Julian began the legend in his soft melodic voice. “As Hamish said, Richmond castle is not far from here. It was built in the eleventh century by a Norman named Alan the Red. It is said to have been built over deep caverns. Well, one day, not long ago, a fellow by the name of Peter Thomas, a potter by trade, was wandering outside the castle walls. He chanced upon a cave with the entry partially covered. Being a curious man, he pushes aside the stones and goes inside..."

Julian paused and grinned, shifting lower into his seat. He was relaxed and amused. She smiled too. There was something wonderful about Julian when he let this side of his personality show.

"Well, when he enters the cave, the first thing he sees is a huge stone crypt; King Arthur's tomb. He knows this to be the case, because lying on the lid of the stone coffin is Arthur's massive horn, and beside it, the mighty sword Excalibur.

"Light glitters off the sword, and it catches his eye. Peter couldn't resist coming closer and picking up the weapon. But the second he does; the room erupts into a thundering racket. The scrape and screech of stone rubbing against stone is all around him as tombs within every corner of the cave began to open. It is deafening. Dust, long undisturbed, begins to swirl around the room. And then the blood curdling clatter of armor begins, echoing throughout the cavern. He is petrified!

"Shaking with terror, he quickly lays the sword back on the stone coffin.

"Yet as suddenly as the racket began, everything stops. All was still, but for the settling dust. And of course, an awful and eerie silence. Well, he spins around determined to high tail it out of there as quick as his feet can carry him.

"As he flees, the gravelly rumblings of an ancient voice booms, 'Potter Thompson, Potter Thompson, hadst thou blown the horn, thou had been the greatest man, that ever was born.' Well, poor old Peter runs even faster for his life, stopping only to cover the entry once more with stones, blocking the entrance so no one else could stumble upon the sleeping knights."

Madelyn looked at him appreciably, "That's a marvelous story. And is it all true as well?"

Julian chuckled. "It is." For a second, they smiled at each other, the functioning side of his lips curling into a wide grin, before Julian turned to look out his window. "Oh, but now I see the rain has stopped. Hamish and I will be needed to help with the wagons and horses. It will be a battle getting them through this mire." Julian half rose and knocked on the coach ceiling. They came to a sliding halt.

"Oh aye," Hamish smiled. "But we're almost home missy. We might just make the rise before sundown."

When Julian and Hamish stepped down from the coach, it was as though the energy had been sucked out with them. The amber coach light no longer radiated the warmth it had. As the coach ambled forward yet again, she pictured Julian sprawled comfortably across from her with his hat pulled down low to shade his scarred cheek, while telling his story with relaxed ease. This was the husband she wanted to know.

Her thoughts were interrupted when the coach

took a jarring skid sideways. She wiped the mist from her window once more and peered into the darkening landscape. They were climbing a rise, on a narrow trail. The valley behind them was smothered in a misty fog, gray clouds cloaking the heather and brambles below. The sun had set, and night was rushing in under the stormy skies. Low rumblings of distant thunder warned that another downpour may be eminent. She pulled her wool cloak around her, leaned back, and huddled against the chill.

A horse whinnying and a man shouting had her back at the window, trying to look behind the coach to see what had caused the fray. The carriage stopped. She could make out distant shapes, struggling with one of the wagons. A baggage cart had slid from the trail and leaned precariously into a steep ditch.

Julian rode up to the coach, his black cloak swirled around him, as he spun to a stop and spoke to the coachman. She slid open her window to hear.

"Carry on Briggs," he shouted up to the man, "take my Lady up to the Manor. We have lost a wheel and will be some time." Then he glanced at her from beneath his brimmed hat. "You are only a few miles from Montrose. Briggs will see you safely home." And he touched his hat before turning back to the chaos behind him. He looked for all the world like a highwayman, dark and mysterious against the night sky. Madelyn could not suppress a shiver.

The coach moved forward up the incline at a slow pace. The rain started again. Heavy raindrops could be heard intermittently hitting the coach roof as a flash of sheet lightning lit the sky. At the crest of the hill Madelyn slid her window open to look back once more at the wagons below. She could see several lanterns bobbing in the dark and hoped they would be able to right the wagon before the upcoming storm.

She peered forward as the carriage levelled out atop the rise. She could see a figure up ahead struggling in the mucky road. The heavy drops had begun to hit the roof with increased frequency as another flash of sheet lightning illuminated the road.

A woman was hunched over into the gusting wind, keeping to the edge of the road to avoid the worst of the mire. As they approached, she slid a little, almost losing her balance and falling into the path of the coach.

Without thinking, Madelyn rose and rapped firmly on the trapdoor of the carriage, then returned to her seat and pulled back her window to holler at the coachman. "Stop! Stop. She will need a lift."

The woman waited by the side of the road until the coach rolled to a halt, then walked the few paces to the door. Madelyn flung it open, and the woman wordlessly pulled herself up into the carriage. She plopped down on the seat, carefully opened her cloak, and pulled out a bundle, wrapped in a thin cloth and knotted to make a bag. She set it carefully on the seat beside her.

The coach jerked forward once more. Madelyn watched curiously as the woman pulled back her hood, revealing a wizened old face—tanned and wrinkled. Startling white-blue eyes gazed at her as the the old lady smiled. "Thank you for taking me out of the storm deary." A crash of thunder interrupted her, and she waited for the echoes to fade away before continuing. "It was in the nick of time."

As if to validate her statement the rain began to drive against the coach with renewed vigor.

"My name's Elizabeth Heeds. But people call me Old Bess, and I like the title. I do a little midwifing and doctoring with herbs and such to cure whatever ailments my people have. And who might you be?"

"Madelyn Stallridge, Lady Montrose." It was her first time using the name, and Madelyn was pleased she had practiced it. "I am journeying to my new home."

"Ah. I thought as much." The woman leaned forward with interest, taking in her appearance. "We'd heard his Lordship had gone off to London to find a bride. And here I am the first to meet her." She chuckled, her eyes sparkling in the amber light of the carriage. "A pleasure to meet you, a pleasure indeed."

"Thank you."

"You've the look of a city girl about you, dear. 'Twill be a change for you to be out here in the wilds, I'm sure." The woman cackled, "Aye, quite the change. You won't find much city life out here."

"No, I think not. But it is a beautiful land. I look forward to becoming a part of it. It's to be my new home and I know I will love it."

"Oh, it's beautiful, that's true m'lady." Old Bess looked at her critically. She felt as though the woman was assessing her in some way. "But it can be mighty lonely. Especially for a young girl in your position."

Madelyn's stomach clenched with her words. "In my position…?"

"There are few young women of your class in the area. Not a lot of neighbors. Of course, you'll have the Stallridge cousins across the way…Edwyn and Henry." The old lady suddenly smiled. "Oh, I'd forgotten. There's Anne. She's widowed now and will come home to live with her brothers." She nodded. "She'll be some company for you. She's a quiet lass from what I remember, but always had a good heart—an oddity in that family." The thunder rumbled and she paused once more. "…But Anne would have at least a decade or two on you, still, I think she'd make a fine friend."

Madelyn was pleased to hear there would be someone for her in this desolate place.

"Aye," the old lady continued, "And you may need a good friend, given the curse that hangs over the manor."

"Curse?" The coach lit up with eerie white light, followed by a loud clap of thunder which shook the coach.

The old woman again waited for the noise to dim, before saying, "Where's my head? It's not the time, nor a night to be sharing old wives' tales. And that's all it is. Old legends die hard in this country."

"A curse! But now you must tell me."

The old woman shook her head. "Nay, it's just an old tale...nonsense really."

"Oh please. You cannot just leave it at that. I must hear it."

Old Bess sighed. "I suppose someone will share it eventually. But mind, you're not to take it seriously."

Madelyn thought of the tales of King Arthur, and the giant Wade. She grinned. "I promise it will just be a story for me."

"All right. It began almost two hundred years ago. The Lord of Montrose had lost his first wife after many years. His children had grown; his daughters married, and his sons off to fight in the wars. He found himself to be lonely and decided to take a new bride. In the next county, he met a young woman who struck his fancy. But she was too young for him...too young and too beautiful to be the wife of a lonely old man. Like all old men, he was too proud to admit his age, and took her to wife anyway."

The woman grinned at this. "'Tis the folly of many an old man. Anyway, the marriage began well. The young miss was a gentle soul, who nursed his ailments and graced his days with much joy. Katherine was the lass' name. It's said she was a healer, though some say she was a witch. Well, over time the young woman did indeed fall in love with her husband, despite his age, and cared for him as no other ever had."

Thunder rattled the carriage again, forcing the woman to pause. The rain was coming down harder now, pounding on the roof of the carriage. Old Bess was forced to raise her voice to be heard. "There came a day when Katherine was called down to the village. A young man had been gored by a boar and needed her ministrations. Katherine took her herbs, needles, and thread, and tended to the man. 'Twas a long healing, requiring Katherine to come again and again to drain and clean the wound.

Now it was around this time that Katherine had fallen with child. At first the Lord was happy. He invited everyone in the village to join him in a feast to celebrate his good fortune."

Old Bess stopped and looked at her, hesitant to continue. But Madelyn was engrossed in the story. "Please go on," she urged, expecting a tall tale like the two she had been told earlier tonight.

"Well, his joy didn't last long. Rumors began to circulate that the child wasn't the Lord's own. It was said the Lord was too old to accomplish such a feat. Therefore, the baby must be the handsome young man's from the village. And sure, hadn't the two spent hours alone together in his hut.

"When the old man got word of the gossip, he was furious. He confronted his wife. And she, a proud woman too, began at first by refusing to answer such slander. The old Lord, of course, took this as her admitting to the deed.

"Now, it so happened that there was a crew of bricklayers in the home, just finishing the repair of a crumbling fireplace. Maybe that's what put the worm into the Lord's head. In a fury he ordered his young wife immured—bricked into a cell of some kind in the dungeons to suffer a long and painful death. Too late Katherine tried to deny the accusations. Lost in his anger and damaged pride, the old Lord wouldn't rescind the order. He directed the workmen to a hidden location in the dungeons, and they began the gruesome task."

Old Bess sighed. "'Twas said that as the last bricks were laid, the young wife uttered a curse. No Lord of Montrose would find love or happiness in a marriage until she was released from her tomb. And should a woman dare to love a Montrose man, she too would find an early death.

"Well, the old man was sickened by shock and grief. He took to his bed that night and was dead by morning. The servants tried to find the hidey hole and release Lady Katherine, but the house contained many secret passages and hidden rooms. All their efforts were in vain. The brick layers were itinerant laborers, and horrified by their part in the ghastly deed, had quickly moved on. The poor lass, she was never found."

There was a long silence as Madelyn sat wide-eyed in horror. This was not the tall tale she had expected. This was a curse; an affliction which spoke directly to her. She had married a Lord of Montrose.

"I shouldn't have told you this. At least, not on your first night. I must be getting old and foggy in the head. Forgive the ramblings of an old woman." Old Bess reached over and patted her clenched hands. "It's just an old wives' tale, not to be taken serious dear."

Madelyn swallowed, suppressing a shudder. “And have all the marriages since been unhappy ones?” Her voice sounded strange even to her, distant and high-pitched.

Old Bess refused to answer. She shook her head. “No more of that now. It’s sorry I am to have told you that old story. Every big house has one, and this one’s just yours.” She looked away for a moment, glancing out the coach window. “And see, the rain has stopped in good time too. My lane is just ahead. Briggs will drop me here; he knows the place well enough.”

Madelyn shook off her lingering feelings of trepidation. Old Bess was right. It was just a story. It must have been the storm which chilled her so.

Old Bess reached over and patted her hand once more. “In time you'll be happy here. I’m a wise woman and I know these things.” She smiled, and Madelyn noticed her startling blue eyes again. They twinkled with mischief. “Some say I’m a seer, and that’s what I see for you.” She nodded, looking her over once more. “It’s pleased I am to have been the first to meet you. You seem a fine young woman and good too, offering a ride to an old woman. My cottage is just across the lake. Come visit for a spot of tea once you’re settled.”

“Oh, I will,” Madelyn answered. Despite the unsettling story, she liked the old woman. Old Bess had a kindness about her.

The coach slid to a halt. Old Bess picked up her cloth bag. “My precious herbs,” she said, her clear blue eyes twinkling once more as she tucked the bundle under her cloak, "always best picked before a storm." The older woman opened the coach door, and slid down to the muddy earth, closing the door behind her.

The coach lurched forward once more. Madelyn slid back the window and raised her hand in farewell to Old Bess. She turned to look forward, peering into the distance, hoping to see Montrose Manor. But night had swallowed the views, and she could see nothing but dark shadows ahead.

Her new home, and the life she would make there, were a mystery. She hoped Old Bess was correct; that she would find happiness here. Her mind wandered to the curse of Montrose. She shivered, before quickly banishing the thought. Surely it was just as Old Bess had said, an old wives' tale.

CHAPTER 3

TWO WATERCOLORS DEPICTING GARDENS OF LIGHT

Lightning lit up the sky as the coach passed slowly through a stone archway, rattling across a cobbled courtyard. It came to a stop at last. A high stone wall, dark and massive, was all she could make out of the building beside her. She stayed in the coach while the driver braved the rain, going to the door to sound the knocker.

There was a long wait before dim lights illuminated a pair of windows on each side of massive double doors. Finally, one of the doors opened slowly.

Madelyn tried to prepare herself to meet her staff. She adjusted her bonnet, tucking stray hairs back within its cuff, then smoothed what she could of her crumpled skirts. It was a hopeless enterprise. The long journey and the damp had taken their toll. She feared she would make a bedraggled first impression.

But there was no time to fuss. The driver pulled

open the coach door, set down the step, and held an umbrella for her to alight, though it did little to shield her from the gusting rain. Somehow, she managed to step into a wide puddle of water. It was ankle deep, drenching the hem of her skirts and cloak before she hurried up several steps and through the open door into the hall. The massive door slammed shut behind her, with a hollow, reverberating echo.

The entry was dark, but for two lamps. One stood at each side of the doors, freshly lit, and just beginning to give the room light. Further into the hall, on the left, a wide staircase curved into a high ceiling, and another fluttering lantern sat on an end table at its base. The recesses of the room were cloaked in shadows. Only the outline of a fireplace sat across the great hall to her left, unlit and cold. The impression was one of vast barren space.

A woman stood before her, wearing the black and white livery of a servant. Her hair was pulled back into a severe bun, and covered by a securely fastened, small cotton cap. She had an angular face, set in firm disapproving lines, with dark thick brows furrowed, and a thin mouth pressed tightly closed.

The woman's eyes travelled the length of her person, resting on the hem of Madelyn's sodden cloak, which oozed a brackish pool beneath her. The housekeeper's brows furrowed further into a disapproving scowl, making the woman look even more forbidding. Madelyn had to bite her lip to keep from apologizing for the mess she was creating.

"Welcome Lady Montrose." she said in a perfectly precise voice, raising her eyes, then dropping into the stiff bob of a curtsy. "I am Mrs. Waldron, the housekeeper."

Before Madelyn could reply, the door swung open again, with a gust of wind and rain. The coachman dragged her chest into the entry, then unceremoniously tossed her soaked carpet bag onto the floor beside it. He wordlessly turned and left, pulling the massive door shut behind him once more.

Mrs. Waldron ignored the interruption. "We were not expecting you tonight my lady. All is not as prepared as I would have hoped."

Madelyn was momentarily distracted by the scurried entry of two young girls, who she took to be maids, and a young man, with his tunic misbuttoned. They lined up next to Mrs. Waldron, who turned to glare at them. The poor lad quickly refastened his jacket under the watchful eyes of the housekeeper.

"For tonight, you will meet only those who will attend you. Tomorrow is time enough to greet the rest of the staff." She had a voice which brooked no argument, not that Madelyn was so inclined. She was feeling exhausted and chilled to the bone. Her fingers trembled as she undid the strings to her bonnet, unsure if it was nerves or the cold.

"This is Annmarie, and Annmargaret. They will see to your personal needs and act as parlor maids." The two girls curtsied in unison. Madelyn noticed they were identical twins, both with soft brown eyes and sandy hair. Each gave her the same shy smile.

"Pleased to meet you," they chorused. Even their words were synchronized. Annmarie stepped forward, taking her heavy cloak, and bonnet.

"And this is Ned, a footman. He can help with any of the heavier tasks, beginning with carrying your bags up to your room."

Madelyn nodded at the young man, "Ned," she repeated. He blushed scarlet and immediately moved to the trunk and hefted it up.

"Now then, I am sure you are much in need of some warm food and a rest after your long journey. There will be plenty of time to show you around the manor tomorrow. Annmarie will bring a tray to your room… Annmargaret will attend you." Both girls hurried off. "Also, I will send a hot bath up to your room."

"Thank you. That would be much appreciated." For all that the woman looked forbidding, Madelyn was thankful for the quick assessment of her circumstance. She was in no mood to tour the house tonight. As Mrs. Waldron had so bluntly stated, there would be time tomorrow to get acquainted with her new home and the other staff.

"If you would follow me." The housekeeper said and led her across the room, where she picked up the waiting lantern before briskly mounting the wide staircase. Madelyn was so intent on hefting up her skirts to avoid leaving a muddy trail, she had little time to take in her surroundings. She could only register that the staircase was made of carved ancient oak, abnormally wide, and looked as if it went on forever.

From the balcony, they turned into a spacious hallway. Wall sconces intermittently placed along the corridor provided feeble light. Portraits of men and women lined the walls, their eyes glowering down at her from above. There was no sound other than the crisp footsteps of Mrs. Waldron.

"The upper hall," Mrs. Waldron announced without turning back in her direction. "The family's rooms are traditionally in this wing. You will see the portraits of the Lord's ancestors as we go." The paintings varied in size. They passed a huge picture of a fierce figure in full armor, with his sword raised as though to cut down intruders.

And that is exactly how Madelyn felt at this juncture—like an intruder. There was nothing in the rich stark features of this house to remind her of home. It was cold and filled with dark shadows. Surely it would look different in the light of day, she assured herself. This feeling and the chill would pass as the storm moved out.

Madelyn was thankful when Mrs. Waldron stopped halfway down the corridor and opened a large oak door. Bundling up her heavy wet skirts, to keep from smearing mud across the house had become an awkward burden. "The Mistress' suite. This is your sitting room," Mrs. Waldron announced. Madelyn stepped into the room, staying close to the door. The fireplace had been lit, and though the room was still cool, the flames promised future warmth.

It was as though they had entered an entirely different realm. This room was well lit after the gloom of the entry and the hall. There was a pair of cozy cream-colored chairs, strategically placed by the fire, with a small serving table between them. One had a soft knitted coral blanket draped over its back. A desk and bookshelf, loaded with novels, sat next to a draped window.

"To the left is your bathing room, and dressing room. Your bath will be delivered to you there." Mrs. Waldron walked across the room and Madelyn took a few steps, still carefully holding up the offending gown and peering over the housekeeper's shoulder. She had time to note a tub pulled up to a glowing fire before Mrs. Waldron walked briskly back across the room.

"And your bedroom is here on the right." This time she followed the woman through an open archway all the way into the room. It too was done in soft colors. The bedding was coral and cream, beautiful and silky. A hint of watercolor green was skillfully used as a second accent, evident in the tiny floral print of the drapes, a fluffy cushion, and the velvet covered chair by the fire. She could not resist running her hand across the bedspread.

"It is beautiful," she said, and meant it.

The woman gestured to another door. "The adjoining suite of Lord Montrose," she said.

Julian's bedroom, she thought. Mrs. Waldron opened the door on the far-right wall, but only partially. Madelyn used the opportunity for a quick peek inside. There was a huge masculine bed in rich browns, and heavy oak furniture so different from the delicate pieces in her rooms. The housekeeper pulled the door firmly closed. Madelyn blushed at the implication of intimacy.

"It is all quite lovely. Thank you for decorating it so tastefully," she said, hoping the housekeeper would not notice her embarrassment.

The woman gave a little snort. "It wasn't me that decorated it. It was done by the former Lady Montrose, poor lass. She had little time to enjoy it. We had most of her possessions removed and tidied up for you. However, a few of her things that we thought might be of use were left; books, a few robes, and the like. No point in letting them rot."

With the doors all opened and aligned at the end of the rooms, Mrs. Waldron was able to look through all the way to the dressing room. "Ah, I see your bath water has arrived. Once you finish, a hot meal will be waiting in your sitting room. I trust everything is to your liking."

Madelyn had time to only nod before the woman continued. "As I said, tomorrow, we will do a tour of the house and introduce you to the staff." Mrs. Waldron walked through one of the bedroom doors opening directly into the hall. Without a further word, she left the suite.

Madelyn stood for a moment assessing her surroundings. Whoever had decorated these rooms had done so lovingly. The rooms were both tasteful and comfortable. After the cold, dark walk through the lofty house, this suite was a haven.

A young maid appeared in the archway. "Your bath is ready ma'am."

"Thank you. Annmarie?"

"Annmargaret ma'am."

After a luxurious bath, Annmargaret helped her into a warm robe. She made her way to the sitting room where she sat by the fire to dry her hair. She could hear Annmargaret bustling about in the dressing room, unpacking her things. It was new to her, to be so pampered. In London, there had been only Milly to attend her mother and the four girls, which meant that most of the time they looked after themselves.

The door to the hall opened, and Annmarie, at least she thought it was Annmarie, entered with a tray. "I brought you a light soup. Cook warmed up some biscuits, and there is a little cheese with some warm milk. I hope it is to your liking milady." The girl set a tray next to her on the serving table.

"Thank you." Again, Madelyn was impressed with the pampering. At home, if one missed a mealtime, it was a long wait until the next meal. There were no staff for coddling of any sort. She smiled. This circumstance she could get used to in this foreign world—Yorkshire. She enjoyed every bite of the meal, feeling much spoiled.

Annmarie stepped into the room, apparently finished with the unpacking. "If you need anything ma'am, there is a bell next to the fireplace. You need only pull it, to summon me or my sister."

"What time does the staff retire for the night?"

Annmarie wrinkled her brow. "I don't rightly know ma'am. Annmargaret and I are new here. His Lordship brought us up from the village before leaving for London. He wanted everything ready for his new bride. Isn't that romantic?" She grinned. "We're in training. Mrs. Waldron says we're not half ready to serve. But my sister and I decided since there are two of us, that makes a whole, if you know what I mean." Her eyes twinkled mischievously.

"Excellent notion."

"I will just take this away, then prepare your bed. By then Annmargaret will have found your nightgown."

Madelyn slid her chair closer to the fire and began brushing out her hair in the heat to help it dry. It really was a cozy sitting room. There were tall windows, now draped for the evening, lining the exterior wall, which would surely fill the room with light during the day. She smiled as she envisioned the view she would have of the moors in the valley below. Again, she thought of the woman who had occupied this room over a decade ago. She must have loved this space.

Across the room, a pair of watercolors graced the wall. Setting the hairbrush aside, she went over to examine them. They both depicted views of a garden. The first was a rendition of a rose arbor—red roses, with white clematis intertwined amongst its stems. The arch sheltered a bench, set against a gray stone wall. The second was a garden of wildflowers, featuring daisies and light purple blooms against a thick green hedge. Both were well done with light brush strokes and soft blurred backgrounds. They left an impression of light and warmth. The same style was reflected in this suite, a tangible feeling of comfort and peace. The name Alice was written with the date in a delicate hand at the bottom of each painting.

Annmargaret stepped in from the dressing room, with Madelyn's new cotton nightgown in her hands. "I chose something warm for tonight. Will this do or would milady like something a little more..." she blushed.

"It will be perfect." Madelyn was quick to respond. She turned back to the paintings once more. "Annmargaret, do you know the name of the previous Lady of Montrose?"

"Well, she was gone long before I took an interest in the affairs up here on the rise. My sister and I would have only been girls when she came here to live. But I most certainly heard of her. People still whisper about her in the village. Lady Alice was her name."

Her suspicions about the artist were correct and she nodded thoughtfully. "I know only that she died young, but no one has told me how she died. What happened to her?"

Annmargaret looked down for a moment, then

returned her gaze with wide eyes. "I am not sure I should talk to you about her, though I suppose you will hear about it all soon enough. It's not a secret after all." She paused again as though debating her next words. "Lady Alice was here less than a year. I was told she was rather delicate, and very homesick for her family in the south."

"Was she ill then?"

"Ah, nooo..." Annmargaret began twisting Madelyn's nightgown nervously in her hands.

"I will hear of it eventually as you said, Annmargaret," Madelyn said, curious now.

"It is said she jumped from the old tower," she whispered, then looked behind her as though expecting someone to admonish her for speaking of the tragedy. "I heard the master was devastated. But all of that is long in the past."

Madelyn's throat was constricted; she could only swallow the shock which washed over her. She stood stoically as Annmargaret helped her into her nightgown. *Why was I not told? Could my mother have known this and kept it from me? Would it have made a difference? Likely not,* she concluded.

Suicide. A terrible sadness weighed her down. She numbly allowed herself to be led to the mirrored little table and sat down. Annmargaret brushed her hair, then began weaving it into braids.

"I should not have told you. It was so long ago; I am sure it is almost forgotten by now..." Annmargaret's apologies faded away. She could only hear the word suicide as it echoed through her consciousness.

When her hair was done, she stood. "Thank you, Annmargaret. I am very tired, and will go directly to bed," she said woodenly. She walked into her plush bedroom, with the covers folded back invitingly and crawled into bed.

Annmargaret spent a few moments banking the fire, dousing the lights, and turning her bedside lamp to low before quietly leaving the room.

Madelyn lay in bed thinking about what she had just learned of her predecessor. How could a woman, so obviously focused on all things light, become so dark and depressed that she threw herself off a tower to her death? It made no sense.

Her mind wandered to the old woman's tale of the curse upon the house of Montrose. Despite the warmth of the room, and her thick covers, a shiver chilled her. Perhaps the wives of the manor were indeed cursed, and she too would fall into a dark melancholy.

No, Madelyn silently reprimanded herself, she would be happy here. She was the Lady of Montrose. She had a strong young man for a husband and was much privileged to live a pampered existence here in the house. She could not wait to write her sister, Beth, and tell her she had not one, but two ladies' maids to see to her comfort. Beth would be green with envy.

But the image of the vast landscape of the moors—lonely and mysterious, filled her mind as she tried to find sleep. And then there was the house itself. The manor was cold and dark, the only respite being the pastel softness of this suite. Yet even here, surrounded by light, the previous wife of Montrose had found no comfort. She could only wonder if she would suffer the same tragic fate.

CHAPTER 4

LORD MONTROSE MAKES HIS PLANS

Julian was relieved to enter the warmth of his bedroom after a long night. Poor old Hadley, his personal butler lay sprawled on the chair by the fire. He woke him, and sent him to bed, after assuring him he could manage on his own.

When he had left the army, only a few months ago, and returned home, he was surprised to see Old Hadley still at his post. Hadley had been with him since he was a child. He reminded himself to have another serious talk with the man about retirement. Hadley had refused to leave his service. Even the offer of a cottage of his own, with a decent pension had not swayed him.

Having finished washing up, he wrapped his robe around himself and walked into his bedroom. The door to the adjoining room loomed in front of him. He wondered if his bride lay asleep in her bed next door. Unable to resist, he gently opened the door.

For a moment, he took in the soft amber glow of

the room, purposely avoiding a glance at the unfamiliar lump beneath the bed's covers. The fire had died down, and he added a scoop of coal and a log, then stood back, satisfied with the burst of flame.

It smelled different. The room was alive with the fresh scent of the woman; a lingering odor of rose soap, presumably from her bath, and beneath it, the crisp lemony scent he knew to be strictly her own.

Finally, he turned and faced the bed. It drew him close. He found himself standing over her. Her soft auburn hair lay in a thick braid across her pale neck. There was a smattering of freckles on her nose and upper cheeks, that he had not been aware of, and he leaned in close to examine them.

She was beautiful. There was a fresh innocence about her as she slept; she looked like a young girl, not a woman. He had clearly been wrong when he had judged her to be simply acceptable.

She groaned and rolled to her back. He arched away, afraid she would awaken to find him here, but thankfully her eyes did not open. He stood by her bedside for a minute longer, wondering how he felt about this new bride.

The only emotion he could identify was confusion, and perhaps, an aching fear; a fear he knew to be a terrible yearning. Despite the fact he had firmly decided to keep a wife for the sole purpose of producing an heir, he knew that deep in his heart, he wanted the future a bride could bring. He secretly hoped his bride could give this lonely place some joy. But his stomach knotted with a kind of dread, too.

For the first time in many years, he allowed the memories of his first wife to creep into his consciousness. He remembered the boyish enthusiasm he had felt upon his marriage, discovering the wonders of their marriage bed, and his fascination with everything about the feminine creature that was his to love and protect. He recalled too his efforts to have Lady Alice as the companion he always longed for—a longing that stemmed from his daydreams as an only child. Despite his efforts none of his dreams had come to pass. He had tried too hard, too soon. Closing his eyes, he banished the painful thoughts.

This time he was determined not to make the same mistakes of his past marriage. The eager boy of a decade ago had been lost with the tragedy of Alice's death and the long years of bloody battle that followed.

This time he would keep his distance until Madelyn had settled in. He wanted her to find happiness here, to make this her new home, but he knew he could not risk giving his heart to her. Never again would he subject himself to the pain brought from the death of his first wife. He had failed Alice.

This time there would be no such mistakes. He would protect his wife carefully, but most of all, he would guard his own heart.

Julian returned to his room, closing the door firmly behind him.

CHAPTER 5

A TOUR OF AN ANCIENT HOUSE

Madelyn was awoken by the sound of someone shuffling about in her sitting room. For a moment she was disoriented and wondered if it was Milly.

One of the twins stepped into her view. "There you are. I didn't want to wake you, milady, but Mrs. Waldron is itching to show you the manor." The girl pulled back the drapes, filling the room with bright sunshine. Madelyn squinted into the shock of light.

She closed her eyes for a minute. "Good morning, Annmargaret?"

"Annmarie. I brought you some breakfast. Would you like it here or in your sitting room?"

Madelyn smiled to herself. She could have breakfast in bed. Another tidbit to add in her letter to Beth.

She glanced at the door to Julian's room. "The sitting room will be fine, thank you. Does Lord

Montrose also take his breakfast in his room?" she asked, thinking she might share a meal with him.

"Oh no, ma'am. The master rises early. He is usually with the horses by six, then comes in around eight for breakfast. He has a routine, the Lord does." Annmarie smiled. "And it's almost noon."

"Oh dear." She thought of the formidable Mrs. Waldron waiting for her all morning. Not a propitious start for her first day. At some point today she would have to assert herself as the Lady of the manor. In London, the household had only a cook, and one maid, their Milly. She and her sisters had helped with the cleaning and laundry. While her mother spent her time balancing the accounts, and squeezing what she could from a meagre budget.

She hurried through her morning ablutions, then quickly ate a muffin with cheese. When she was ready to go down, Annmarie was nowhere to be found. There was nothing to do but find her way alone.

The hallway was as she remembered it. Only this time a large window at the far end of the hall, next to a narrow stairway, provided more light. She looked up at the portraits lining the walls as she walked. The faces of the Montrose ancestors, as Mrs. Waldron had labeled them, were no less intimidating in the light of day. Their dark eyes appeared to say she was unworthy, an impostor amongst this prestigious crowd from the past.

She reached the balcony with a sigh of relief. "The walk of doom," she muttered, then quickly assured herself that with time she would become accustomed to it.

From the balcony rail, she could see the cavernous hall below. She stood for a moment to absorb it. Taking a deep breath she faced the entry, where two heavy doors dominated the view. They were huge, at least twelve feet high and made of heavy oak, aged a deep brown. Tall windows on each side of the door framed the entry. The same dark wood made up the wide staircase, the railings, and the balcony. The floors were some sort of stone tile. The overall effect was one of ancient masculine power. It would be impossible for anyone to come through those monstrous doors without a sense of awe.

She ran her hand along the banister as she walked to the landing. The wood was polished to a perfect shine.

Mrs. Waldron's crisp footsteps could be heard from below. Madelyn picked up her skirts and hurried down the stairs to find the older woman.

The housekeeper wore the same black and white uniform, with the same disapproving frown as last night. "Ah. There you are at last Mistress." She clapped her hands. Immediately a line of servants formed to her right. Madelyn had the impression they had rehearsed this ritual.

In addition to the twins, and Jimmy, who had attended her in York, there was Ned, a cook, who was an elderly robust woman, and her assistant, a scullery girl, an old fellow named Hadley was introduced as

Julian's valet, a cleaning woman named Gertrude, and Mrs. Waldron. Madelyn greeted each one in turn.

"We keep a small staff here in the house, but that may change now that the master is home and with you as mistress. We have already opened parts of the house which have been closed for some time. I brought in some temporary help for Gertrude these last few weeks." Mrs. Waldron said. "We recently hired two gardeners, and of course there are the stable hands, which you will meet at a later time." At the housekeeper's nod, the servants retreated as quickly as they'd lined up.

Mrs. Waldron handed her a key ring, with scores of heavy iron keys. "We generally only lock the east wing, and those are the larger black iron keys, so you'll not need to carry these. Now then, shall we begin our tour?" Mrs. Waldron did not wait for an answer, instead she indicated the entry. "This section of the house is the oldest in use. The foyer is part of what was the old keep. The doors were brought in from Rome by a Lord of Montrose in the fourteenth century," she said with not a little pride. "The house itself was built by the Normans around 1180. Of course, parts of it have been torn down, updated, or even added to over the years."

She walked to the large double doors leading to the east wing, and using her key opened them. They swung wide revealing a stone and oak room much like the entry. She and the housekeeper took only a few steps into the room. Like its western counterpart, this room had stone floors, with heavy weathered oak trim. The windows were shuttered, and there was little else to see, except ghostly sheet covered furnishings in a high-ceilinged room.

With an expression of regret, Mrs. Waldron walked a few more paces into the room, her shoes echoing on the stone floors. She rested her hand on the dark mantle of a huge stone fireplace. "This wing of the house was partitioned off about 100 years ago. It was too much upkeep for its use.

"At one time Montrose was a stronghold, a fortress here in the North, originally built of stone and a crucial part of the Norman defense. The manor housed a contingent of soldiers, officers, and the like. It was said that Henry the second once stayed in its rooms. Then again, the place was active during the reign of the Tudors, with the wars against the Scots, and finally the battles of the seventeenth century."

She sighed, running her hand lovingly along the mantle, then brushed the dust off her fingers onto her skirts. "This room was used for balls and entertainment. But those days are past. Now Montrose serves only as a country house. Besides these days the family does little entertaining out here in the wilds. There really is no point, and too much expense in maintaining the east wing." Mrs. Waldron looked around the room once more and mournfully shook her head. "It is a shame really. The place could be one of the great country homes."

Madelyn recognized the deep attachment Mrs. Waldron had to the manor. It softened her impression of the woman, humanizing her. For whatever reason, this show of emotion had lightened her worries about working with this intimidating woman. She was glad to have seen it.

Mrs. Waldron's voice became crisp once more. "There is access here to the cellars, which would have housed troops, and of course, the dungeons of old. They run the length of the house. She lit a lantern from the mantle. "We can take a quick peek, but there is little to see below. Thankfully, it is very dry, thus we use some of the space for storage, but not much else."

Mrs. Waldron led the way to a heavy oaken door tucked into an alcove behind the fireplace. She pushed open the door. Madelyn was expecting a narrow-cobwebbed stair. Instead, a wide stone staircase appeared, with a narrow window partway down, presumably at ground level, lighting the way. It led to a large stone room. Several narrow windows provided only a muted light, and Madelyn was thankful for the glow of Mrs. Waldron's lantern.

The floor was swept clean. To the right, sheeted furniture, and wooden crates were stacked high against the stone walls. On the left was a wall of brick. Mrs. Waldron walked crisply to the rear of the space, where the walls on each side opened to arched hallways. "This room would have been a hall of sorts where the soldiers could gather. And to the right, beneath the old wing, is a long hallway opening to a line of separate quarters. Each room would have housed one or several soldiers—a barracks of sorts. They have been cleaned out and are empty now…just stone and dust, I am afraid."

Madelyn looked around the tidy room. "It is not what I expected. I envisioned a dungeon of sorts, something more..." she tried to find a word which would not offend and said, "…eerie, I suppose."

Mrs. Waldron chuckled dryly. "Oh, we have that too. Montrose has its secrets like many old houses." She flashed Madelyn a smile, which appeared to twist in the lantern's glow, then walked briskly to the arched doorway at the left of the room. Madelyn followed.

Holding the lantern high, the housekeeper indicated a dark corridor. A few paces forward and the narrow stone walls opened into another wide room. Again, high narrow windows emitted faint light. A figure of a man materialized just in front of the housekeeper. Madelyn could not contain a startled gasp.

Mrs. Waldron chuckled again, a hoarse rasping sound. "This is the armory. There are a few pieces left. Old treasures I call them." She moved forward and lightly brushed the full suit of armor which Madelyn had mistaken for a man. There were piles of armor and decaying knickknacks along the walls, having fallen from metal hooks still holding scraps of what looked like decaying leather. Another full suit of armor was braced against the far wall, leaning precariously into the corner. "You'll not want to venture far in this direction. There are no neat entries lined along the long hall like the barracks on the east side. This hallway," she stated as she gestured to one of two arched entries near the back of the room, "here, leads to the dungeons. Really a big gathering room, the torture chamber I call it." The housekeeper gave a dry chuckle and said, "Followed by a series of cells connected by hallways leading off in different directions."

They stood silently while Madelyn took in the scene. Spider webs and creepy piles of ancient armor filled the space much as she had expected when she first came down the wide staircase. Madelyn's mind flashed to Old Bess' story of Lady Katherine and the curse of Montrose. She shivered at the thought of being buried forever within these dark stone walls.

Mrs. Waldron spoke again, thankfully interrupting her thoughts. "This is the 'eerie' you expected," she said, and chuckled. "You will not want to come down here alone. Past the torture chamber lies a maze of dark hallways and stone rooms. I will not be showing those to you today. Take my advice and stay clear of them. A person could easily become hopelessly lost."

With that final comment, the housekeeper turned abruptly, walking crisply back to the main room and the wide stairs. Madelyn hurried behind her, not sorry to leave the gloom of the cellars behind her.

Back on the main floor, after locking the double doors to the east wing, Mrs. Waldron walked down a narrow hall behind the stairs. "The servants' staircase, and the only access to the tower rooms. You will find this staircase on the upper floor as well," she said, then shot her a hard look. "I also suggest you avoid the tower. Nothing up there but storage." An image of the former Lady Montrose plunging to her death invaded her thoughts. Yes, she nodded her acquiescence and suppressed a shiver, best to avoid that fate. The house of Montrose had not been kind to its former Ladies.

Mrs. Waldron continued, "The kitchens and linen closets are back here. The kitchen itself has been updated, with all the latest amenities." She pushed a swinging door open. Madelyn had a quick glimpse of the activity inside before they moved on. "The servants' quarters are down this hall. They're actually part of the old east wing. My rooms are here. And you will see my suite tomorrow, when we meet to discuss the week's menu and any other household issues, if that suits you?" Mrs. Waldron turned to her and glowered as though prepared for battle should she object.

"That will be fine." Madelyn quickly answered. She had no idea how to run a manor, in fact she didn't have a clue how to manage a household of any size. She was relieved to accept the appointment. She stole a glance at the formidable woman. For all her stoic countenance, thus far the housekeeper had been quick to anticipate her needs. She obviously had a firm grasp of what the mistress' role was meant to be. Madelyn was more than willing to accept the older woman's direction.

They returned to the entrance foyer. "The west wing holds the common rooms of the house in use." She turned and opened double doors into a pleasant large parlor. "These doors can now be left open," she said, and indeed the light and color brightened the dark entry. The housekeeper turned toward Madelyn and continued, "The former Lady Montrose designed the updates for these rooms and her plans were followed. Sadly though, she was not here for the completion of the project. As a result, you will find the rooms are untouched, and still new in fact. The work was done while the master was away. We did a thorough cleaning recently which was all that was needed to bring them up to date." She frowned. "With the Lord away at the wars, we kept a skeleton staff here. I myself supervised the work on the updates." Her lips twitched with the slightest curve, which Madelyn took to be a smile.

Madelyn walked around the sitting room. Here too were the airy designs she so loved in her suite. The far wall had a series of windows, framed with soft light green drapes. The furnishings were tan with accent cushions picking up shades of green in the room. The wall was papered in paisley patterns of wildflowers. A set of glass doors opened to the gardens, with a full-length window on each side. She walked to the left window. The view was of the drive, and the hills beyond.

"It is lovely," Madelyn said. And indeed, it was. After the gloom of the cellars, and references to the fated tower, the sitting room felt like a whole new world. The air smelt of a crisp, lemon-scented cleaner. She took a long breath, feeling her shoulders relax.

Mrs. Waldron nodded with just the hint of a smile. "Windows were added all along this wing, and the floor above. It needed improvement. We call this room the green parlor."

Next, she was shown a smaller parlor. Mrs. Waldron called it the family room, and it had also been redone along with the formal dining room, a breakfast room, and a library. The library was at the back of the house. It too had double glass doors, this time accessing the rear gardens, with matching windows on each side. There was an intimate arrangement of furniture across from the windows before a lit fireplace. To the left were shelves of books with a massive desk placed before them. On the right, a piano stood against the far wall, with music laid out as if it had been recently played. Of all the rooms shown to her, this one was the most appealing to her.

"His Lordship prefers the library. His evenings are usually spent here."

Madelyn walked to the double doors and looked out at the rear gardens. It was a beautiful view. The stables sat to the far left, with the pastures in the distance.

"There you have it." Mrs. Waldron concluded. "Simply stated, the east wing is closed, with the entry separating the two wings. The west wing houses the common rooms on the ground floor, with the family rooms off the balcony above. The servants' quarters and kitchens are behind the main stairs, with some of the rooms jutting into the east wing."

They circled back through the kitchen area and finally to the entry with its wide stairway to the second floor. Madelyn had to scramble to keep pace with her on the stairs. At the upper landing Mrs. Waldron paused.

"Along this hall are the guestrooms, the nursery, and as you know, the suites for the master and yourself." She opened a door on the left. "All the guest rooms are similar." Madelyn caught a glimpse of a standard bedroom, done in soft pink. "This is the rose room. The others are all different shades." She took a few more steps down the hall.

Madelyn stopped in front of the portrait of the warrior brandishing his sword and ran her finger over a small brass plate beneath it. Mrs. Waldron, seeing the gesture, explained, "The paintings have a label beneath with the name and date for each. Someone in the past was thoughtful enough to add them and the tradition has been kept up with each generation."

Further down the hall, directly across from the door to her bedroom, the housekeeper opened another door. "The nursery," she said, allowing the door to open only a crack before pulling it closed, her lips in a firm line. Madelyn was immediately curious and resolved to explore it herself later in the day.

"I will leave you here, next to your suite. Just a reminder that the house runs on a country schedule. Mr. McGowan generally joins his Lordship for breakfast at eight, luncheon is served at one, and dinner is in the formal dining room at seven. Afternoon tea is at your request."

Madelyn wondered if this was a criticism of her

rising late today and her cheeks burned. Tomorrow she would be up and in the breakfast room at eight. "Thank you for the tour, Mrs. Waldron. The house is magnificent."

Mrs. Waldron nodded in response. "Luncheon will be served informally in the breakfast room in thirty minutes." For a moment she looked as if she were about to say something more but changed her mind. She turned abruptly and retreated down the hall, her shoes sounding a sharp staccato in the silence.

Madelyn leaned against her door, reviewing the rooms of her new home in her mind. Directly across from her was the door to the nursery. She stepped across the hall and opened the door.

Heavy drapes blocked the light. Even in the shadows, it was clear this room too had been touched by the former Lady Montrose's hand. She walked across the room and pulled back the curtains of a large window along the far wall. Light filled the room, bringing it to life.

The walls were a variety of pastels, accented with cheerful wallpaper in flowered motifs. All the furnishings were draped in white sheets and coated with a decade of dust. The form of a bassinet was obvious beneath its cover standing by the window. She pulled off the sheet revealing a light birch cradle. It was decorated with tiny hand-painted buttercup sprays. She reached down and set the cradle to rock, watching as it reflected the light.

A brown paper parcel sat within the baby's bed.

Madelyn sank to the floor beside the cradle and removed the package. She untied the bowed strings and folded back the paper with care. Inside was a soft yellow blanket and matching cushion. Hand embroidered along the edges of each was a delicate trail of green ivy, with tiny blue and pink forget-me-nots. She ran her hand along the intricate pattern lovingly stitched into the borders of the pieces.

The pillow was complete, but the border of the blanket was only finished on three sides. One side of the blanket had only its green foliage. She held the blanket up to be sure her eyes had not deceived her. Along the right perimeter of the blanket only three tiny flowers had been added to the hem. She let the blanket fall to her lap.

Had Alice been pregnant? The cloth was soft and pliant, its color still bright and unfaded. She carefully folded the pieces back into their brown wrappings and set them in the cradle again, then pulled the sheet back over the bed. But covering the cradle did not still her racing thoughts.

The woman who had so lovingly designed the improvements to this house, Lady Alice, had created peace and light in her surroundings. Her gentle touch was blatantly obvious in this nursery with its tender details. Was her death really a suicide? She rested her hand on the shrouded cradle, setting it in motion once more and watched its sheeted form rock slowly back and forth. None of it made any sense.

There were too many questions and no answers,

but who could she ask? Talking with her young maids about the former Lady Montrose, of whom they knew only by lingering gossip, would produce no results. Approaching Mrs. Waldron or Julian was unthinkable. The image of Old Bess flitted across her mind. It might be time to visit the woman for tea and a long talk.

Madelyn rose abruptly from the floor and lifted her watch brooch. It was almost one. Luncheon would be laid out in the breakfast room shortly. She wanted to at least see her husband. She hurried from the room and down the hall, reviewing the location of the breakfast room as she went. It would not do for her to be tardy for a second meal today.

She tried to dismiss the thoughts of her predecessor as she went. Perhaps her curiosity was intrusive. *The former Lady Montrose has little to do with me,* she assured herself. *I must let her rest in peace.*

It was time for her to concentrate on her new husband. She lifted her skirts to make her way down the massive stairs, planning possible conversations with Julian in her head. It was unfortunate she knew so little about the estate. She resolved to determine his interests and at least attempt a repartee with the man.

But the vision of the shrouded cradle rocking in the nursery lingered. Like her, Lady Alice had come to Montrose as a young bride. What could possibly have happened to drive this woman of light to the tower on that fateful day?

CHAPTER 6

THE HIDDEN GARDEN

The breakfast room was used for all meals except dinner. It had a full window overlooking the back garden. Madelyn sat over her empty plate and watched two laborers in the distance attempt to rescue an overgrown hedge from the wild, while she contemplated her situation.

There was only one place setting at the table. Julian was obviously not going to join her for the meal. She wondered if this was his habit or if he was purposely avoiding her.

One of the twins came in, "Would you care for tea ma'am?"

"No, thank you, Annmarie," she said, taking a guess at the name. "Is it his Lordship's habit to come to the house for luncheon?"

"I don't know ma'am, being new here and all. I know cook is preparing a basket to be taken out to the stables today."

Madelyn tossed her napkin down, abruptly leaving the breakfast room and headed for the kitchen. The first thing she noticed upon opening the swinging doors was the warmth in the room. The next was the scent of fresh baking—the cook was busy taking a rack of buns from the oven above a smoldering fireplace. Through a wide archway to the left the household staff had gathered for lunch and chattered at their table. Directly in front of her the scullery maid, Midgie, was placing a faded tablecloth over a basket of food, sitting on a worn wooden worktable. Ned stood at the back door, prepared to deliver what she assumed was the food for Julian and Hamish.

"I thought I might take the meal to the stables today," she announced. The room quieted, even the chatter from the dining table in the adjacent room was stilled. She was sure her desperation to gain her husband's attention must be evident to all.

For a long moment no one spoke. Finally, the cook bustled over to the worktable. "Now then, that is a fine idea. It's a lovely day. We'll add a bit more food." She turned to her scullery maid. "Midgie, get a decent blanket for a picnic." Cook tossed back the cover and examined the contents of the basket with a frown. "Her ladyship, it will just be a minute."

Moments later, she was trudging across the yard, carrying the basket in one arm and a kettle of lemonade in the other. Just beyond the stables, she could see Hamish leaning against the fence rail, while

Julian worked a horse in the pen. She made her way toward them.

Hamish turned and smiled as she approached. "Ah. Good day ma'am."

"I brought lunch." she said and smiled in return.

"And in perfect time too. I'm ready for a bite." He left the rail and helped her lay out the picnic in the grass along the fence line.

When they had settled on the blanket, Hamish opened the basket. "Let's see what we have in here." Inside they discovered a packet of sandwiches, cheese, fruit, and even a tray of strawberry tarts. Madelyn helped him arrange the food.

Hamish helped himself to a sandwich while Madelyn poured him a mug of lemonade. He smiled again as he accepted it.

Julian stood in a corralled pen, a sleek black horse on a leading strap circling him. She could hear his soft voice reassuring the animal. As the horse circled, he turned with it, his shoulders and arms working the reins in an age-old rhythm. Even from this distance she could sense the quiet strength of her husband. For a while she sat mesmerized by the spectacle.

There was a gentle manliness about him—a calmness. Even the horse sensed his controlled presence. He gradually shortened the reins until the beast was brought close. She watched, entranced as he stroked its sleek black neck, whispering to the creature softly. Madelyn's heart ached with a sort of longing. Her marriage was just over a week old, yet she had shared only a few words with her husband. Except for the morning of the proposal, she could not recall a time when he had touched her.

Hamish cleared his throat interrupting her thoughts. She reluctantly turned to him. "A fine strong animal that one." He grinned, and she reddened, wondering if he had guessed her thoughts.

"Do you ride Lady Madelyn?" he asked.

"I took riding lessons when I was a girl. But that was long ago, and I am not sure if I could manage anymore. In London, we were unable to keep horses."

"Ah. Once you are back on a horse it will all come back to you."

Madelyn turned to watch Julian return the horse to the stable then stride toward them. His work clothes suited him. He wore a loose faded tunic of sorts, open at the neck and cinched at the waist by a wide leather belt. His trousers were stretched taut over strong thighs and tucked into high brown leather boots. He moved with grace uncommon for so large a man.

Unable to take her eyes from her husband as he approached, she responded, "I would love to ride again."

As Julian settled himself on the blanket next to her, Hamish remarked, "A fine little filly that one. She is taking to the halter well."

Julian helped himself to a sandwich, then leaned back, stretching out his long legs. "She's a beauty for sure."

The sun was warm on her back, though the air still

held the cool bite of spring. All around her, the land was green and fresh from the recent rain. It was so different from the foggy congested air of London.

Madelyn listened to the men's conversation about the various horses they had purchased in London with interest. It was not the topic so much as the relaxed countenance of Julian which held her attention. He was obviously pleased with his recent purchases. The conversation was animated and enthusiastic. Julian was in his element here with the horses.

She filled the mugs with lemonade and silently handed them over to the men without interrupting them. She looked curiously at the land behind the stables. The pasture was fenced with a herd of at least a dozen horses grazing, some with foals. Wanting to contribute to the discussion she asked, "Is breeding horses the main focus of the estate?"

For once he did not turn away from her or carefully present only his unscarred profile. Instead, he faced her and gave his twisted smile before turning to the pasture and his horses. It was a rare privilege and she immediately smiled in return.

"Horses are a new investment here. For the most part, we raise cattle." He pointed to the high land off in the distance. "Further out on the rocky dales we run sheep. Wool has carried this estate for generations. You will have to take a ride out, so you can see this new home of yours."

"Your wife tells me she has not ridden in many

years. You may have a task ahead of you in getting her back in the saddle," Hamish said.

"Is that so?" Julian asked, his voice soft as his gaze settled on her. Having his attention focused on her, with his lips curling into a lazy half smile, had her stomach quivering.

She met his gaze, and answered him, careful to keep her tone nonchalant, "I am afraid I will be terribly rusty. But I would so love to be able to explore the land on horseback. It is beautiful here."

Hamish grinned and his eyes sparkled mischievously. "Well now, I believe instructing you is a task for your husband. We have a young mare which may do. Is that not so, Jules?"

Julian shot Hamish a glance, lowering his brows. When he turned to her again his face was serious. "I suppose we could arrange a few lessons, if that would please you."

"Yes, that would be wonderful!" She clapped her hands together. "Can we begin right away?"

He chuckled, resting his hand lightly on her shoulder. "Tomorrow will be time enough," he said. But Madelyn could barely hear the words. Her mind focused solely on the feel of Julian's touch. The warmth of his hand could be felt through the material of her gown, both reassuring and exciting. "We could start you on Queeny," he was saying, and she forced herself to concentrate on his words. "She is a gentle girl and won't give you too much trouble. Then we will see how you go from there." He grinned, withdrawing his hand

and Madelyn bit her lip to squash her disappointment at its loss.

She would be able to ride. In London they had been unable to afford the expense of keeping a horse. Even the cost of hiring one from a livery stable had been out of their reach. It had been many years since she'd had this opportunity. Riding was an extravagance much mourned when her father had lost their country house in a failed business venture.

Remembering she had no riding gear, her elation quickly turned into painful disappointment. It could be weeks before she would have a proper riding habit made. She felt as though a lovely gift had been snatched away and her eyes began to burn. "However, I am afraid I have nothing to wear."

Julian appraised her serviceable day dress, his face expressionless. She became acutely aware of how shabby she must appear to him. In London, money had been too dear to spend on day wear. As a result, her dress was faded and much mended. She was sure he would find her attire completely inappropriate for the Lady of the manor. Yet there was little she could do about it. There had been no funds for a proper trousseau, and no time to create a wardrobe even if there had been. She had the bolts of cloth she had bought in York, but it would take time to have new clothing made.

"Speak to Mrs. Waldron." His face hardened as his eyes travelled over her body again as though assessing her size. "There are several chests of clothes which you should be able to make use of. Tell her I said you may have them." From his dark expression, she assumed the clothes were those of his first wife, Alice. Her stomach did a little flip.

Julian rose abruptly, his easy attitude gone. "And now, it is time for us to get back to work," he said, reaching out to take her hand and help her up. "Thank you for the lunch." He did a little formal bow then walked away toward the stables. She stood and stared at his stiffened back as he left.

While she was distracted, Hamish packed the picnic. He picked up the basket, then handed her the blanket with a gentle nudge. "Would you like to meet your mare before you go? Jules has her in the stable, and I think we might be able to find a carrot or two to help you win her affection."

"That would be marvelous," she said, shaking off the sadness that had dampened the comfortable atmosphere.

They walked into a well-kept stable where Hamish found a few carrots for her from a bin by the door. He then led her to a stall where a chestnut mare whinnied softly as they approached. "Here she is. You'll find she is a gentle soul once you get to know her," he said.

The horse moved forward stretching her glossy neck into the aisle. Madelyn stroked her downy nose. "Hello Queeny. Oh, you are a lovely beast," she said softly, smiling as the horse gobbled the carrot she offered.

Hamish handed her a second carrot. "With a little

patience and attention, you should find she'll serve you well. It is the way of most animals. A little patience and time, and they all come around."

When she glanced at Hamish, he winked at her. Madelyn got the impression he was talking about more than just the horse. She ran her hand down Queeny's neck and patted her front shoulder. "I will see you tomorrow my love." She said, handing the mare a final carrot before turning again to Hamish.

Taking the basket from Hamish, and tucking the empty kettle inside, she began her trek back to the house. From this angle she faced the east wing. It was a tall grey stone structure, and unlike the remodeled west wing, had kept its narrow medieval windows. The central tower, squared with exaggerated turrets at its corners loomed above.

Unable to face the massive front doors, she made her way to the back of the house, through the gardens. Workers continued their endeavor to wrestle the expansive yard from the wild. The hedges that circled the back had been trimmed, and the two men were now working on a fountain, tearing away vines which covered it in a green snarl.

She kept close to the wall of the house where the grass was trimmed, on a brick walking path which meandered along its base. Further along, the path veered outward to accommodate a thick, overgrown hedge, towering over her head and softening the stark walls of the house.

Where the central tower jutted out from the gray

stone east wing, she noticed a break in the wall of green and paused to peer into what must have once been a secluded garden. On two sides of the enclave were the tower and east wing walls, both intermittently covered in shrubs and vines, with the overgrown hedge completing the enclosure. Directly ahead of her, against the gray walls was an ancient stone bench. An iron trellis arched over it, covered with knotted browned vines.

The scene was familiar to her. She gasped softly when she recognized this neglected alcove as the rose arbor from the watercolor in her room. Picking her way through the tall grass, littered with blooming daffodils and wild daisies, she made her way to the bench. Despite being careful, her dress caught on the prickly branch of a dead rose bush, and she tugged it back from its grasp.

Setting her basket on the dusty bench, she examined the trellis. It was indeed the scene from the painting, hardly recognizable in its neglected state. A single red rose pushed through the blackened stems of the forsaken vine. She smiled, somehow it had survived. With a little care the arbor could be beautiful once more.

She spread the picnic blanket down on the grimy bench and sat to take in her surroundings. How lovely this hidden garden must have been. A private place to relax, read, or simply withdraw for an hour or two and enjoy the beauty. She closed her eyes, listening to the hum of bees and imagining what the garden might have been for Alice when she had painted it a decade ago.

A gust of wind rippled the tops of the hedge, producing a low keening whistle, interrupting her thoughts. It was a hollow lonely sound, gradually fading as the wind stilled. She opened her eyes and tried to identify its source, but it had died away.

When next the breeze ruffled the top of the hedges, it began again. Had it not been for the over-grown hedge with its gangly boughs bent and swaying with the wind, she would not have connected the sound to the breeze. She decided there must be a vent of some sort which caught the wind at an angle producing the strange wailing sound. It would be impossible to find it with the garden in this neglected state. It would likely be found along the base of the house, hidden in the tall grass and snarled shrubbery.

She decided to speak to Julian about restoring this hidden garden. The workmen were busy with the main grounds, but perhaps she could hire a few men from the village to help her. At any rate it was time to head back to the house.

She sighed. It would be awkward asking Mrs. Waldron for the chests of clothing Julian had mentioned. Her lack of riding habits was an obvious indication of her former poverty. Furthermore, the idea of wearing the late Lady Montrose's clothes was disconcerting. But she was determined to spend an afternoon riding with her husband and no small embarrassment would stop her. She hurried back to the house.

Thankfully, Mrs. Waldron only nodded when she hesitantly requested the chests. When she tried to explain her lack of riding habit, the housekeeper interrupted, "No point in wasting the fine clothes."

Madelyn stood self-consciously as the woman eyed her from top to bottom. "Hmm," she grunted, "It seems there should be minimal if any adjustments to be made. Annmarie and Annmargaret are skilled with a needle; however, I will send to the village for Mrs. Snell. She is a fine seamstress. They certainly will have you outfitted in at least a riding habit by tomorrow afternoon. The chests will be brought to your room immediately." Her lips curled into a thin smile. "You will find an assortment of gowns as well. The girls can be kept busy making a few alterations to each of them, and they will be as new. With the housework caught up, there is little enough to occupy the two of them." She snorted, clearly disapproving the necessity of two lady's maids for her use.

Only minutes later, young Ned dropped the third and final trunk into the dressing room amongst a flurry of activity. Dresses and fripperies were strewn around the room as the twins searched through their contents for riding habits. Exclamations of excitement followed each discovery. There was an assortment of gowns in every imaginable shade and material. Alice had certainly not come to Julian without a substantial trousseau. For the next hour, the three of them rummaged through the chests.

Three riding habits were found. Annmarie helped her into a dark green one. After fussing with the tailored jacket, both girls stood back to admire the result. "How wonderful. It fits perfectly. I don't think a single alteration should be made." Annmarie gave a happy little giggle. "The Lord will not be able to take his eyes off you in this."

Madelyn walked to the full-length mirror and looked at herself. Outside of pressing and perhaps a little brushing there was little that needed to be done. It was disconcerting to think she and Alice were matched so perfectly. The more she learned about Lady Alice, the more perfect the women became, and the less worthy Madelyn felt. No doubt Lady Alice had also come to Julian with a substantial dowry; she had come to the Lord at a cost.

She ran her hand over the finely woven dark wool. It was beautiful—she was beautiful in it. The green set off her auburn hair and light complexion to advantage. It had been a long time since she had worn anything this lovely. But still she frowned, remembering the grim expression on her husband's face when he had suggested the clothing. The idea of wearing an exact outfit of Alice's, which was sure to trigger sad memories for Julian, disturbed her.

Mrs. Waldron appeared at the door with a small, humped woman, who she introduced as Mrs. Snell, a seamstress from the village. "I see the habit fits. Good."

She nodded at Madelyn. "The former Lady Montrose was not a woman to ride," she snorted. "That outfit was seldom, if ever worn. It will get some use at last."

Madelyn glanced at Mrs. Waldron's stern face, wondering if she had recognized her discomfort in wearing the outfit, and was attempting to relieve her worries. She was beginning to suspect that Mrs. Waldron was not the tyrant she portrayed.

She turned back to the mirror and ran her hand down the lapels of the jacket. "I wonder if we could make some changes. I purchased a bolt of light green satin. Could we replace the lapels and trim with light green? And something with the skirt, but I am not sure what. I need it to be different...mine."

"Excellent idea." Mrs. Waldron said. She looked at Mrs. Snell who nodded her agreement, not taking her eyes off the habit.

Mrs. Waldron walked to the open chest and pulled out the second tan riding habit. "And this one is too light as it is and can be dyed. I think a nice chocolate brown."

"Yes, yes." Mrs. Snell agreed in a raspy old voice.

Mrs. Waldron let the dress fall back into the chest and addressed Mrs. Snell. "I will leave you to it. We expect the green one to be ready by tomorrow afternoon. The girls will assist you. Also, there are the gowns, and several bolts of cloth for new. There is plenty to be done here. The twins will help, but I suspect you will need to bring in young Mary from the village to complete the task." She turned toward the door.

"Thank you, Mrs. Waldron," Madelyn said. "But before you leave, I wanted to ask about the little overgrown garden I found today in the back gardens. I am thinking of having it restored."

The room fell silent. Even the twins were frozen in place.

Mrs. Waldron glowered at her. "I would not bring that up if I were you, and certainly not to his Lordship. It is to be left as it is." The housekeeper gave a brisk nod, as though the subject was closed, before leaving the room.

Mrs. Waldron's abrupt dismissal of her plans was both confusing and annoying. *How dare the woman,* she thought, *I will speak to Julian about it this very night.* Around her the twins and Mrs. Snell went back to their work, refusing to meet her gaze.

She had expected to help with the work, but Mrs. Snell shooed her from the room. Madelyn reluctantly left, retreating to her sitting room. She had a little time to herself before she dressed for dinner. Listening to the sound of the muted voices from the next room left her feeling homesick. She pulled back the drapes and took in her view.

From her window she could see the back gardens, with the stables on the far left, then the pasture and finally the moors beyond. The house sat on a rise, with a full panorama of the valley and dales beyond. With the spring rains the hills were covered in blooming heather. It was beautiful, but there was a stark loneliness to the scene.

It was difficult to conceive of this place as her new home. She could not imagine a time when she would take in this scene and feel the comfort of familiarity.

She pulled her chair next to the window and gazed far into the distance, imagining her home in London. At this time in the afternoon, she and her sisters would also have been in the sewing room; busy darning, ironing, or sewing. There would be constant chatter, some of it bickering as they went about their work. Her heart ached for those noisy afternoons.

Gradually her gaze focused on the corrals near the stables and the men who worked there. Even from this distance she could identify the figure of her husband, tall, with his broad strong back, and his easy movements.

She wondered if she would ever be able to penetrate the stiff distance he kept between them. Her girlish dreams of a future with a husband who cared for her, perhaps even loved her, were tattered and torn. The man she had wed took pains to avoid her. She was alone in a foreign land. Her view from the window underlined her isolation. Was it this loneliness which had affected poor Alice? Or was it the ancient curse dooming the marriage before it had really begun? Could she too be cursed?

Tears of self-pity began to gather in the corners of her eyes. She squeezed her eyes shut to hold them off. I am homesick, that is all, she assured herself.

Tonight, Julian would join her for dinner and then tomorrow they would spend time together riding. She was determined to charm him. The man was her husband. Outside of the servants, he was all she had in this isolated existence. Somehow, she would break down the barriers around him, and build the relationship she had always wanted in a marriage. And as to curses, let them entertain the folks of Yorkshire as they always had. Surely, they could have no effect on her.

CHAPTER 7

A SHARED KISS

Julian stood and gave a formal bow as she entered the dining room. He was dressed for dinner in a dark suit, his hair pulled back into a queue and tied with a ribbon. He looked very much the Lord of the manor, handsome and sophisticated. She had debated wearing one of the beautiful gowns from Lady Alice's trunk. But she could not bring herself to do it, not until the alterations had been made. Rather than trigger painful memories of his former wife she had chosen instead to wear her pale-yellow gown, the one she had worn to her last ball. It would have to do.

In the subdued light, with his scarred face and stoic expression he looked forbidding at the very least. To make matters worse, the place settings were at opposite ends of the long dining table. A tall candelabra stood at its center, reflecting an amber glow onto the dark polished wood of the table. Other than that, only two wall sconces lit the room. An unlit fireplace took up most of the wall to her right, and above it a huge painting of a knight seated on a rearing stallion did nothing to soften the atmosphere.

The other walls were covered with oak paneling, darkened with age, and swallowing the light. The one large window was heavily draped.

Ned and Julian's ancient valet stood in formal attire, prepared to serve the meal.

Madelyn took her place in silence.

Julian looked to his servants and announced, "You may begin."

However, Madelyn was not about to eat in the formal gloom. "No," she said. She felt her cheeks heat as three pairs of eyes turned to her. "Could we open the drapes? There is still light to be had this time of year." Ned and old Hadley looked at Julian as though waiting for his approval.

There was a moment's pause before Julian nodded his approval. She worried she had once again been too blunt; a character flaw her mother was forever trying to correct. But the pleasing color which permeated the room was well worth her effort. She glanced at Julian. His face had twisted into the now familiar half smile. She was tempted to gather up her place setting and move to a position beside him. But that was too much too soon, and she instead satisfied herself with the small change she had made. Patience and time, she repeated Hamish's words silently.

The meal was served in silence. Madelyn searched for a way to scale the barrier between them. She settled on the topic of the overgrown garden. "I found a lovely spot today, near the tower in the main garden. However, it is quite overgrown."

Julian looked her way at last. "The rose garden I assume?" His expression was forbidding.

Despite his dark look, she pressed on. "It is surrounded by a thick hedge and was quite hidden by the foliage. There is a lovely stone bench near the wall."

Julian nodded, his lips curling into a grimace. "That would be it. I haven't seen it since I returned." He lowered his eyebrows, as though willing her to close the conversation. The scars added to his ability to intimidate, with the ravaged side of his face twitching as if attempting to match its counterpart.

Madelyn again ignored his stern expression. She continued, "As I said it is overgrown. I know the gardeners are busy with the main yard, but I was wondering if I might hire some folks from the village to help me restore it?" Her question was met with grim silence. Julian concentrated on his dessert, refusing to meet her gaze. As the silence ticked by into a painful minute, she began to wonder if he was going to ignore her request completely.

Finally, she could endure it no longer. "It would be lovely...so protected and secluded there against the house," she added, hoping to convince him to approve the project.

He raised his head at last. There was no mistaking the expression of closed pain on his face. *The rose arbor must have been a place dear to Alice,* she thought. A spark of anger flushed her cheeks. She could not be expected to forever tiptoe around the ghost of his former wife. She was, after all, the new Lady of Montrose and this place was her home now.

"I love the hidden garden," she persisted, "I very much want to see it returned to its former beauty."

He sighed. "I will speak to the gardeners. Willy is the head man. You can share your plans with him. He will bring in help if he needs it."

"Thank you." She gave him her widest smile and received only a grunt as a response.

The room returned to its former silence.

After dinner they retired to the library. Julian had brandy, and she a glass of madeira. Madelyn held her glass with both hands, hesitating as she watched Julian take a chair by the fire. The thought of seating herself across from him and struggling to find a topic of conversation was too much to bear. It was with some relief that her eyes fell on the piano.

Setting her glass on an end table, she walked to the instrument and ran her hand delicately across the keys. "May I?"

"By all means." he answered, sounding relieved. It appeared he too was at a loss for words to share with his new bride.

One of her talents had always been the piano. She sat on the bench and examined the sheet music resting on the music desk—Bach. Beautiful, but she chose instead to play folk songs, the scores of which she knew by heart.

She began with, 'All in a Garden Green,' singing softly to the music. After a few minutes she sensed his presence beside her and looked up at him to smile a welcome. As she began, 'Early One morning,' she could hardly contain her joy when his soft baritone joined her. She kept her eyes on the keyboard, careful not to break the tentative connection they had made through the music.

For her next song, she boldly chose 'Clyde Water,' it was normally sung in a male/female duet. To her surprise he sang his role, this time with swagger, his voice a perfect complement to hers. When she played the final bars, she looked at him, unable to contain her elation in their perfect harmonies, and laughed. He laughed with her.

"Do you play?"

"I do. But unlike you, I need the music."

She slid over as he took a seat beside her. A familiar sensation of warmth and comfort permeated her consciousness. The physical contact relieved the awkwardness between them, and she allowed herself to relax.

The book of sheet music was opened to, 'Badinerie.' After running his fingers up and down the keyboard, he began to play. She watched his hands as they moved gracefully along the keys. She was able to catch the beat and the two of them played together. He continued to increase the tempo and she went with it, her fingers flying across the keys to keep up. Finally, he defeated her; she was unable to stay the course. She pulled back her hands and laughed. For the second time that evening he joined her, laughing at his victory as he played a few more bars.

"You play well," he said. He was amused, turning to her to share his half smile.

Again, she felt as if she had been given a gift. She had become accustomed to his ravaged face. It was a part of him and somehow made him even more appealing. "But not as well as you," she quipped, purposely remaining playful, not wanting to spoil his mood.

He slid a second book of music onto the music rack and began to play. Madelyn let herself lean against him. She could smell his tangy cologne combined with a touch of minty soap, and beneath it all his own rich scent; safe and manly.

THEY SPENT the evening together at the keyboard. After a while, her eyes began to droop, and she no longer tried to play. But she was loath to leave the closeness they shared. Soon, she was unable to suppress a yawn.

He finished his piece with a flourish, stood, and held out his hand. "It's time I took you up to bed."

She took his arm. Together they traversed the staircase and the long hall. This time the hall did not spook her as it had in the past. Her mind was focused on the feel of her husband's arm as he led her to her room. All the fatigue left her as she thought of the night to come. Would this be her wedding night?

Her mother had told her of the physical side of

marriage and what would be expected of her. At first, she had not believed such a thing was possible. In a household full of girls, there had been whispers of what transpired between lovers, but the information allowed to reach their virgin ears was sketchy at best. Her mother assured her that such relations expressed the love between a husband and wife. Still, she now felt her stomach twirl with apprehension.

At her door he turned to her, resting his hands on her shoulders. For a long moment he simply looked down at her. The lights were dim, highlighting the white jagged scars on his rugged face. But it was his eyes that held her attention and appeared to ask a question.

She leaned forward, not taking her gaze from his, willing him to kiss her. And he did. Very slowly, he leaned down and touched his lips to hers. She shivered with the contact, raising her arms to his broad back.

His lips were gentle, softly brushing against her lips. His touch brought a sizzle of tingling excitement. And then there was the nearness of him, the warmth of his hard body and his natural manly scent which drew her closer to him. She encircled his back with her arms and pressed against him, wanting more.

He deepened the kiss, and she gasped. His tongue pressed through her parted lips, shocking her with its intimacy as he explored her mouth. Her hands gripped his back as an unfamiliar headiness left her knees weak and her heart pounding in her chest.

She had been kissed before, stolen kisses, by tentative suitors, but nothing like this. Never had she felt this wild weakness, this insatiable need to pull a man close. Julian's hands were running the length of her back, and she tried to do the same, feeling his rippling strength beneath her fingers.

Then he slowly withdrew from her, and she opened her eyes, unaware she had closed them. Her breath came in short gasps as she forced herself to meet his gaze. His eyes were dark pools, hiding his emotions, but his lips betrayed him. They twisted into a half smile, as if he shared the same heady experience.

She leaned forward to kiss him once more, but he quickly stepped back, one hand firmly grasping her waist while the other opened the door to her room. "I think it best…we say goodnight," he said, his voice strangely hoarse. "Tomorrow, we will have our ride." He kissed her lightly on the lips, then nudged her gently into her room.

The door closed behind her. She leaned against it putting her hand to her lips. His touch held some sort of magic. Though she had limited experience, Madelyn knew the passion she had just experienced was uncommon. There was something between them; some powerful attraction that took away all of her reason. The idea was both exhilarating and frightening.

She prepared for bed, still shaken by her body's response to the man she called husband. Laying quietly in her bed, she listened to him moving about in his room. For a few minutes she thought he might come to her. Her heart pounded wildly in her chest as her imagination plagued her with thoughts of his strong hard body next to hers.

But the door to her room remained closed, a stark reminder of the wall between her and her husband. Tomorrow is another day, she thought, a day to build upon their relationship which had begun so tentatively this evening.

CHAPTER 8

A PORTRAIT OF A YOUNG MAN

Madelyn lifted her skirts and hustled down the stairs, determined to catch her husband at breakfast. Mrs. Waldron stood at the end of the hall, wearing her usual disapproving frown. Clearly the lady of the house was expected to be more decorous, moving gracefully about, and perhaps breakfasting in her room. She ignored the housekeeper's glower. This Lady Montrose would be joining her husband for the morning meal. She paused briefly outside the arched entry. Taking a deep breath she smoothed back her hair, pulling her heavy auburn braid forward onto her chest, before walking into the room, in what she hoped was a sedate manner.

Hamish and Julian looked up at her with identical expressions of surprise. "Good morning," she said, forcing a smile as they rose awkwardly to their feet. "Sit down, sit down. I hope I am not interrupting."

Without waiting for an answer, she took a dish from the sideboard and began to fill her plate. She could feel their eyes on her back as they muttered their response.

Julian sat at the head of the table with Hamish on his right. She took the chair across from Hamish who gave her a wide smile and a wink while she settled into her place.

Julian cleared his throat. "We generally discuss the business of the day at breakfast."

Madelyn waved away his words. "Don't let me stop you. I promise to sit quietly," she said, reaching for the jar of jam and applying it to her scone. "Perhaps I will learn a little more about my new home." She turned to Julian with a wide smile.

Julian shifted uncomfortably in his seat. Finally, he gave her a tentative half smile. Hamish chuckled. After a moment of awkward silence, Julian resumed their conversation. "As I was saying, the roan will need more time on the leading strap..."

The men soon relaxed into a conversation of horses, fields that would be seeded, and rental agreements. After several minutes Julian glanced uneasily in her direction. Her heart fluttered when his blue-gray eyes met hers. "I am afraid we have bored you with all this talk of business," he said.

She gave him a reassuring smile. "No. It is quite all right. Please do not feel you need to entertain me." He responded with his usual twisted smile, before turning back to Hamish.

She let the soft rhythm of Julian's voice wash over her as she concentrated on the busy day she had planned. It was enough to set a precedent; she intended to start each morning with Julian. Several times Julian looked uneasily in her direction, and each time Madelyn smiled in response. She interrupted their conversation only once to offer and serve them more tea from the carafe on the sideboard. By the time the men left to begin their work, Madelyn felt they had accepted her presence at the table.

Immediately after breakfast, she made her way to the rear of the main staircase and the heavy oaken door which Mrs. Waldron had deemed the entry to the housekeeper's suite. She took a deep breath before knocking.

Mrs. Waldron opened the door, stepping aside to reveal a small office area. An archway led further into what she assumed would be a sitting room and adjoining bedroom. There was a tall narrow bookcase to the left of the desk, sparsely decorated with various knick-knacks, including a collection of small porcelain angels. One shelf held a circular frame containing the portrait of a young man. Next to it several smaller frames were arranged. A vase of dried flowers graced the top of the shelf, its flowers faded with age. On the wall behind the desk a large painting of Montrose Manor dominated the small room.

Mrs. Waldron did not offer a tour of her suite, and Madelyn did not intend to request one. "Ah. Thank you for your promptness, Lady Montrose," she said, indicating a cushioned chair set before the wide desk, dark with age. "Please sit down. I have the menus for the week laid out for your approval."

Madelyn settled herself into the seat. She found it difficult to take her eyes off the painting. It showed the manor house, stark and barren against a stormy sky. Its gray walls with the original narrow windows looked forbidding and impenetrable. The manor's original role as a garrison, a stronghold for the armies of the past, could not be more evident.

Mrs. Waldron noticed her gaze. "It is a lovely painting. The former Lady Montrose removed it from the main hall. When I asked to hang it in my rooms, she had no objections," she said as explanation.

"It is...it certainly makes a statement," Madelyn answered.

Mrs. Waldron walked to her desk with crisp steps, leaving the door to the hall open, and took her seat, flipping open a ledger. "The daily meals," she announced. "I took the liberty of settling this week, but if you have suggestions, we can make alterations." This was said with such a forbidding frown, Madelyn decided that unless broiled eel was served daily, she was not likely to object. She nodded her agreement with each day's repast.

"Now then," Mrs. Waldron said, closing the ledger. "The next order of business for the week is to set a date for a dinner party. The neighbors, specifically the Stallridge family will be expecting an introduction and—"

A discreet knock sounded from the hall door. The cook stood at the entry, clutching her hands nervously. "I am sorry to interrupt ma'am. The tinner is in the kitchen. He wants his account settled and says he won't be waitin'."

"Harumph!" Mrs. Waldron snorted, rising from her desk. "Please excuse me, Lady Montrose. I will be just a minute."

Madelyn sat in front of the desk, trying to avoid staring at the bleak rendition of Montrose Manor directly in front of her. Her eyes wandered to the only other furniture in the room. The little porcelain angels looked so out of place lined up on the shelf.

In a moment of curiosity, she rose to examine them. Each little figurine was perfectly formed and delicately hand painted. Carefully picking up one of the ornaments, she turned it over to check its mark, New Hall porcelain. They were beautiful pieces, from an expensive maker. That the formidable Mrs. Waldron collected miniature angels, softened her view of the woman, and she smiled as she carefully returned the angel to its place.

The shelf above held the oval portraits. The subject of the little paintings was a male, starting with images of a small boy and progressing to the larger four by eight-inch oval of a young man. Something about the young man was familiar. Madelyn picked up the frame to examine it more closely.

"My son," Mrs. Waldron said from the doorway.

Madelyn flinched at the sound of her voice and

almost dropped the picture. Appalled to have been caught snooping, she froze, her cheeks red with embarrassment.

Mrs. Waldron walked to her and gently took the portrait from her hands, setting it carefully back in place. "This is Charles," she said. "I was married, then widowed young, just before I arrived at Montrose. It was all very difficult at the time, but I have my Charles to show for it."

"Oh—oh…I'm sorry. I had no idea," Madelyn stuttered.

"Yes. Well, few do know of him," she said softly, running a finger along the frame. "With my husband gone I was forced to take a position, and of course, there was no place for my son here. He stayed with my sister for a bit, then was away at school so it all worked out for the best. Charles is studying law at Cambridge and will soon approach the bar."

"You must be very proud of him," Madelyn said.

"I am," Mrs. Waldron replied, her firm voice back in place, as she returned to her desk. "Now then, shall we plan an evening of entertainment. A small guest list, I think. The Stallridge cousins will do for your first time entertaining. Your other neighbors are further afield, and we can plan a soiree at a later date to include them."

Madelyn allowed the housekeeper to make the plans without disagreement, thankful the woman had the arrangements well in hand. She could not help but be relieved when the meeting was completed. Finally, she could begin to concentrate on what interested her more, the hidden garden.

Madelyn met Willy, the head gardener, and several village men in the secluded garden to discuss the plans for its revitalization. Willy was a short man, and wiry from years of labor. They stood together by the alcove while three young men began to tackle the obvious chores—trimming the hedge and hacking down years of dead grass and weeds.

"Aye, well, the place was a rose garden…once," the elderly man was saying, "And it's surprised I am that you'll be wanting to restore it. I'd 'ave thought with the whole business, the Lord would just let 'er grow over."

"But it's beautiful…" Madelyn objected, "why would you think it should be left to ruin?"

Just then the wind caught the tops of the hedges and the strange hollow sound echoed through the garden. The men stood still at their tasks. A young man on top of a ladder cutting the outer hedge rotated to look at Willy with an expression akin to horror. His ladder wobbled with the abrupt movement. He was forced to pause in his work to steady himself.

Willy turned to her with a squinty expression on his weathered old face. He waited until the sound had faded away. "It's the god-awful wailing ma'am." He looked down and kicked a tuff of dried grass. She could hear him muttering, "Misery of…godforsaken ghosts...the likes of those poor women…" When he raised his head again his expression had contorted into a grimace. "Mayhap you should leave well enough alone Lady. This'll not ever be a place to sit and relax, what with that constant moaning."

Madelyn laughed. "But it is only the whistling of a vent of some sort."

"Aye, well, so you say. But we all call it the wailing wall. Some say it's the crying of the wives of Montrose. Don't know if I agree with that myself, but I'm not the kind to be playing with the other world, so to speak. The way I see it, those poor ladies should be left in peace. I said the same to the former Lady. She didn't listen and just look where it got her—here with all the others!" He squinted up at her again, this time with a hopeful expression. "Leave it be, I say."

"A vent Willy. That is all it is. The rest is all nonsense." Despite the certainty that she was correct about the air vent, she felt a shiver of dread, and gave a little laugh to dispel the knot in her stomach. A wailing wall indeed, she thought wryly, reminding herself that superstitions and wild tales died hard out here on the moors. "No, Willy. I want the garden restored. It will be a rose garden once more. And since you were here for the last construction, you already know the layout. We can go with the original plans."

The breeze picked up again, and as if in protest, the low whistle began once more. Willy winced in response. He gave her a final warning glare before he moved off to help the men with the work, his back stiff with indignation.

Madelyn sighed. There would be no convincing the man. Perhaps when the garden was beautiful once more, he would change his mind. Or maybe if she found the vent, she could prove to the fellow that the whole business was an architectural anomaly. She made a mental note to venture down into the cellars to find the source of the wailing. The position of the jutting tower wall on the side of the garden meant the vent was probably on the far wall of the armory in the cellars—either there or very near it. Thankfully, she would not have to travel far into the gloomy caverns to find it.

She could not help but be curious about the famed dungeons of Montrose. She supposed they had been a necessary feature, given the house's history as a military outpost. During the wars, the cells certainly would have housed political prisoners. And then, of course, there was the story of the immured Lady of Montrose. She shuddered at the memory of the tale.

Lady Alice had done much to lighten the mood of the ancient house with necessary renovations and updating décor. Though her death had only added more to the sinister legacy. Wouldn't it be wonderful to find the famed tomb to end once and for all the superstitions surrounding the wives of Montrose? If Lady Katherine and her fabled demise had actually occurred, she amended silently.

But there was no time to search for the vent or evidence of Lady Katherine's existence today. She would have to hurry back to the house, change for her riding lesson, and then head to the stable. A tremor of excitement rippled through her. To be able to ride once more was pure joy. She would certainly add this news in her letter to Beth.

Best of all, she would be with Julian. This was an ideal chance to charm her handsome husband.

CHAPTER 9

A GRAY HAZE ON THE HORIZON

Madelyn arrived at the stables just as Julian led two saddled horses out of the barn and looped their reins onto the hitching post. One was a huge black stallion, part Percheron, who snorted and pawed the ground impatiently. Beside the stallion was a roan mare, looking dwarfed next to the massive beast.

The stallion was beautiful, its inky coat catching the light as it arched its head in an imperious stance. Strong, and powerful like its master, she thought. How appropriate that Julian should have such a horse.

Madelyn could not resist teasing Julian. She gestured to the stallion. "You will have to get me a mounting block, he is a bit tall for me."

There was a moment where he believed her to be serious, and he looked at her, astonished, before he chuckled. "No, my dear. Pagan will take no rider but me." He led the mare to her. "Queeny, however, will be a fine horse for you. She is spirited, but gentle."

Julian began his lesson by using the leading reins to have her circle him in the corral. After only a few minutes he grinned at her. "You seat a horse well. I think we can safely move to the small pasture."

Madelyn could not resist a glowing smile in response to his praise. The second she had been hefted up into the saddle, all her riding skills had returned. She patted Queeny affectionately while she waited for Julian to mount his horse.

Once in the pasture, she was disappointed to note that Julian still held a leading rein. He glanced at her as they headed out and saw her disappointed frown.

"Better to be safe, my dear. I don't want you to take a tumble on our first day. Shall we try a trot?"

When Madelyn nodded, he urged the horses forward. After a turn around the small enclosure, Madelyn found her rhythm. They progressed into a slow canter. Two more rounds found them back at the corrals. Julian pulled up beside her and unhooked the lead. She was flushed with pride from her accomplishment. It had been such a long time since she had the privilege of riding, that she feared she may have forgotten how. But it had all come back to her.

"We will keep to the small pasture today. Tomorrow will be time enough to venture out, and try a gallop," he said, when he saw her look longingly at the gate.

Together they circled the pen in a slow canter. Occasionally she glanced across at Julian and they shared a smile. He watched her carefully, occasionally nodding at her progress. She was struck by her husband's quiet patience. He was a fine teacher.

After an hour they walked the horses to the stables. He slid down from his horse and helped her dismount, his hands resting on her waist once she reached the ground. "You did very well. You'll make a fine horsewoman."

His strong hands were warm on her waist. She remained still, not wanting to lose his touch. "Thank you. It was wonderful to ride once more."

He nodded, stepping away to take the horses by the bridle. "Now comes the most important part. You must look after your horse." He led the horses into the barn, with her keeping pace at his side. "We have many stable hands. But if you are to ride, then you must learn to care for your mount yourself."

Madelyn had never saddled or groomed a horse before. She watched carefully as Julian loosened the cinch on his horse, then followed the same procedure with Queeny. Finally, he lifted the saddle from his horse and slung it over the rail. She attempted to do the same, but the bloody thing was awkward. She gave it a hefty tug and found herself sprawled on her backside with the saddle atop her.

To make matters worse she had landed in a suspiciously soft mound. She looked sharply at Julian. If he dared to laugh at her she would be tempted to slug him.

He didn't laugh. Instead, he carefully lifted the

saddle from her, with one hand and offered the other to help her up. To her surprise, once she had dusted the debris from her behind, he held out the saddle.

"Hold it here," he said and gestured, "and just here. You won't need quite as much force that way." She lifted the saddle, surprised at how easily she was able to maneuver it to the railing. Next, he showed her how to rub the horse down and brush Queeny's glossy coat. When she was done, she led the horse into her stall.

Queeny immediately gave a series of snorts and nudged her shoulder.

Julian chuckled. "I believe she expects to be rewarded for her patience with a little oats, and I quite agree." He showed her where to find the oats in a stall at the rear of the barn. It had been converted into a storage room of sorts, with a mound of hay and several sturdy barrels of grain.

Madelyn stood back and watched Queeny enjoy her treat with some satisfaction, pleased that she had managed the whole business well. She glanced at Julian and smiled. "You are a fine instructor," she said, and meant it. He was a patient man, and a gentle one she added silently, watching him pat a farewell to his horse.

"And you have been a fine student," he answered.

She grinned at him, "We make a good pair then, you and I."

He suddenly became serious, the relaxed attitude of the lesson replaced with his more familiar stiff demeanor. She reached over and took his arm as they left the stables, ignoring his discomfort. "I cannot wait until tomorrow. In London I would often dream of galloping once again, and now it is a reality." She smiled and squeezed his arm. "Thank you for this Julian. But now I must go back to the house. I am scheduled for a fitting with the seamstress." She leaned forward, standing on her toes to kiss his ravaged cheek, before leaving him and heading to the house.

About halfway across the yard, she turned to look back. Julian still stood where she had left him, watching as she made her way across the yard. She smiled to herself, lifting her arm to wave. Last night at the piano and again today with the horses, she felt as though they had made progress in their relationship. She was beginning to know him. Whatever his reasons were for keeping a barrier between them, she was not going to allow it without a fight. And the more time she spent with him, the more she enjoyed his company.

The next week was spent in a whirlwind of activity. Each day she met Julian and Hamish in the breakfast room. Julian gradually became more comfortable with her presence. Determined to learn what she could about the estate, Madelyn listened attentively to the talk of its management, careful not to interrupt their business meetings. She began to feel as though she was learning about her new home and her role within it.

Mrs. Waldron had her going over the household accounts. The woman kept a meticulous ledger of all expenditures, and the responsibilities of staff members.

The housekeeper had a definite model of each person's duties in the house, including hers. Though she was still an intimidating figure, Madelyn was thankful for the direction. With Mrs. Waldron's assistance, she was beginning to grasp the workings of a household as large as Montrose Manor.

Then there were the constant fittings and designs for her new wardrobe. Making do with borrowed clothes would not do. Mrs. Snell had to hire an assistant to redesign the clothing in the chests and start putting together a wardrobe worthy of the Lady of Montrose. Materials were ordered, dress designs appraised and adjusted, and fittings were required.

What time was left of the morning she spent in the rose garden. Each day more of the space was recovered from the wild. Willy, the head gardener, had grudgingly accepted that the restoration was inevitable. Though he still winced each time the wind blew, he had begun to express some enthusiasm in the project. It was impossible not to enjoy its secluded beauty, and even Willy was not immune to its charms.

"At least it is the right time of year for a project," he admitted as they decided upon the plantings that would need to be done. "I'll be making a trip to York. Can't trust the boys to do the buying. Between the Lord's plans for the main yard, and now this, there's plenty to be done. And if it's to be kept up, there'll be another lad to hire, that's certain."

So, a trip to York was planned. Between the bolts of

cloth, the fripperies, and accessories needed for her wardrobe and now the new plants for the rose garden, Madelyn's list of items was long and expensive. Spending money did not come easily to her after years of frugal living. She had no idea what budget she had and dreaded Julian's reaction to the expenditure. She vowed to continue learning more about her home, its workings, and its income.

Julian quietly approved her purchases. If he found her extravagant, he did not say. They spent evenings together. Some nights they played the piano together, and she cherished those moments. There was an intimacy in sitting side by side and one of the few times he touched her.

Except when they rode. Each day she ventured out with him, exploring more of the land around her home. He was a quiet presence at her side. But he always helped her dismount. He would step in close to her, holding her firmly by the waist to help her down. At first, she thought it accidental that he pulled her body close enough to brush against him. To test her theory, yesterday she had purposely leaned into him as she dismounted, relishing the feel of his strong body against hers.

He held her against him for a moment when her feet touched the ground. She chanced a glance up at him to see that his eyes had widened with surprise. She gave him her cheekiest smile.

And he laughed. Giving her a quick peck on the

cheek he said, "You best get back to the house my dear or there will be little work accomplished by me this afternoon."

Each day she appreciated his gentle nature more. His love of the land and its livestock was evident in everything he did. Today they galloped far from the usual pastures. It was a clear spring day, with a breeze still holding the bite of recent winter.

He led them across the fields of fresh green grass, and up a rise to a knoll, where he reined in and stopped. Madelyn pulled up beside him.

The view from the rise was breath taking. The moors below were covered in purple heather, dotted with the dark shapes of grazing cattle, where the land was firm enough to hold them. Bluffs of trees stood out stark and freshly green. To the far right a small lake glittered blue and silver, its banks sheltered by dark woods.

For long minutes she took in the scene. From the rise, the horizon was a distant blue haze, and the rolling hills appeared to stretch out forever. Its stark beauty overwhelmed the senses.

She looked at Julian. He was a massive figure atop his black steed, standing out sharply against the backdrop of his land. His black cloak had been flung back, its dark navy lining a silken glow, rippling in the wind. He rested his gloved hands on the saddle horn holding the horse in check effortlessly. Black knee-high boots and leathered thighs completed the picture.

Julian's face was impassive; his scarred cheek facing

her as he surveyed his holding. Madelyn was once again reminded of the ancient warriors of times past. There was fierce pride in the man as he looked out over his estate. He was a product and a part of this stark wilderness.

Madelyn's heart beat a familiar tempo as she took in this vision of her husband. She was painfully aware of a consuming attraction. Even now her heart ached with an unquenchable longing. Hamish's assurance that all would be well with patience and time was wearing thin.

"While I was away, I often dreamt of this view," he said without turning to her. "Our land stretches as far as the eye can see. And beyond that, there are the dales, the land where we raise sheep. It is a full day's ride to reach the hunting lodge, from where we manage the outer regions." He took a long deep breath. "This is one of my favorite spots."

Madelyn's heart lurched. It was the first time he had confided in her his feelings. She was almost afraid to break the spell by answering him. "I can see why. It is stunning. I had no idea it could be so beautiful." She struggled to find the right words to aptly define the expanse before her. There was a barren loneliness to the moors—no comfortable quaint cottages or winding roads. "It is so free and uninhabited."

He turned to her and gave her a half smile. "Just there in the valley are the bogs. You must always avoid them. In some places a horse and rider can disappear beneath the peat, never to be found. Always, always, stay on the trails," he warned.

Then he was quiet for a moment, while he again surveyed the scene before he added, "There are those who find this land too vast…too isolated, but for me it is everything. It is my dream to keep it as it is." He frowned and turned his horse to the left, gesturing with his hand that she should maneuver her horse forward to join him.

"From this angle everything changes." He pointed to a cluster of houses in the distance. "The village of Redding is just there. To the right is the lake, with Old Bess' cabin hidden among the trees."

Madelyn interrupted, "Oh, I promised to visit Old Bess. Now that I am a more capable rider I must do so."

Julian nodded. "If you look closely, you can see the road you'll need to take."

Madelyn followed the line he pointed out, looking back at Montrose in the distance and tracing the route. "I think I could manage it." To her surprise, just to the east of the manor, in a bluff of trees she noticed the tower of another estate. "Who lives there, just across the way? I had no idea we had neighbors so close. It is certainly not visible from the manor."

"That is the Stallridge cousins, who I am sure you will meet soon enough. The house was once the dower house and sits less than a mile from Montrose. Henry Stallridge will return from London soon, having fetched his newly widowed sister Anne home. I expect he will be over in the next day or two."

Turning back to the view over the rise, she noticed what looked like a smudge of smoke in the distance, just east of Montrose lands. "Is that a fire Julian?" she asked, pointing to the gray haze.

Julian's lips thinned into a fine line. A dark scowl transformed his features, and even the scar on his cheek crumpled in distaste. "It is a coal mine. Henry is stripping the land bare to make his fortune. He wants to extend the business onto Montrose lands. It will never happen as long as I draw breath."

He looked at her, his eyes black and determined. "It's why I married you. I need an heir. The place is entailed. Should I die without offspring, male or female, Henry will have Montrose. And if I let that happen, the land as it is will be no more."

Without another word, he nudged his horse and turned back toward Montrose at a canter. It felt like a dismissal. Madelyn was left to follow behind, her thoughts in turmoil. His words hurt. Though she knew their marriage was arranged to produce an heir, to hear it so blatantly expressed in all its lackluster was a blow.

It tarnished all her pretty dreams of a true marriage; one she had hoped would be based on love and companionship. He wanted nothing from her. Only the heir to secure his true love—Montrose.

She could not stop her tears. They overflowed from her eyes, and were pushed, flat and cold, to her hairline by the wind. Once at the stables, she dismounted without waiting for his assistance. Her tears had dried, but her anger remained. She wordlessly completed her tasks.

Having fed Queeny her oats, she turned to him. "I shan't bother you to ride with me tomorrow. I will be visiting Old Bess on my own," she said, then moved abruptly to the door.

"Madelyn—"

But she didn't wait for his words. She rushed from the barn and, lifting her skirts, ran back to the house. All the way to the house she considered her position. Perhaps her best way forward was to give up on the marriage she wanted. She considered their evenings together the past week. Though he had not kissed her again, each time she touched him she'd felt a tingle of awareness. Surely, he too could feel the passion between them.

By the time she reached the patio doors to the library, she had begun to calm her inner ranting. Yet, it was as though everywhere she turned there were barriers to the life she had planned for her future, and the relationship with Julian. Starting with the legacy of Lady Alice. It was as though the woman still hovered over them, smothering any hope of the happiness she craved. There had to be a way to lift the shadow of her fateful death from this house.

Lady Alice had fulfilled the curse of Montrose. Perhaps she too was destined for an early death. Madelyn repressed a shudder. Nonsense and superstition, she reminded herself, this land of dark mystery was tainting her very thoughts.

Her blunt, practical nature had not served her well in the drawing rooms of London. But here in this land of ancient myths, it was those very qualities which she would rely on to lift the dark clouds which hung over this house.

CHAPTER 10

A VISIT TO THE TOWER

As she hurried up the stairs, she considered Lady Katherine from so long ago, cursing the wives who had dared to follow her. I doubt the woman existed, she thought to herself. It's my guess the thing that plagues this family is a streak of insensitivity running through the male line.

She stopped at the landing and looked at the rows of portraits in the hall. She had always hurried past them keeping her eyes lowered to avoid the disconcerting presence of their all-knowing eyes. The first picture was of a young woman dressed in a soft white gown and seated by a window of light. Her blonde hair was worn up, with curls escaping a braided coronet to frame her face. Everything about her was delicate; her features were perfectly symmetrical and even her fingers which held a piece of embroidery were slender and feminine. Her wide corn-flower blue eyes held within them a hint of sadness.

Madelyn was almost afraid to look at the name beneath it. She knew who it was. Her fingers touched the brass plate embedded in the frame. Lady Alice Montrose, with a time of death a decade past.

She stood for a moment taking in the vision of her predecessor. Had Lady Alice been a victim of the bloody curse? Lady Alice had been in Montrose only a year, yet she had left her mark on every piece of this ancient house. Even its Lord was forever changed by her short life.

There was a quietness about the likeness. Without having met her, she was sure she would be soft spoken and gentle. Again, she wondered what could possibly have driven her to the tower.

The husband Alice married would have been different than the one she'd left behind. Julian had been a young man, only twenty years old. It was almost painful to picture the man Alice had for a husband; so handsome and strong, with his gentle nature contrasting a strong physique. It would have been impossible not to love that man, she thought to herself. Even now, with his scarred body and mind, the man was hard not to love.

Alice was everything she was not. She imagined her as being correct in every way. The young lady her mother had always hoped Madelyn would be, an ideal she could never quite accomplish. Julian still suffered from her loss. It was her death which had driven him away from the land he loved to fight in the British army. Julian's scarred face was a direct outcome of her fatal decision. She should hate Alice for the choice she made.

But she did not. Instead, she felt a strange connection to the woman. She looked again into the blue depths that were Alice's eyes. The artist had captured a calm serenity about her. He had chosen to have her sit by a window of light. It was exactly the impression Madelyn had of Alice. She was a young woman who appeared to have delighted in light and beauty. The quiet joy she found in her surroundings was evident in the changes she had made in Montrose. The designs for the west wing, airy and bright with new wide windows and her suite, done in soft pastels, all indicated a woman who saw a future here for herself. Madelyn thought briefly of the cradle with its bedding so lovingly embroidered and closed her eyes to banish the thought.

It seemed impossible this woman chose to end her life. It made no sense.

She looked away from the picture and down the long hall which ended in the narrow servants' staircase; a staircase which would take her to the tower room. Alice must have accidentally fallen from the window. It was the only explanation.

She marched down the hall and without hesitation began to climb the narrow stairs. So intent was she on discovering the truth about Alice that she failed to notice a figure reach the landing behind her. She picked up her skirts, and hurried forward before she changed her mind.

The tower had been a defensive structure in bygone days. The steps were narrow and built of stone with thin shutters closing off the windows and shrouding the darkened landings at each floor. She quickened her pace.

Madelyn was breathless by the time she reached the top. On the final landing, she paused for only a moment, before purposely striding across the dark room to where a gap in the shutters let in a narrow band of light. She grasped the shutters and pulled them open, immediately filling the room with sunlight.

The entire space was constructed of stone—ceiling, floors, and walls. The windows were designed for archers of an earlier time, thin slits only a little over a foot wide with frames of thick stone. But for a few forgotten trunks littered in the corner of the room, it was an empty cube of solid rock.

There were two shuttered windows, identical to the one she had opened, on each wall. She examined the window in front of her. There was no glass, only shutters to block out the cold. Its base was at her chest. Her heart sank as she realized it would have been impossible for someone to accidentally fall. One would have to climb up onto the sill and purposely squirm through the foot deep stone gap to plunge to their death.

She leaned into the window, standing on her tip toes, and grabbed the exterior of the frame to pull herself forward. Only after edging herself ahead until her feet left the floor could she see below. The secret garden was directly beneath her. Far below, the men were busy digging up fresh beds for the roses which would soon arrive.

She knew with sickening certainty this was the fateful window Alice had forced her way through.

There was a noise behind her, a choking gasp. Before she could get her feet onto the floor and turn, she was yanked back and spun around. Julian glared at her; his expression dark with anger. The scars on his damaged face twitched menacingly. He pushed past her and slammed the shutters closed.

"Julian, I—" She was not able to finish her explanation. He picked her up, swung her effortlessly into his arms, and began an immediate descent down the stairs.

His arms held her in a fierce grip while he negotiated the stone steps at a dangerous pace. Afraid the two of them would tumble to their deaths, she put her arms around his neck and hung on tight.

Only when they reached the hall's safety did she loosen her hold and try to explain. "I was not trying to jump Julian." She arched back from his body and tried to meet his gaze. But he refused to look at her and tightened his grip. "I only wanted to see if it was possible to accidentally fall."

They reached the door to her room. He swung it open, strode in, and tossed her onto the bed.

He stared down at her, his eyes piercing her with fury. His strong hands were fisted at his sides. "You are never to go into the tower. Never. It is off limits to you. Is that understood?" His voice was dangerously soft.

Madelyn slowly rose from the bed, her face burning. She straightened her dress before looking up at him. Julian angry was a fearsome sight. He looked like the savage warrior from the portrait in the hall; dangerous and brutal.

Despite her trepidation she forced herself to stand tall and speak to him in a clear, firm voice. "I only wanted to be sure a person could not accidentally fall from the window," she repeated. "I had no intention of jumping, I assure you." She walked towards him and rested her hand on his arm. Looking directly into his eyes, she added, "And I never will."

Her words calmed him; his eyes no longer blazed. He put his arms around her, pulling her tight to his chest. She could feel his body tremble slightly, his muscles contracting as he squeezed her hard against him. For long minutes, the two of them stood silently together. Madelyn rested her head on his shoulder, running her hands up and down his back until the rigid stiffness left his body.

She realized she must have given him a fright. Finding his second wife squeezing through the very window from which Alice had leapt to her death would have been a terrible shock.

"How did you know I had gone up to the tower?" she asked, without lifting her head from his shoulder.

"I followed you back to the house. I wanted to apologize for offending you. It was thoughtless...what I said to you on the height of the land. I meant only to explain my love of the land and did not intend to comment on our marriage agreement."

She smiled against his shoulder before raising her head to meet his eyes. *Not completely insensitive,* she thought to herself, *there is hope for us yet.* "Thank you for that," she answered.

He looked down at her. "I do want you for my wife," he said. Madelyn found herself mesmerized by the dark pools of his eyes. Lowering her gaze to his lips, she leaned into him, wanting him to kiss her.

And he did. The first gentle touch of his lips to hers brought the familiar shiver of excitement. For a few seconds he kissed her softly, tentatively. But then it was as though a flood gate opened. His arms tightened around her, and he became fierce once more. His hand gripped the back of her head, and she opened her mouth to him.

She could only hold on to him as he ravaged her mouth. Her knees became weak with a dizzying sensation. She clung to him, willing him not to stop. She took a step back, shifting to brace herself against the wall.

Julian groaned. His mouth left hers and trailed to her neck. She could feel his warm breath as he hungrily nuzzled her, his mouth wet and hot. His body was pressed hard against her, his hips pushing against her rhythmically, and she could feel his swollen manhood on her belly. She vaguely registered the sound of her bodice tearing as he tugged at the shoulders of her gown. She wiggled her arms out of her sleeves, not wanting to lose his touch, even for a moment.

She gasped when his hands found her breasts. He

kissed her mouth once more, his body still pressing against her. She was lost, clinging desperately to him, and wanting more, but not sure what it was she so needed.

A sudden loud crash was followed by a shrill squeal. Julian jerked back from her. He turned, then spun around to shield her with his body.

"Oh dear, I am so sorry. So sorry."

Madelyn peeked around Julian's shoulder to see the young maid crouched on the floor. She was picking up the pieces of a broken tea pot from the floor, amongst a puddle of tea, cream, and sodden biscuits. A cup, miraculously unbroken, was spinning at her feet.

Madelyn quickly slid her arms into the sleeves of her gown and attempted to close the bodice. A rip from the shoulder to the breast had the front of the dress gaping wide. She clutched the pieces of cloth together with her hand.

Julian turned and looked into her eyes, then his glance trailed to her hand where it held the front of her dress together. His eyes filled with aching regret. He touched the hand clasping the dress and leaned close to her ear. "Forgive me," he whispered, then strode abruptly from the room.

Madelyn tilted her head back, resting it against the wall for a second and closed her eyes. She took several calming breaths to still her beating heart before she reopened them.

One of the twins was on her hands and knees, busily trying to clear away the mess. "I am so sorry.

Heavens! I had no idea the Lord was visiting your rooms. I thought to bring your tea. After riding you always take tea in your room. I—I thought to—"

"It is all right Annmarie," she said, interrupting the poor girl's prattling. Reaching down, she picked up the surviving cup and added it to the tray of broken porcelain with fingers that still trembled slightly.

"It's Annmargaret ma'am. Please let me get this. I will have it all cleaned up and fetch you a new tray."

Madelyn left her to it and stepped into her dressing room to stand in front of the full-length mirror. Her hand still clutched the pieces of her torn dress together. Her face and neck were flushed, grazed by the rough stubble of Julian's jaw. Her eyes were wide and dark as they scanned her person.

Passion, she thought to herself. This is the feeling whispered about by her and her friends behind gloved hands. And she knew so little about it. She only knew she wanted Julian.

Madelyn slowly removed the torn gown. Her body was alive; her skin prickled with awareness at every touch, every rub of material as she pulled the ripped gown down and stepped out of it. Looking into the mirror once more, she tried to define the strange new feelings, but she could not. She knew only that they were both exhilarating and torturous, if such a thing could be possible. She knew too that Julian had the same desperate desire.

Julian, however, appeared determined to erect a wall between them. She had only begun to understand the traumas of his past. But that was the past. She wanted to be his future. The damage done to his heart was an enemy she would defeat. This passion they shared might be the bridge between them. *Tonight, I will have my wedding night,* she vowed. If Julian did not come to her, she would go to him.

CHAPTER 11

A STRATEGIC RETREAT

The wind bit into his face as he galloped past the rise and into the valley below. It would be hours before they reached the high country and his hunting lodge on the outer perimeter of his estate. Hamish rode silently at his side. Hamish had reacted to the sudden change of plans and the immediate trip to the nether regions without comment. He had only raised his eyebrows and said, "Aye, then I'll be packed and ready within the hour."

"Make it a half hour," Julian had replied. Yet even with the quick departure, they would have to keep a steady pace to reach the manor house out on the dales before nightfall. They had galloped past the rise, and now were forced to take a slower gait to keep the horses from being winded.

His thoughts returned to his new wife and the disastrous events of the afternoon. Madelyn would be sitting down to dinner about now. He imagined her surprise and disappointment when she realized he was gone. But it could not be helped. He had been forced to make a strategic retreat.

His plan with his new wife had been to move slowly. He had no intention of leading their relationship into the abyss of the last one. He would not make the same mistakes. Alice had been forced into the role of wife and expectant mother too soon, with disastrous results. He had been too young to understand or even see the challenges she faced.

Alice had been a lady in every conceivable way. Her interests revolved around homemaking, with pursuits appropriate for a woman of her class. When the image of her came to mind, it was always one where she sat in quiet repose; painting, sewing, or designing new plans in her sketchbook for the east wing. She seemed to blend softly into the background of Montrose, unobtrusively going about the business of managing the house.

He always knew the physical part of their relationship had been a chore for her. He winced when he remembered how he had been with her; too young and lustful to consider her delicate nature. He was convinced it was entirely his actions, and the too-soon pregnancy, which had driven her to the tower on that fateful day.

This time he was determined to avoid those mistakes. He had laid out his plan like a battle with a precise timetable. For the first three months he and his new wife were to become acquainted. He would develop a friendly relationship with her, not letting his heart be engaged. Only after that would he introduce her to the responsibilities of the bed chamber. And even then, he would be careful not to impregnate her until after the first year.

Everything should have proceeded according to his strategy. But Madelyn was not behaving in the way he had anticipated, not at all. She undermined his battle plan at every turn. First, she was not the reticent creature Alice had been. Madelyn did not blend into the background. She was everywhere, involved in all aspects of life on the estate. From breakfast to evenings in the parlor, she invaded his space at every turn. Breakfast, a time he and Hamish spent planning the day, found her there, avidly listening, and occasionally asking questions. Then there were the daily rides and evenings together.

Madelyn laughed easily, and loudly. She seemed to share with him a love for the moors. He pictured for a moment her face as they rode to the rise, her cheeks rosy from the cool air and her eyes so alive with excitement. Alice had hated the moors, and mourned the loss of society, sometimes even being tearfully homesick for the busy world of the city. Whereas Madelyn had embraced life at Montrose. He had been afraid of what Madelyn's reaction to the estate would be, living so far away from all she knew. Her easy adjustment had been a relief.

The worst part of the whole experience was that he wanted her with him. Each day he waited to see her face in the morning, anxious she might not make it down for breakfast. And he was always sure to be working near the stables after lunch, eager to go with her on their daily ride. He knew she could ride on her own now, but didn't want to give up precious time together.

Evenings were the most trying. After a day spent in her presence, he ached with wanting her. Sitting beside her on the piano bench was both a joy and a form of torture. He closed his eyes and breathed deeply. Even now he could smell the clear fresh scent of her and feel the touch of her body against his. Each night he battled to hold himself back from bursting into her room.

And all of that had culminated in the scene in her bed chamber this afternoon. He grimaced when he remembered her wide-eyed expression as she held the pieces of her torn gown together. He had done exactly what he had been determined to avoid. He had been a brute.

It was the scene in the tower which had led to him losing his usual restraint. Seeing Madelyn wedged into the window frame as though ready to jump to her death had shaken him. For a moment it had been as though the whole nightmare with Alice was being replayed. It was his darkest fear.

All his efforts to keep Madelyn on the perimeter of his life and to keep himself from once again being vulnerable to the horrible agony of loss, had failed. He could not lose her now. Somehow, in these few short weeks, she had wriggled her way into the shadowed corners of his reality.

He groaned aloud.

"Is it as bad as that?" Hamish asked.

Julian slowed the pace to a walk. The trail here began a long slow climb through a wooded section, with room for two horses abreast, or a single coach, as it meandered through the thick forest. Once they reached the crest of the hill the trees would give way to rocky formations, jutting from the earth to display their thick dark veins of black coal. It was this very hill which his cousin Henry was convinced held a fortune beneath its foliage and if he had his way this rise would be stripped and mined.

He patted his horse, Pagan, and turned to Hamish. "If not for the entailment on the estate I wouldn't have taken a wife. I should never have subjected a woman to this lonely place or to me."

"Aye well, you have. And it seems to me the woman is adjusting fine to the moors, and to your wicked self." Hamish answered, softening his words with a little chuckle.

There was silence for several minutes as they crested the hill and began the trek down its bald rocky backside. Hamish cleared his throat and continued as though the long gap in their conversation had not occurred. "It seems to me you have this woman mixed up with someone else. And we both know who I am speaking about. You never want the name mentioned, and up until now I have respected your wishes."

Julian grunted. "Does this mean you'll not be respecting my wishes now?"

"Aye it does. Lady Alice made her choice, and though I don't for the life of me understand her reasons, I say it is time you left her in peace. This new wife of yours is not the quiet little lass who came here a decade ago. She is a woman. And from what I have seen, she is not a delicate Miss who needs to be wrapped in sheep's wool to survive."

"Hmm. You have had your say then?" Julian asked. He was not surprised to hear Hamish voice his opinion on the matter. It was not in his nature to let matters rest. What surprised him was he did not experience the familiar gut-wrenching nausea at the mention of Alice's name.

"I have," Hamish replied, "And you'd do well to mind it."

"Hmm," Julian responded. They had reached the flats. He urged his horse to a canter and Hamish followed suit. The conversation was over, but the topic still swirled around in his mind.

Madelyn was indeed not at all like his first wife. He pictured Lady Alice now, still surprised that the image brought no pain. Alice had had an ethereal quality about her. She was quiet, going about her day with a gentle lassitude. He tried to remember a time when she had ventured out to the stables, or ridden with him, but he could not. When Lady Alice had left the house, she could be found in the secluded garden, sketching, or planning her renovations for the interior, her domain.

When he tried to compare this image with Madelyn, he concluded that Hamish was right. Madelyn was an entirely different character. His new wife had invaded every corner of his consciousness, despite his best efforts to keep her at bay. She was an unusual woman. He reached up and touched his gloved hand to his ravaged cheek. It was strange that not once had he seen the usual repulsion in her eyes—not even on the occasion of their introduction.

He shook his head to banish her image and forced his mind to focus on the task ahead of him. The far reaches of his estate, where the rocky dales provided pasture for his sheep would be the focus for the next few days. He would leave the unsettling business of wives and emotions behind. And when he returned, he would go back to his original plan of attack for this marriage—if the woman allowed him.

CHAPTER 12

A VISIT WITH OLD BESS

Morning came with the same empty disappointment of last night. She had asked Annmarie to bring a tray, seeing no purpose in spending another meal alone at a table. Julian had left her with only a brief note, informing her that he would be away for the next several days.

She sighed. There was no point in mulling over his motivations for leaving so abruptly or mourning his absence—she had done enough of that last night. Instead, she made a mental list of what she could accomplish while Julian was away. There was plenty to do, beginning with her promised visit to Old Bess.

After meeting with Mrs. Snell and adjusting several pieces of her new wardrobe, she went to the kitchen to collect the baked goods she had requested as a gift for Old Bess.

Once astride Queeny, all her despondency melted

away. The morning was crisp, but the skies were clear, and the winds were still. She took a deep breath of the clean fresh air as she veered her horse to the left onto the road. It circumvented the village and the lake, heading toward the cottage Julian had pointed out from the rise.

Just past the rise, trees lined the lane. Beyond their thin blind, freshly planted patchworks of fields and meadows could be glimpsed, with cows grazing as the new calves romped. Here the boggy land of the moors had retreated, allowing fields of arable soil for the small farms.

Beyond the village, the trail narrowed and meandered through a stand of mature pines. Occasionally to the left, she caught sight of the glittering surface of the lake. Old Bess' cottage came into view as the lane opened into a clearing. A freshly planted garden plot was sheltered at the rear of the property by fruit trees in full bloom filling the air with their sweet scent. There were several outbuildings tucked against the forest, fenced and housing chickens and pigs. A cow, heavily pregnant, grazed on a strip of grass to the far right, behind a rickety log fence.

Near the house, two old wooden chairs and a short tea table sat amongst bright orange poppies and dark purple pansies which had forced their way through cracks in a rough rock patio of sorts. The cottage itself was smothered in tall lilacs, also in full bloom.

Madelyn slid from her horse and led Queeny to the

garden gate where she looped the reins around its corner post, smiling as she took in the pastoral sight. The homely atmosphere suited the kind woman she had met in the coach.

Before she could make it to the front door to knock, it burst open. "There you are at last. I've been wondering how you settled in," Old Bess said, giving her a welcoming grin from the doorway. "By the look of you, you've done fine deary."

"I have. Bess, I brought you a lemon cake. Cook said it is your favorite." Madelyn handed her the tin she had been given in the manor's kitchen.

"Oh aye, and so it is. It'll be perfect with a cup of tea." Old Bess took the cake, her startling blue eyes shining. "Come in, come in. I've just made a pot. We'll have some tea with this lovely cake." She gave her a wide smile. "It's good to see you looking so fit. Are you liking it here in the wilds then?"

"I am. I already love this open land," she said, stepping inside. It took a moment for Madelyn's eyes to adjust to the dim light in the cottage, after the bright sunlight of the spring morning. Thus, her first impressions were of scent. The air was saturated with both spicy and floral aromas, so thick it almost overwhelmed her. As her eyes focused, she saw the reason. Hanging in clusters from the open-beamed ceiling were plants of assorted varieties—drying. A long wooden table was braced against the wall near the fireplace, its top littered with jars of dried herbs. A bowl and pestle sat on its surface, with a few bunches of dried herbs lying next to it.

Old Bess chatted happily as she prepared the tea. “It warms my heart to hear that. I’d a feeling you would be good for this place, and it for you. And as I said before, I’m seldom wrong.” She laughed a little, then indicated the scattered herbs on her worktable. “I’ve been making a tonic for Mauve in the village. She can’t seem to shake a congestion of the lungs,” she said as she filled a teapot. “’Twas a bad winter for the woman and I hoped with spring she’d clear up. But sadly no.” She reached up and took down two matching teacups from the cupboard next to the stove, handing them to Madelyn with careful reverence. “We’ll take our tea outside. It’s a lovely day to enjoy a little sun.”

Madelyn took the cups from her hand and followed the older woman through the doors to the furniture clustered on the leveled stone in front of the house. They each took a seat in the wooden chairs. Old Bess poured the tea and served each of them a slice of lemon cake.

“What a lovely tea set," Madelyn commented.

Old Bess smiled, pleased with her compliment. “’Twas a gift from the Lord’s mother, Lady Abigale Montrose. It’s my most prized possession. She and I became fine friends.” Bess sighed. “Such a sad case. Got a lung infection, she did. The weather here didn’t help with the illness. Poor woman wasn’t long for this world.”

"Another unhappy wife of Montrose," Madelyn muttered, taking a sip of her tea.

"Oh no," Old Bess interjected, "Lady Abigale wasn't an unhappy woman. Quite the opposite. Right 'til the end she was a loving and giving soul. Everyone loved the woman." Old Bess shook her head, lost for a moment in her memories. "When she married the Lord, he was much older, and not long for this world himself. Lady Abigale managed the place and raised young Julian on her own. It was not unusual to see her riding about, looking after the estate. A strong fine woman, until she got caught in a winter storm and took sick."

"Was Lady Alice here at that time?"

"Aye, she was. 'Twas just before the wedding. Lady Abigale had arranged the match you see. When she became ill, she was adamant about the couple keeping to the date, wanting no delays for a period of mourning. I always wondered if perhaps they should have waited, but they kept their promise to her."

Old Bess paused to eat her lemon cake. The ladies were quiet for a moment while they enjoyed the treat. A bee buzzed around Madelyn, and she brushed it away. The spring sun was pleasantly warm, and the air sweetly perfumed in their sheltered spot in front of the cottage. She glanced down at the rocky patio floor, where a purple pansy had pushed through a space between the flat stones, its face smiling up at her.

Madelyn was desperate to have Old Bess tell her more about her predecessor. To understand Julian, she needed to know more about the disaster of his first marriage. She had decided to trust Old Bess with her concerns about her marriage and simply ask.

When she raised her head, Old Bess was watching her with interest. "I want to know more about Lady Alice," Madelyn said. Though she was uncomfortable with sharing the private challenges in her marriage, Old Bess was the only avenue by which she could find the answers to her many questions. "Lady Alice seems to..." she paused unable to find the right words. Her cheeks burned with frustration.

Old Bess set down her teacup and leaned forward patting her hand. "I understand. 'Twas a trying time, one that still haunts the folks up at the big house, I'm sure. However, I'll tell you what I can." The older woman was thoughtful for a moment. "…Best to begin at the beginning I always say." She took another sip of tea, then set the cup down carefully, and looked out toward the garden as though gazing into the past.

"As I said, Lady Abigale arranged the marriage. She wanted a young woman for Julian who could bring both a substantial dowry for Montrose and please her son. At the time Henry, the Stallridge cousin, was pushing for a marriage between Julian and Anne to unite the estates. But Lady Abigale would have none of it. Anne was at least a decade older, not the handsomest woman, and painfully shy. She didn't think the two would suit.

"Lady Abigale journeyed to London, intent on finding the perfect bride. An arrangement was made with Lady Alice's father, a wealthy merchant, and Lady Alice was brought to Montrose. The couple decided to honor the arrangement and the wedding was planned. Then sadly, Abigale took sick after being caught in that storm. It was a grim time for all of them at the house. But as I said, Lady Abigale on her death bed, had them promise not to delay the wedding. It was always my belief she feared Henry's interference..."

Old Bess paused to top up her tea, then looked to Madelyn to see if she wanted more. Madelyn nodded, not wanting to interrupt her tale. The older woman chuckled and continued, "And indeed Henry Stallridge was furious. It was the best part for me, I'll admit. I do not like the man." Old Bess sobered and sighed. "The young people married. Poor Anne was sent off to marry an old fellow on the coast. And perhaps Lady Abigale was wrong, the way things turned out. But who was to know at the time?"

Old Bess took a sip of tea and set her cup on its saucer with exaggerated care. She released a long sigh. "As I said, the couple went ahead with the wedding, but it was a sad start to the marriage, what with the death of Abigale and all. Yet things seemed to go well at first. In fact, I thought it was a fine match. I don't know what happened up there to make the young woman so unhappy." She shook her head, meeting Madelyn's eyes with a puzzled expression. "I'd visited with Lady Alice in the days before her death. She came here for a tonic. She was very excited and pleased. She told me about—" Old Bess stopped abruptly.

Madelyn's stomach twisted. "The baby?" she asked, feeling heartsick. So, her suspicions had been correct.

Old Bess nodded sadly. "The whole thing made no sense. For a while I was sure it was an accident, but Florence…Mrs. Waldron, assured me it could not have been." Bess shook her head once more and made a tut-tutting sound. "'Twas true that Lady Alice was home-sick. She detested the isolation of Montrose. She missed London society, and then of course, there were few women here for her to mix with."

There was a long silence, punctuated only by the sound of the bees busy at work on the lilac blooms against the cottage.

Madelyn tried to envision the reaction of Julian, still touched by the loss of his mother. "And Julian," she said, "must have been devastated. He left to join the British forces shortly after."

Bess leaned back in her chair, with a long sigh. "'Twas a terrible time. The young Lord was incon-solable. He was gone before the month was out. Hamish managed the estate, and Mrs. Waldron went ahead with the house's renovations—no surprise there. That Florence has always been so wrapped up in the place. They redid much of the house from what I hear. Always waiting for the young master to come home, but it would take almost a decade before he returned."

"Did no one hear from Julian for all those years?"

"Oh no. The Lord kept in contact with Hamish, helping to manage the place from afar. Lord Montrose has always loved his lands."

"It is true he loves the land," Madelyn agreed.

Old Bess scowled. "Then there came a time when no one heard from the Lord. Hamish received word from his commander that Lord Montrose had been injured. Henry Stallridge was sure Julian had perished from his wounds and tried to take over the place, even planned to move in. I believe it was that which brought the Lord home at last. The young Lord had barely unpacked his cases before going off to London to fetch a bride. And here you are." Old Bess smiled at her as though attempting to end the sad story on a positive note.

Madelyn took a sip of tea, contemplating what she had learned. She thought of her predecessor, so alone here. Maybe it was the isolation which had driven young Alice to the window that fateful day. But then she remembered the blanket, so lovingly embroidered. She closed her eyes and forced the image away. It was a painful tale even now.

Madelyn considered the other details of the story. "Why do you hate Henry Stallridge so much?" she asked.

Old Bess thought for a moment. "I don't hate the man, but I do dislike him. Henry is very much the Lord at Stallridge. He was married at one time you know. But his poor wife was sickly. After a decade of failed attempts to give the man an heir, she finally perished from her efforts. I can't quite forgive the man for it." The older woman looked down at her teacup, turning it slowly between her clasped hands, lost in her memories for a moment. Old Bess was a midwife and Madelyn was certain she would have made every effort to nurse the woman back to health. But difficulties with bearing children were often fatal for women.

She continued, "And then he controls his siblings with an iron hand. Poor Anne was always much put upon. The only one to escape Henry's machinations seems to be the youngest, Edwyn. That boy is a wild one. Even Henry is unable to rein the lad in. But he spends most of his time in London these days." She took another sip of tea, and continued dryly, "Though I am sure the rascal is still getting into scrapes in town."

Old Bess sighed and set down her cup. "But back to Henry. The man is obsessed with the Montrose lands. It all started with Lady Abigale. He pursued her relentlessly after the death of the old Lord. He didn't have much luck. Lady Abigale had her heir; Julian was ten at the time. She didn't want a husband and was determined to manage the place alone. Henry was quite put out."

She chuckled. "But I suppose it started even before that. Henry's father and Julian's were twins you see; not identical, but born only minutes apart. Julian's father inherited Montrose and Henry's dad got the dower house and a piece of land to set up a lesser estate. For a time, Henry was the heir to both, being the oldest of that clan and with the Lord here so late to marry. Henry was fifteen before Julian was born. I think it went to his head."

"I don't suppose he was happy with the birth of Julian then?"

Old Bess laughed. "That he was not."

The sun went behind a cloud, leaving a sudden chill. "Thank you for sharing all this with me Bess. It helps to have a better understanding." Madelyn set down her cup and rose. It was time for her to return to the manor.

Old Bess stood with her. "All of it is passed. Take my advice and don't linger much on these things. It's a new time now, and for certain a change is needed up there at the house." She glanced back at her cottage door. "Will you be going by the village? I have a packet of herbs for Mauve. I wonder if you could drop them by. It'll save the poor woman a trip out to get them. She'll be found behind the counter at the village shop."

"Certainly."

"I'll just grab them. I won't be a minute." Old Bess said and hurried inside.

Madelyn unfettered Queeny and brought her around to the door. Old Bess handed her a small leather pouch and helped her mount. "I'm pleased you came today. You must come again deary. And be sure to tell Cook I much enjoyed the cake."

"I will," she said, "and thank you for tea. I promise to return soon."

Madelyn walked her horse beneath the pines on a slow trek to the village while she considered all she had learned. She had suspected Lady Alice was pregnant at the time of her death. Now, she was sure. The knowledge left her feeling ill and confused.

It was ghostly quiet. Even the sounds of Queeny's hooves were muffled, cushioned by an accumulation of pine needles over many years. The sun filtered through the upper boughs of the trees in random beams, casting Madelyn in light, then shadow, with a hypnotic effect.

The forest around her blurred, fading as she pictured the image of the young woman in the portrait, lovely and serene. Lady Alice was bent over her sewing. And then the strangest thing happened. The vision of Lady Alice lifted her blonde head, piercing Madelyn with her cornflower blue eyes. A nauseating horror washed over her as the woman's lips moved, pronouncing the word 'never' in a soft whisper.

Queeny shied, neighing, while bucking a staccato of side steps, then rearing into the air. Madelyn was initially taken by surprise, almost sliding from her saddle; only just managing to take a firm grip on the reins before the horse burst into a gallop. They were almost at the village before she was able to calm the beast. And still the horse fidgeted, with its ears pressed back and its head held high.

Madelyn patted the horse's neck, as they left the pine forest behind them. "Easy, girl. Whatever spooked you, Queeny, is long gone," she murmured, gentling her until the rooftops of the village were visible through the trees. She forced aside her thoughts of the vision, assuring herself it had been only a passing fancy; an illusion brought on by all the talk of Lady Alice and her sad fate.

After rounding a copse of trees, the village came into full view. The trail evolved into a cobbled street. It was not straight, but wound through the row of houses and up a rise. At the end of the lane at the highest point a steeple rose above the town, dominating the skyline.

Madelyn walked her horse slowly past a blacksmith shop; its wide doors open and the sound of metal clanging against metal indicating someone was busy at the forge. Next was a bake shop, filling the air with the smell of fresh baked bread, and alongside it a small shop that declared itself to be a lawyer's office, a printer, a telegraph depot, and a newspaper.

After passing several more cottages, and a leather works, she found the general store. Out front a cluster of elderly men sat on the benches near the door, enjoying the spring sun. She slid off Queeny and wrapped her reins around a hitching post, conscious of half a dozen eyes looking at her suspiciously. Pulling the small leather sack containing the herbs from her pocket, she glanced up in time to see the old fellow on the far left crossing himself, as though she was an apparition. Her cheeks burned as she hurried into the shop.

Directly in front of her was a long wooden counter, where an elderly woman was serving a lady dressed in all black. A lad stood behind the woman ready to gather whatever purchases she made. The woman turned and looked at her as she approached.

She was tall and angular, with a long sad face partially covered by a black lace veil, attached to a matching plain bonnet. She stood slightly stooped, as if to deny her height. Madelyn estimated her age to be about forty years, with wrinkles around her eyes and a down-turned mouth suggesting that not all of those years had been happy ones. Her clothing, and the presence of a footman meant she could only be Anne Stallridge.

Madelyn decided to introduce herself. "Good day. You must be Lady Anne, who I have heard so much about. I am Madelyn Stallridge, the new Lady Montrose."

"Yes," the woman answered in a soft voice, hunching even further, while dropping into a sort of half curtsy. Anne was very tall for a woman, and thin. There was a gangly awkwardness about her. Her face began to color, and Madelyn remembered Old Bess' description of Anne as a painfully shy woman.

She gave her a bright smile, extending her hand. "I am so pleased to meet you. We are neighbors, I believe. I hear you have just returned to Stallridge House." The woman's hand felt cool and boney in hers before she quickly pulled it away.

"Yes." Lady Anne bobbed her head. "Henry fetched me. I arrived home only yesterday."

"I am glad to have a neighbor. I do so hope we can be friends. Mrs. Waldron and I have sent an invitation to your household for a dinner party. I hope you will come?" Madelyn asked.

"I am sure Henry will accept. He is eager to meet you." She smiled at Madelyn; a smile which softened her sharp features, making her face almost pretty.

Madelyn found herself eager for female company. "But perhaps you could come for a cup of tea and a little visit before then? Lord Montrose is away just now, and I would so love the company."

"I would like that," said Anne.

The woman behind the counter had finished wrapping her parcel, and Lady Anne slid it to the lad at her side. She nodded at Madelyn, before moving to the door in long manly strides. Madelyn watched her leave. She was not a handsome woman, as Old Bess had implied, but she appeared pleasant enough, if a little awkward and shy.

When the door closed, Madelyn stepped forward to the counter. "And you must be Mauve," she said, handing her the little leather bag. "Old Bess asked me to drop off these herbs."

"Oh aye. So, you are the new lady up at the house," she said, tilting her head, to eye her critically. "And how are you settlin' in? Homesick and heartsick I reckon in that godforsaken place." She looked at Madelyn with an almost hopeful expression.

"No, actually. I quite love it here." Madelyn gave her a wide smile. "You live in a beautiful land."

"Hmm," the woman snorted, then mumbled, in a voice not intended for Madelyn to hear, "...we'll see how long that lasts." But Madelyn had heard it, and she looked back at the woman sharply.

Mauve tilted her head to the side once more and gave Madelyn a sly look. "I can't imagine the place holds much interest for a city girl such as yourself." Her gaze took in Madelyn's new boots and the green riding habit, with its silken lapels and trim. She looked smugly satisfied with what she saw. "It's not been the best of times for the ladies of Montrose, ye kin." She leaned forward, looking as if she was eager to share a few tidbits with her.

Madelyn did not give her the opportunity. "Old Bess sends her regards and hopes you feel better soon. I best be off."

Once outside, she deftly mounted her horse, then turned to the old fellows who watched her curiously from their bench. "Good day to you gentleman," she called, nodding purposely in their direction.

She received a chorus of responses, "Oh aye, good day, my lady, ma'am," and a series of half bows. Even the gentleman at the end gave her a toothless grin and a nod. She smiled with satisfaction and nudged her horse into a canter.

It was apparent the village people had decided she would be another sad victim of the curse, she thought grimly. A new bride of Montrose must have revitalized the old superstitions surrounding the estate. She supposed there was nothing better than a well-told tale, complete with magic and curses. A new chapter, with another gruesome tragedy to add to the legend could only be a titillating prospect.

"Well, they will not be getting it from me," she said

aloud, and spurred Queeny into a gallop. She had learned today that Lady Abigale had been happy here at Montrose. She had loved the land and its people, and they had loved her back. It was her, not Lady Alice she would emulate.

She galloped through the wooded lanes and up the rise. The wind took her bonnet from her head, and it slid to the back of her neck. She made no move to secure it, enjoying the brisk air against her cheeks.

She pulled Queeny back at the height of the rise and gazed across the open plains to where the gray walls of Montrose stood out starkly against the rugged land, its central tower jutting into the clear spring sky. *Home,* she thought. And for the first time she knew the word to be a truth.

She sat atop Queeny and looked at the long lane leading to the manor. She could understand why the woman in the village had labelled it 'godforsaken.' It looked forlorn and barren, alone on a stretch of plain. A stone archway just before the lane turned into the courtyard was all that remained of ancient walls which must have once encircled the place. In the past, keeping the expanse in front of the stronghold clear would have been essential for its defense. But those days were gone. In her mind's eye she pictured towering oaks sheltering the road, giving the approach to the house a more prestigious and pleasant appeal. She smiled, deciding to speak to Willy about buying saplings to plant on each side of the lane.

She wished Julian were home so she could speak to

him about it. Bundles of saplings would be inexpensive. Though it would be many years before they matured enough to be even visible from the rise. But I will have many years to leave my mark on Montrose, she assured herself.

The last time she had sat on a horse upon the rise, Julian had been beside her. She smiled at the picture he had made, strong and warrior-like as he surveyed his lands. He and Montrose were hewn from the same stone, she decided. Both were suited to this wild land, and both were fortified against intruders, with thick impenetrable walls. But I can be the perfect invader, neither will withstand my assault. The comparison made her smile.

But the haunting image of cornflower blue eyes meeting hers in the forest still lingered on the edge of her consciousness. Lady Alice's suicide had scarred her husband more than the blade which had torn his face. The guilt and confusion such a death had caused would be a hard burden to carry. The more she learned about Lady Alice, the more she suspected all was not as it appeared. The single word 'never' still echoed through her mind. She believed it. Something had happened to Lady Alice, and she was becoming convinced it was not suicide.

If it wasn't a suicide, and it wasn't an accident, there was only one other option. That was something she refused to think about.

She nudged Queeny forward, beginning her trek back to the manor, pushing aside her suspicions for now. It would be enough to make friends with her neighbors. Anne was the only female company around for miles. There should be plenty the women would have in common.

Henry did not sound like a character she wanted to know. Old Bess had painted him as a controlling bully. But he lived at Stallridge House and surely, he could have little effect on her life at Montrose.

CHAPTER 13

VISITORS AT TEATIME

Madelyn had worried the days would drag on with Julian away, but the opposite was the case. Once Willy, the gardener, had grudgingly approved of her idea for the line of oaks along the lane, he got whole-heartedly behind the plan. He declared the trees would grow best if they did not have to compete with the grasses and sage, ordering a strip of land on each side of the lane plowed in readiness for the oak saplings. Three teams of horses and plows were brought in to properly work the soil.

"Well, if you're convinced the master will welcome the change, who am I to argue it," he had growled. "But if it's going to be done, it'll be done properly. We'll do two rows with trees spaced intermittently on each side."

It was Mrs. Waldron who expressed her disapproval of the planting. Immediately after breakfast they met to set the week's menu. The meeting was more tense than usual. The housekeeper's grim expression was unwavering. She avoided eye contact and her lips remained compressed in a thin line. Finally, after the weekly menu had been set, Madelyn asked, "Is there something bothering you Mrs. Waldron?"

Mrs. Waldron looked up at last, her dark eyes glittering with disapproval. "There is," she said. "I have been informed of your intention to reconstruct the front lane. I would have hoped you would consult me before making such a drastic decision. His Lordship will not be pleased."

Madelyn laughed nervously. "I would hardly call it a reconstruction, Mrs. Waldron. I am only planting a few trees." She looked up at the forbidding portrait of the house dominating the wall behind her housekeeper. "I am sure Lord Montrose will welcome the change."

Mrs. Waldron snorted. "Harumph! That I doubt. Willy returned from York late last night with the trees. But there is still time to change your mind." The woman leaned forward and added firmly, "I suggest you find an alternate location for the planting. The Lord will not be pleased with your interference."

Madelyn rose, the sting of anger from the housekeeper's words colored her cheeks. Mrs. Waldron's disapproval had the opposite effect. Now she was more determined than ever to have her trees. "Thank you for your advice, Mrs. Waldron."

Madelyn dismissed Mrs. Waldron's disapproval and hurried to the garden sheds. The news that Willy had returned yesterday from York with the saplings and other plants for the hidden garden meant the day would be a busy one.

Willy wanted the saplings in the ground before the roots could dry out. More men from the village were hired to plant, stake, and water the new trees. Madelyn too, wanted everything done as quickly as possible—before Julian returned. Despite Mrs. Waldron's grim prediction, she was sure the change would be a happy surprise for her husband.

She was unable to resist mounting Queeny and riding up and down the lane, supervising the planting. Her role evolved into the task of ensuring the planters were supplied with bundles and stakes, keeping the process flowing smoothly. Thus, she spent the day riding up and down the lane. It was a hard day's work to complete the job in a single day, but she had the kitchen prepare hearty meals and treats for teatime, bringing them out to the crew herself to keep them motivated.

At the end of the day, she sat her horse at the top of the drive and surveyed the finished job. The worked soil made two twenty-foot black stripes, framing each side of the lane. The oak whips were invisible, but the lines of stakes stood out plainly against the rich dark soil. A team and cart, loaded with workers returning to the village after the long day clattered past, their voices and laughter clear in the still twilight. When they passed her, they doffed their hats. Madelyn pulled her bonnet from her head and returned the gesture with an exaggerated bow, eliciting more comments and laughter from the crew.

Madelyn stayed at the top of the lane long after the wagon's clattering had faded away. She pictured the lane as it might look in the years to come and was pleased with the image. She had made a permanent change on Montrose.

She grinned when she realized Montrose had returned the gesture. The woman who sat astride Queeny at the end of the lane was far removed from the young girl who'd spent her days sewing in the parlor in London. It was a fair exchange.

The next morning found her stiff and sore after her long day in the saddle. She decided to forego her usual ride to spend the afternoon reading. She had yet to study the book of British Architecture in the 16th century which she had purchased in York. She brought the heavy tome downstairs to the library and set it on the tea table next to the glass patio doors, pulling her chair up close to read. It was pleasant in the light, with a view of the back gardens and Julian's horses next to the stable.

While paging through the book, she came upon a chapter about hidden rooms. During the conversion to Protestantism in the Tudor reign, many families, particularly in the North of England, renovated to create hidden chapels and priest holes. She looked around the library, wondering if Montrose too held those type of secrets. It certainly had the space for it.

She had yet to explore the bottom floor which housed the dungeons of old.

One of the twins interrupted her musings from the doorway. "Lady Anne and Sir Henry Stallridge are here to visit you ma'am. Shall I ask them in?"

"Oh, lovely. And it is almost teatime." Madelyn rose and walked to the cluster of furniture by the fireplace. It was comfortable and warm there with a cheerful fire burning in the grate. "We'll serve it here I think Annmarie."

"It's Annmargaret ma'am. I'll bring them in. Cook has some lovely biscuits we can serve."

Before Madelyn could respond a gentleman burst into the room. He was a short, heavy-set man, of about fifty years with dark hair and thick matching sideburns covering his cheeks.

"Ah there you are. I have been curious to see this new bride of Julian's." He hurried to her side and took her hand. "Sir Henry Stallridge," he said, "And you must be Lady Madelyn." He brought her hand to his lips and brushed it with the perfunctory kiss. "You've been making quite a stir in the community. I have heard your name bandied about more than once. I must say, I have been rather curious."

"Pleased to meet you, Sir Henry." She was unsure for a moment how to respond to his comments. "I too have heard your name bandied about," she said, and smiled at his raised eyebrows.

"Well now. Not the shy Miss like your predecessor I see." His eyes narrowed while he appraised her, scanning the length of her body. Madelyn was thankful she had worn her new day dress, and that Annmarie had spent extra time this morning to coil her auburn braids up into a pleasing knot. "You look as though you have settled in well," he added.

"Thank you. I have."

She turned to where Anne hovered uncomfortably in the doorway. "Come in Lady Anne. I am so glad you accepted my invitation." Madelyn went to the woman and took her hands before leading her to the settee. "Please sit down. I was about to have tea."

The ladies sat on the sofa. Sir Henry had declined a chair and walked to the fireplace where he casually rested his arm on the mantle. Madelyn noticed his clothes were the finest cut, a dark gray morning jacket with black silken vest and black trousers. For a country gentleman he was impeccably dressed. He resembled Julian in some ways. He had the same dark coloring and wide shoulders, but with Sir Henry's squat height and thick waist he looked bulky rather than powerful.

"I noticed the new plantings as we drove up the lane. A fine idea. I have always wanted to do the same. But I was wondering why you chose such tiny saplings? It will be years before they are large enough to make an impression. I would have chosen more mature trees."

"My gardener Willy assures me that smaller plants root much faster and will outgrow trees even a year or two older. Besides, I have plenty of time," Madelyn answered, concentrating on keeping her smile intact. She was proud of the planting. Sir Henry's criticisms were not appreciated. One of the twins entered with the tea service and an assortment of treats on a tray which she placed on the side table. "Ah, our tea."

"Shall I pour ma'am?" the young maid asked.

"Yes. Thank you, Annmargaret."

"It's A-Annmarie," the maid stuttered, noting Madelyn's quick glance. "Cook included some special biscuits. Miss Anne's favorite she said." Annmarie carefully poured for the ladies, then a third cup for Sir Henry which she carried with slow and careful steps to the fireplace.

Madelyn realized this would be Annmarie's first experience serving guests, just as it was her first time entertaining in her own home. She waited until the girl had served Henry his tea to smile at her. "That sounds lovely. Thank you, Annmarie."

Offering Anne a biscuit from the tray, she said, "You are my first guest. But if Cook knows your favorites, you must have come here many times before. You will have to tell me how I fare as a hostess."

Anne smiled. Madelyn again noted how her face softened with the expression.

"I—" she began.

Henry interjected, "Of course, she's been here many times. We all have. Montrose is our family home after all." Sir Henry leaned back puffing out his expansive chest. "Grew up here on Montrose. Our father and Julian's were twins and inseparable. Anne and I spent as much time here as at Stallridge House," he said, then glowered at the ladies as though prepared to defend a denial.

With a final nod to emphasize his point, he took his cup and saucer, and walked to the patio doors. He sipped his tea while gazing out at the view. "Of course, things have changed since that generation passed, but we still consider Montrose Hall our true home, don't we Anne?"

"Well, I—"

Sir Henry again interrupted, "Unless I am mistaken, Jules has purchased more horses. Hmm..." He set his cup down on the tea table next to her book. "I think I will take a walk down to the stables and see them for myself." Without another word he opened the patio doors and hustled out across the back gardens toward the stable.

Madelyn was taken aback for a moment by the man's rudeness. She glanced at Anne who had colored slightly.

"Henry forgets himself I know," Anne said, her cheeks flushed with embarrassment. "He sees Montrose as his home...I do not think he means to offend," she apologized. "And then, with Julian away all those years, he began to think of Montrose as his responsibility."

Madelyn glanced out the window at the figure of Sir Henry bustling across the expanse of the back lawn toward the stable. "It does give us time for a little visit," she said, then smiled and offered Anne more treats from the tray. Anne chose two of the jellied biscuits.

"Are you pleased to be home at Stallridge?" Madelyn asked.

She shrugged her thin shoulders, sitting a little taller. With her brother's exit she had become more animated. "It is good to be back home, but I do wish Edwyn was here—my youngest brother. He is much younger than Henry and me. Edwyn is the baby in the family, only twenty-two." She laughed a little. "I think he was a bit of a surprise for my parents. I have always been more of a mother to him than a sibling. Henry says he will be coming up for a visit soon." Anne blushed, as though such a long speech was difficult for her.

"Are Edwyn and Henry quite different then?"

"Oh yes, Edwyn is a bit of a rascal, but he has a good heart." Madelyn noticed that Anne's face lit up when she talked of Edwyn. "He is a handsome fellow, and quite loved by everyone. I think it is his charm which gets him into so many scrapes." She laughed a little, with the comment. "It drives poor Henry to distraction."

Madelyn refilled their teacups. "We have much in common. I have younger sisters, three of them. I do miss them. But of course, London is so far away, and it is not likely I will have the opportunity to see them often."

Anne made a tut-tutting sound, tilting her head sympathetically. "That is unfortunate. I suppose I was luckier than you. My husband, God rest his soul, lived only two hours ride from Stallridge. I was able to visit often. And I did, especially when Edwyn was home."

Madelyn noticed that when Anne talked about her brother Edwyn, she was relaxed and almost giddy. She chatted happily about Edwyn's various escapades. Apparently, despite some issue involving an inappropriate liaison, the young man had finished his education at Eton and had taken up a commission with the British forces. Anne was enthusiastic about his advancing career. "He will be successful. He is, as I said, a charming young man, which will serve him well. When he returns to Stallridge, you will have an opportunity to meet him." She paused and repeated, "He is not at all like Henry."

Madelyn contemplated asking Anne about Lady Alice. If Anne was home frequently, she must have known her. But then she remembered Old Bess' tale about poor Anne, forced to waste ten long years of her youth for Julian to come of age, only to be discarded. She must have resented the new Lady of the Manor. But perhaps she would have some insights into what had occurred. Madelyn decided it was worth the effort to ask.

"You must have met Lady Alice then. What was she like?"

Anne shifted uncomfortably in her chair. She raised her cup and saucer, then sipped her tea before answering. When she finally looked up her face was serious. "I did know Lady Alice. She and I were friends. It was I who found her there in the rose garden," she said quietly. Her eyes filled with tears. "I never quite forgave myself for that morning. I should have come by sooner. I knew she was in danger, you see." It was an odd choice of words. Anne's cup began to rattle in its saucer, and she set it down carefully.

"Had Julian and Lady Alice been quarreling then?" Madelyn asked.

Anne shook her head and continued, "Oh no. Lady Alice was not the type to bicker. Julian had gone to the high lands for a few days, and I had promised to visit. When Alice could not be found in the house, I went to the hidden garden. It was her favorite spot, you see." Her long face crumpled a little. "But I was too late..." She looked around the room as though searching for an escape. "Today is the first time I have dared to come back to Montrose. I am afraid it has made me a little emotional."

Madelyn reached over and patted Anne's hand. "Enough of this talk. I did not intend to make you sad…" Madelyn searched for something to say to lighten the mood. "You must not have seen the renovations. Would you like a tour?"

Anne wiped her eyes with hands that still trembled. "I would," she said, straightening her shoulders.

Madelyn led Anne through the salons with their large windows and soft color palettes. While Anne appreciated all the changes, Madelyn could not help but think about the morning of Alice's death. Hearing that Julian was away at the time was a welcome relief. Until Anne made mention of that particular fact, she had not realized she harbored a dark suspicion about Julian's role in his wife's death. At the very least, she assumed there had been a quarrel. But apparently that was not the case.

After completing a walk around the west wing, they returned to the library. Sir Henry had returned and sat in her chair by the patio doors, flipping through her copy of 16th century Architecture.

"Ah. There you are," he said, rising as they entered. "I wondered where the both of you had got to."

The ladies returned to their former seats. Madelyn noticed that Anne appeared to shrink into her corner of the settee. Her shoulders had slumped inward once more.

Madelyn was struck again by how different Sir Henry was from Julian, despite their relationship as first cousins. Henry had the look of a businessman. Even his clothing, impeccable and of the latest fashion, was more suited to a club in London than the wilds of Yorkshire.

"I am surprised at your choice of reading material. I too am interested in architecture," he said, closing the heavy book. "I always wondered if Montrose had a priest's hole." Sir Henry stood, picking up the book and tucking it under his arm. "I think I will study this book if you don't mind." He strolled over to the bookshelves and ran his free hand along the dark wood of the first shelf. He chuckled, "I might even find our legendary Lady Katherine. To me the library always seemed to be the perfect place to begin the search."

"Actually, I have not finished studying the book." Madelyn said.

He laughed again. It was a dry humorless sound. "Not to worry my dear. I'm sure I will have it back to you in a few days." He turned to Anne as though the topic was closed. "Time for us to leave Anne. I've plenty to accomplish today. Thank you for tea my dear." With a quick nod in Madelyn's direction, he strode out the door, her book tucked under his arm.

Anne stood abruptly, "Yes, thank you," she muttered, already turning to leave.

Madelyn caught her arm. "Do come again," then she added in a quieter voice, "Do you ride? Perhaps you could come by on your own?"

Anne nodded before scurrying after her brother, Sir Henry.

Madelyn stood for a few seconds staring blankly at the open door. "What an extraordinarily obnoxious man," she murmured aloud. That he bullied poor Anne was glaringly apparent. She walked to the patio doors and glancing at the table where her book had sat, scowled. She would have to find something else to occupy her time.

This afternoon's visit was not a promising one in terms of building a piece of society here in Yorkshire. Anne was pleasant enough, but Henry was difficult to stomach. A wave of homesickness threatened to overwhelm her.

Gazing out at the back gardens and the pastures beyond, she transported herself to her cozy home in

London. Beth would be taking part in the season this year. No doubt the family would be in frantic preparation, already taking stock of what gowns could be adjusted and what must be purchased. She smiled when she considered her frugal mother, who despite the money provided by Julian, was sure to be stretching every penny. London, and her family were far from her, both in distance and in the reality of her life at Montrose.

She sighed, at least Julian would be back soon. Her stomach flipped as she recalled their last moments together. She imagined her fingers once again grasping his broad back, her lips tingling with the sweet memory of his kisses.

"Come home Julian," she murmured. She smiled when she considered her surprise, hoping he would be pleased when he saw the fledgling oaks planted along the drive. It would be a fresh start to a new beginning of their marriage.

Once he was back at Montrose, she was determined to have a true marriage. She tried to remember what she had learned about the fine art of seduction, but nothing she had ever been taught felt applicable. Dance steps, the coquettish art of maneuvering her fan, lowering her eyes then slowly raising them with a smile, were not useful to her at Montrose.

Impressing him with her arts of seduction was not an option. She would have to be satisfied that her surprise would be enough to win his favor.

CHAPTER 14

THE LORD RETURNS

The moment she awoke, she knew something had changed. She sat up in bed and surveyed the room. There was a faint lingering masculine odor. *Soap, or perhaps cologne,* she thought, feeling her heart skip a beat in her chest.

The door to Julian's room was open. She flipped off the covers and tiptoed to his open doorway to peek in. Hadley and one of the twins were busy making Julian's bed.

"Good morning, my lady," the twin smiled at her, straightening out the bed spread before turning to her. "I left warm water for you in your dressing room. I'll be in to help you dress in a moment."

Madelyn hurried to her dressing room. Julian was home. She rushed through her morning ablutions. If he followed his usual schedule, he would be in the breakfast room by eight.

By the time Annmarie joined her she had given up

on the corset, donned her petticoat, and was attempting to pull her favorite day dress over her head. The dress fitted snuggly with firm stays and would not need the usual corset. It was a lovely blue velvet, and sure to set off her complexion and auburn hair to her best advantage. She wanted to look her best.

"Let me help, my lady," Annmarie said as she pulled the gown down from around her face, "You have made an awful tangle of it."

"His Lordship is home. I want to be down to breakfast with him."

Annemarie gave a little giggle, tugging the gown into place. "Aye well, there is still time. No need to get into such a flurry." She began lacing up the bodice.

"I want to look my best. Can you put my hair up in the style we tried yesterday? The braids wound, with just a bit of hair escaping. Will it take too long?"

"I can. And I'll be quick about it too." She gave Madelyn a wink. The young girl finished the lacing with a crisp bow and nudged her into the seat at the dressing table. She immediately began undoing her thick braid and brushing out her auburn hair. "His Lordship will be unable to take his eyes off you." She giggled again, pleased with the idea of a bit of romance.

Annmarie was true to her word. In only a few minutes Madelyn was hefting her skirts and rushing down the stairs. She paused for a moment outside the breakfast room, adjusting her clothing, then pinching her cheeks for added color. She could hear the muted tones of Hamish and Julian already at the breakfast table. With a deep breath she entered the room.

If she had expected a hearty welcome, she was to be disappointed. All conversation stopped. Her husband glowered at her with the scar on his cheek twitching ominously. She shifted her gaze to Hamish as though hoping for an explanation. He wore a pained expression.

"Good morning. I am so glad you are home," she said brightly, trying to ignore the palpable tension in the room.

Julian grunted, and only Hamish returned her greeting. She stood awkwardly for a moment in the doorway, before walking to the sideboard to fill her plate. She could feel Julian's eyes burning into her back. I am only imagining it, she assured herself, nothing is amiss. But the silence was deafening as she took her seat.

Finally, she could stand it no longer. "What is it? Is something wrong?" she asked.

Julian leaned back in his chair and rested his hands on the table. "We came in after dark last night." His voice was soft, dangerously so. "But this morning when we went out it was difficult not to notice a significant change to *my* front lane."

"The trees. They are a surprise for you, my Lord." Madelyn felt her voice quiver and cleared her throat. "Do you not like them? I thought they made a positive change. We purchased whips, so the expense was minimal. They are little just now, but they will grow Julian.

And then only think of how much improved the approach to the house will be." She realized she was babbling and forced herself to stop. Her cheeks began to burn.

Julian's gaze held hers, but his face remained stoic. She looked to Hamish for some assistance, but he averted his eyes.

"Julian, I—"

"Do you think it might have been wise to consult me before making such a decision?" Again, he kept his voice low.

"I thought to surprise you. And the trees were needed. Why even Sir Henry said—"

Julian slammed his hand on the table with such force the dishes rattled. "Sir Henry! You consulted Sir Henry about changes to my home?"

"No, no. He and Anne visited—"

"Sir Henry has naught to do with my estate!"

Madelyn had had enough. She pushed her chair back and stood. "How dare you raise your voice to me! Sir Henry had nothing to do with it other than complimenting the change. It was meant as a pleasant surprise for you." She took a breath, attempting to quell her rising anger, but she was unsuccessful. All the frustration and loneliness of the last few days welled to the surface. "And furthermore, I was under the impression that this was my home too! Apparently, I was wrong. If you don't like the trees, pull the bloody things out!"

Julian and Hamish wore identical expressions of

surprise. She would have laughed had she not been so annoyed. But she was not done.

She placed her hands on the table and leaned forward to glare at him. "How is it that your former wife, Lady Alice, could remodel the entire house, but I cannot even plant a few trees?"

Her comment brought Julian to his feet. He too put his hands on the table and leaned forward, giving her his most fearsome scowl. "I will thank you not to mention my former wife. That topic is off limits."

Madelyn was not intimidated. She snorted in response.

One of the twins chose that moment to enter the breakfast room and stood uncomfortably in the doorway with a carafe of tea. There was a moment of frozen tension, while Madelyn and Julian stared at each other across the table.

"Well, that did not go as expected," Hamish said cheerfully, breaking the silence.

Madelyn slowly took her hands from the table. Hamish was right. Nothing had gone as expected. Blinking back tears of frustration, she turned away from Julian's glare. "I changed my mind, Annmarie." she said, "I will take breakfast in my room this morning."

"It is Annmargaret ma'am."

"Arrr!" she growled and whirled from the room.

Breakfast was wasted on her this morning, while she oscillated between anger, humiliation, and regret. It was a relief when Mrs. Waldron announced the seamstress had arrived to do fittings for her new wardrobe. Mercifully, she was kept busy until luncheon.

It was only then she addressed her current situation. Her first instinct after this morning's fiasco was to hide in her room and mope. But that option, she decided, would only delay the inevitable. She was still determined to make a success of her marriage, though she admitted, ruefully, she had no idea how to go about it. So far, it seemed as if she had done nothing right.

One of the twins came into the room. "His Lordship sent me up to inquire as to whether you would like to go for your ride this afternoon. He said he will wait at the stables," she said with a twinkle.

"Thank you. It is Annmarie is it not?"

"It is!" she beamed. "I can assist you with your riding habit ma'am, if you will be coming down?" she asked.

Madelyn set her teacup carefully on her dinner tray. "You can," she said rising and moving to her dressing room. If Julian's request were a peace offering, she certainly would not ignore it. She had a few gestures of her own to make.

CHAPTER 15

THE VALLEY OF FLOWERS

Julian was surprised by the ripple of pleasure he experienced when he caught sight of Madelyn making her way across the back garden. He had prepared himself to accept a curt note from the house staff saying she was not available this afternoon.

He turned to the stable hand. "Saddle Queeny, Ned. Her Ladyship has decided to join me after all."

"Aye sir." Ned hurried into the stable, while Julian watched his wife approach. He smiled at her purposeful stride, wondering if she was still in a temper after this morning's disagreement. He had certainly discovered she was not one to be intimidated or cowed by his disapproval. If nothing else, she had pleased Hamish, who spent the morning grinning. Clearly her audacity had impressed him.

Julian was not accustomed to having his authority questioned. Whether on the estate or as a captain in the King's guard, his orders were followed without hesitation. But what baffled him more was her ability to goad him into losing his temper. He took pride in his skill of maintaining control in every circumstance. This morning she had managed to provoke his temper and shatter his usual calm façade with only a few words.

Ned exited the stable, leading a saddled Queeny and looped her reins over the post next to his stallion, Pagan. He checked her cinch and adjusted the stirrups while he considered how to best deal with his wife.

Madelyn was not blending into the background of Montrose as he had assumed she would. She continued to make her presence felt at every turn. Even his estate was not immune to her ruffling effect.

Queeny nudged him and he patted her shoulder. "We must make a peace treaty with your Mistress before she takes over command completely," he murmured to the mare. Queeny gave a soft whinny and arched away from him, distracted as Madelyn walked up with a carrot for her treat.

Even the horse had shifted her allegiance, he thought with an amused grin.

"Thank you for the invitation," Madelyn said, "it is a lovely day for a ride."

Julian nodded while attempting to appraise her mood. Her cheeks were flushed, and her eyes sparkled with emotion, whether from anger, anticipation, or mischief was unclear. She had chosen to wear her green riding habit with a small matching hat set back on her head. A thick auburn braid curled around her neck and down across her breasts. She was lovely, this wife of his.

"Will I do?" she asked.

He could only grunt in response, lending a hand to help her mount. Julian was surprised with how just the slightest touch of her could spark a reaction from him.

"I will take that as a yes," she answered with a grin, settling herself into the saddle.

Unsure of what she expected in response, Julian silently mounted, urging his horse to a canter. They circled the house and proceeded down the lane. The dark cultivated strips of earth with their staked trees stood out clearly against the brambled grounds. He glanced at Madelyn, who had the grace to blush at the source of the morning's dispute.

At the top of the lane, he pulled up and waited for Madelyn to reach his side.

"Will you be pulling out the trees then?" she asked, her eyes on the planting. Her voice was guarded, as though carefully preparing herself for his response.

"No. The trees will stay." He was silent for a moment, considering how best to help her understand his issue without causing a second argument. "It is not the trees I object to." He turned to her and met her eyes. "I will be consulted before further changes are made."

Madelyn gave a loud sigh. "I suppose you are right. I should have consulted you, and next time I will. But they will be marvelous, don't you think?"

It was hard to ignore her enthusiasm. She looked at

him with a hopeful smile, her cheeks rosy with the brisk spring air, and her soft brown eyes luminous. "Marvelous," he said, commenting more on her presence than the landscape.

He looked back toward Montrose, with its gray walls outlined against an open sky. There was a medieval strength—a stark beauty, in its lonely stance on a rise above the moors. But perhaps it was time for a change. The lane would be impressive. And judging by the size of the saplings, it appeared he would have plenty of time to get used to the change.

He turned once more toward his wife, resplendent in her green riding habit and matching cloak. The wind had torn a lock of auburn hair from her braid, and she brushed it back with a gloved hand, her eyes focused on Montrose in the distance. She looked so different from the gay young woman he had watched from the balcony in London. It was as though the moors had claimed her as their own.

She glanced at him and smiled, clearly pleased with the image of the treed lane and his acquiescence in the matter.

Perhaps Hamish was right. Madelyn was not the delicate creature Alice had been. As to the matter of the trees, the issue was closed. She had agreed to consult with him before making further changes, and that was enough.

"Come," he said, turning his horse toward the east pasture, "I want to show you something."

He urged Pagan into a canter. The two of them rode

side by side across the field and into a shallow ravine, where an overgrown path curved around a rocky knoll. A little further down the trail, a small pond of water was captured between the hills, with tall grass, shrubbery, and a few sparse trees framing its perimeter. On its southern side, the hill was awash in color. Bright yellow daffodils and white daises crowded the base of the hill near the water's edge, and a blaze of purple crocuses covered it to the summit.

He smiled when he heard Madelyn gasp beside him. As he had hoped, the hillside was in full bloom.

I will pick a bouquet, he thought, grinning to himself, *a romantic gesture for my beautiful wife.*

"Oh Julian, it is so lovely!"

"It is," he said, dismounting. "Every year they make a showing here. But it is only for a few days, and then they are gone until next spring." He walked to Queeny's side, took the reins, and secured both horses to a tree before holding out a hand to help her dismount.

To his surprise, just as she had done once before at the stables, Madelyn placed her hands upon his shoulders and purposely pressed her body against him as she slid from the saddle. He kept his wife close for a moment, unable to resist leaning down to nuzzle the warm place where her neck escaped her cloak, breathing in the fresh scent of her. His fingers tingled where they held her waist, itching to pull her body even more tightly against his.

Madelyn arched backward and gave him a cheeky smile. He reluctantly took a step away, letting his hands fall to his sides. It appeared his wife could have him lose all reason with just the simplest touch. He would have to be careful to avoid this nearness if he were to adhere to the schedule he had planned for their marriage.

Together they walked to a grassy knoll, rising above the blooming grass, overlooking the pond, and banked by the steep purpled hill behind them.

"Oh, look Julian!" Madelyn pointed toward the pond. A mallard duck, disturbed by their arrival, led a troop of tiny ducklings away from the water's edge. The babies could not have been more than a day or two old—little puff balls paddling heartily behind their wary mother. It was the perfect idyllic scene, and Julian could not contain a satisfied grin.

He unfastened his cloak and spread it on the little rise, thinking first to see to her comfort while he picked his bouquet. "I thought we could stop here for a while."

Madelyn smiled her response and settled herself on the cloak. "An excellent notion," she said.

He immediately set about picking flowers near the water's edge, concentrating on choosing the longest stemmed daffodils and interspersing them with white daisies. Arranging a bouquet was new to him—romantic gestures were something he hadn't done before. He smiled as he worked, both pleased and amused with himself.

He held out the results to assess his arrangement and looked up at Madelyn with raised brows. She grinned back at him. She had pulled her knees up against her chest, wrapping her arms around them, to watch him.

"Something's missing," he said, examining his creation. "Greenery perhaps. What do you think?" he asked. She laughed in response. It was a joyful, heartfelt sound and he smiled back at her.

He chose a few bits of leafy greens and a few spikes of grass to wrap around the stems, holding them in place. Then he took a handkerchief from his pocket, dunked it in the pond and wrapped the cloth around the base to keep them wet.

Satisfied with the results, he climbed back to the grassy knoll. In a final flourish, he dropped to one knee on the cloak beside her and held out the bouquet. "For you, my lady."

"Oh Julian. They are beautiful," she said taking the offering and touching a finger to one of the blooms. When she looked up at him, her eyes were luminous, shining with unshed tears, and a soft smile played upon her lips. He could see the faintest trace of freckles across the bridge of her nose, fading as they neared her windblown cheeks.

His new wife was indeed a beauty. He kneeled before her, resting his hands upon her shoulders and kissed her. He intended to plant a chaste kiss upon her lips. But when she gasped, her gentle breath grazing his cheek, and her mouth warm and inviting, he could not resist deepening the kiss.

He was only vaguely aware of her setting her

flowers on the grass before she encircled him with her arms. He kissed her as he had ached to do every night since she had arrived at Montrose. When she opened her mouth to him, he groaned with the taste of her.

Somehow, she had managed to slip her hands beneath his shirt, and he could feel her fingers running the length of his back, gripping, and caressing him in a rhythm that matched his own. He let his mouth trail from her lips to that special spot where her neck met her shoulders and nuzzled her there. Julian tasted the salty tang of her flesh while he relished the feel of her hands upon him.

He wanted more. He needed to feel his skin against hers. Arching back from her, he took the hem of his shirt, pulled it over his head, and flung it aside. He reached for her. With trembling fingers, he helped her unfasten her cloak, letting it fall behind her, then the jacket of her riding habit, exposing the soft white fabric of the chemise beneath.

He paused for a moment and looked at her. Holding her gaze, he tugged the garment off her shoulders, feeling her slip her arms from its sleeves. Madelyn's eyes were wide, almost black; her cheeks blushed a deep rose. Her lips were parted slightly, and he could not resist leaning in to kiss her again.

Her hands once again found his bare back. Wrapping his arms around her, he became conscious of how slender and soft she felt pressed against him. His wife—a wave of fierce possessiveness consumed him. Holding her close, he rolled them both down onto his cloak, trapping her beneath him. Then, bracing his body with an elbow, he let his lips and hands explore her. Her breasts were the size of his palm and firm beneath his grasp, with sensitive nipples that invited his touch. He kissed and suckled, feeling her body squirm against him. Her hands gripped him close.

Keeping his hands upon her breasts, he shifted his body lower, raining kisses on her soft womanly form. There was only a moment's sanity, a brief interlude while his forehead rested on her belly, when he considered withdrawing from her.

But then, as though of its own volition, his hand reached down to find her stockinged leg. Pushing her skirts up before him as his fingers caressed her thighs, and finally the warm, damp center of her. When he felt her body stiffen in surprise, he shifted, returning to kiss her lips and hold her close, while cupping her nether region with his palm.

He let his fingers explore her, mesmerized by the beauty of her face lost in sensation; her eyes closed, and cheeks flushed. Each time her lips parted with a soft moan he captured it with his lips. He stroked her, his body involuntarily mimicking the age-old rhythm of love, until wet beneath his trembling hands, she arched against him, gasping her release.

He was lost. There was only the warm dampness as he pushed inside her, stopping briefly when feeling the barrier of her innocence. "Acknowledge me, Madelyn," he whispered, "say my name. Tell me you want me."

"Yes, Julian," she breathed against his cheek, "oh yes."

He registered her sharp cry of pain as he plunged into her. But then a madness overwhelmed him. There were only her soft moans and the exquisite sensations of his body as he rammed against her. He felt her legs wrap around his back, and her hands grasp his shoulders to pull him close.

It was too much. He pressed against her, arching high above her while shouting his release. He closed his eyes as his seed pulsed into her body.

Allowing himself to collapse against her, he caught his breath before repositioning them both to their sides so as not to crush her with his weight.

His sanity returned slowly and with it came the realization of what he had done. He had taken his virgin wife—a lady, in a pasture, with only a cloak for a bed. And worse, he had poured his seed into her, fully aware of the consequences of such an action.

She could be carrying his child from this moment. He remembered Alice's tears when she first discovered she was pregnant. She had said she wanted more time to get to know him before becoming a mother. And though, over the next few months, Alice had appeared to accept and even anticipate the coming birth, it must have been a ruse, given the tragedy that had followed.

Madelyn stirred beside him. Knowing he could not face her, at least not yet, he held her head against his chest.

The dreadful certainty that once again, he had let

his passions control his actions filled him with self-loathing. He silently cursed himself.

Glancing down at the auburn head, lying still against his chest, he was sure his new wife must find him the uncouth brute he had proven himself to be. Alice had spent the morning in bed after their first experience together. Madelyn would be forced to immediately ride over a mile back to Montrose.

He sighed. There was nothing to be done except make amends as best he could. And somehow, he must find a way to manage the passion his new wife inspired in him.

MADELYN SHIFTED her head on Julian's broad chest, relishing the warmth and delicious smell of his body so close to hers. She wanted to stay pressed against this man forever. Making love had been a wonderous and exhilarating experience. She tried to find the words to describe her feelings but could not. She only knew that everything had felt so right. She was filled with a languorous lethargy; even her mind was unable to focus on anything but the immediate presence of her husband.

But then Julian shifted away from her, sitting up and donning his shirt. His silent withdrawal confused her after the intimacy of just moments ago. His distant attitude left her feeling desolate and embarrassed. The spring breeze chilled her bare chest, which only moments ago had been so warm against him, and she too quickly pulled up her chemise and reached for her jacket.

"I'll give you your privacy, and fetch the horses," he said, not meeting her eyes.

She was thankful for that at least. Her legs felt oddly weak as she approached the pond and used her handkerchief to clean up. The sight of blood frightened her until she remembered her mother's words on the matter. The water was clear and cool. She took a moment to kneel by the edge of the pond scooping handfuls onto her burning cheeks, before turning to face her husband. He stood holding the horses. Stiff and expressionless, with his face a mask of stoic indifference, he resembled a palace guard.

Something is not right, she thought to herself. She had been so surprised and transported by the experience of making love to Julian. *Perhaps he had not experienced it in the same way?* She remembered his shout at the end —*could he be injured in some way?*

She herself was feeling bruised and sore. That must be it, she assured herself. Obviously, the whole business had taken a physical toll on him.

Julian approached nearer, leading the horses. She quickly smoothed down her braid and rose to meet him. His face was grim, with his scarred cheek twitching as though struggling to match the scowl presented by its right side. It was an expression she was coming to know well, she thought wryly.

As Madelyn walked to meet him, she again felt a

tenderness in her nether regions. The idea that he may be in pain too softened her attitude toward him. She laid her hand upon his arm. “I am sorry if I have hurt you Julian,” she said.

His eyes widened, then to her surprise he threw his head back and laughed. She had no idea what it was he found so amusing, but whatever it was, she was thankful for it. The uncomfortable distance between them melted away.

He reached down, and picked up his cloak, shaking it out before draping it around his shoulders. Next, he picked up the bouquet of abandoned flowers. As he handed them to her, his lips curled in his familiar half smile. “Come wife,” he said reaching out his hand, “you'll ride with me back to the hall.”

Julian settled her across his lap, attaching Queeny's reins to the saddle horn. Madelyn made no objection. Instead, she laid her head against his chest once more, wrapping one arm around him, while holding tight to her flowers with the other.

Julian urged Pagan into a canter as they left the gully. Twisting her body around, she looked back one more time at the valley of flowers, wanting to capture the scene forever in her memory. She smiled at the picturesque setting before Julian tightened his arm around her, pulling her firmly against his chest. She complied, closing her eyes, and breathing in his warm strength—this beautiful man, her husband.

And in that moment, the certainty that she was madly in love with Julian overwhelmed her. The knowledge was both exhilarating and painful. Her Lord of Montrose was unlikely to ever love her in return. He had been damaged, both inside and out. An aching sense of loss permeated her being and hot tears burned her eyes. She cursed Lady Alice for her fateful death, whether it was by her choice or not. She forcibly pushed those feelings aside, concentrating instead on the pleasure of physical closeness between them at this moment.

After a brief ride, Julian drew back on the reins, bringing Pagan to a stop. They had reached the end of the lane with Montrose Manor standing stark and forbidding in the distance. Behind it, storm clouds had gathered, their purple hues ominously contrasting its gray walls. The rows of freshly planted trees did little to soften the view.

She glanced up at Julian. There was a fierce pride in his countenance as he scanned the horizon. For an instant, the medieval picture they must have made flashed across her mind. She lay across his lap, her green riding habit draping Pagan's front shoulder, and her body pressed close against the broad chest of her husband, cloaked in black. Her hand still held the wildflowers. Her whimsical thoughts imagined a warrior, scarred and battle-weary, returning home with his captive bride across his lap. And at this moment, she felt very much a bride.

If I could paint like my predecessor, I would do this painting, she thought, smiling at the contrast her bold painting would make next to the delicate tones of Lady Alice's watercolors.

But then Julian nudged his horse forward, and Madelyn abandoned her passing fancy. She had other more important tasks to focus on. Somehow, she had to teach this Lord of Montrose to love her. She hoped with all her heart it was possible.

CHAPTER 16

LATE NIGHT WANDERINGS

Madelyn tossed her novel aside, pushed back her bed covers, and sat at the edge of her bed. It was impossible to concentrate. Two days had passed since their interlude at the pond. Two days where she had contrived to spend as much time with Julian as possible, while he expertly avoided her at every turn. Since Julian was working further afield there were no daily rides. He no longer joined her after supper, but claimed he had paperwork to do, spending his evenings at his desk.

Madelyn had been so sure the encounter at the pond would bring them closer together. She had gone over the details carefully in her mind. Though much of the experience was blurred by her passion for Julian, she was convinced he had been as overwhelmed as she. The intimacy they had shared was exciting. Even now her body tingled with the memory of his body pressed against hers. It was the piece of their marital life that had been missing—this intimacy. She wanted a proper marriage, and she was determined to somehow achieve it.

Last night she had laid in bed for hours listening in vain for the sounds of Julian returning to his bedroom before falling into a fitful sleep. Tonight, she had found a novel to help her pass the time while she waited for his presence. Though she had no clear concept of what exactly she would say or do when she did manage to be in his company. She had contemplated several options —ranging from an attempt at seducing him, to having a careful conversation about their marriage. But it was now the early hours of morning and still no Julian.

She snatched up her robe and left the room. If he would not come to her, she would go to him.

Halfway down the hall she regretted her impulsiveness. The hallway was cold, and her bare feet stung on the cool tiles. The house was deathly silent. As always there were only two dim wall sconces to light her way down the hall. She kept her eyes lowered to avoid the eerie glares of the ancestors and forced herself to move forward.

She hurried down the wide stairs, across the entry, and peered down the hallway to the library. Light spilled into the hall from its open doors. Julian would be in there, perhaps at his desk. She crept forward, pausing only for a moment to take a deep breath, then stepped into the room.

Standing at the doorway, she scanned the room. Julian was not at his desk. Instead, he was sprawled in a stuffed chair pushed close to the fireplace. His feet rested on an ottoman. Beside him a half empty bottle of brandy and a glass sat on an end table. He was asleep.

For a moment she was simply confused. Then a frustrated anger overwhelmed her. He was so intent on avoiding her, he had chosen to sleep here, uncomfortably propped in a chair, rather than sleeping next to her in his suite. She debated shaking him awake and demanding an explanation. But another glance at the half empty bottle changed her mind.

She spun around to begin her trek back to her rooms and could not suppress a short squeak of astonishment. Standing behind her with a lantern in her hand was Mrs. Waldron.

"Oh! You frightened me," she managed, her heart still pounding in her chest.

"I heard a noise and came to investigate." Mrs. Waldron took in Madelyn's disheveled appearance, her eyes lingering on her bare feet. "You will want to at least wear slippers. You will catch your death wandering about with bare feet."

Madelyn self-consciously attempted to tuck her feet beneath the folds of her robe. "I was just coming down to fetch a glass of milk."

Mrs. Waldron glanced at the open doors of the library. In the dim light it looked as though she smirked, and Madelyn felt her cheeks burn with embarrassment. How ridiculous she must look sneaking downstairs to spy on her husband, who clearly was uninterested in her.

"Cook is sure to have left a little milk in the larder. Would you like me to warm some up for you?" The housekeeper was polite, her tone not suggesting the least bit of ridicule. Madelyn hoped she had imagined the woman's earlier expression.

"Thank you, Mrs. Waldron. Very kind of you to offer, but I can manage. I'll not keep you up," she said with as much dignity as she could muster.

Mrs. Waldron nodded and retreated silently toward her rooms.

Madelyn sighed. She decided a bit of milk might be just what she needed. Taking a glass with her she too returned to her room.

If Julian were determined to avoid her, there was little she could do. But her frustration was tinged with a bite of anger. His rejection after the intimacy they had shared at the pond, stung.

She was done trying to win the man's affection, only to have him persistently turn away from her. Tonight, had been humiliating. It was well past time Julian made an effort to make this marriage work. If her husband found her so displeasing, perhaps she should find other pursuits to occupy her.

Tomorrow was another day, and it would be a busy one. The Stallridge cousins would be arriving for dinner. Despite not appreciating the company of Henry, she was determined to befriend Anne. She was her closest female neighbor, after all. And it would be interesting as well to meet the wayward Edwyn.

She had gotten the impression from Old Bess the man was a rake, or at least a womanizer. She almost hoped he was. It might be a surprise for Julian to see there were men who actually enjoyed her company. A plan began to form in her mind. She could not suppress a smile. She would show Julian how wrong he was to distance himself from her. And even if her husband did not get the message, Edwyn might be a pleasant diversion. Anything to distract her from Julian's rejection would be welcome.

CHAPTER 17

THE INTRODUCTION OF EDWYN

Madelyn checked her reflection once more. The new gown was a soft yellow, trimmed with lovely Queen Anne's lace on the bodice and along its short, off the shoulder puffed sleeves. Unlike the gowns of the last decade, her new dress was cinched tight several inches below her bosom. It was, she decided, the most beautiful gown she had ever worn.

Her hair was done up with a few delicate curls escaping to rest upon her bare shoulders. The gown's bodice was cut low too, revealing a hint of cleavage. She smiled at her reflection, satisfied she presented an appropriate image for the Lady of the manor.

After a brief knock, Julian stood in the doorway between their rooms. He too was the picture of the fashionable gentleman in black jacket and trousers, with a light gray vest and elaborate necktie. He smiled at her, and despite the lingering anger from last night's humiliation, she could not stop her heart from fluttering in her chest.

They walked down the staircase just as the Stallridge family entered from below.

Henry was impeccably dressed. His dinner jacket and trousers were black as was the custom, but his outfit was set off with an elaborate red waistcoat and a stiffly starched white cravat which covered his neck to his chin. "Well Julian, it is good to be back in Montrose again for a formal evening. I must say I was pleased to accept this invitation. A chance to show off your new bride, eh?" he said, reaching to shake his hand.

Julian smiled and replied, "Yes, and you have met my wife, Madelyn."

Henry took her hand, "I have at that." He raised her hand and brushed it across his lips. "Enjoyed tea with her last week. Pleased to see you again my dear. But I have a surprise." He turned back to the entry where a young man was helping Anne with her cloak. "Edwyn has come down from London. He was given a bit of leave from his superior officer."

Edwyn stepped forward and bowed formally. Unlike Julian and Sir Henry, he was blond and slender. He was also shockingly handsome. His blond curls, imitating Lord Byron's in cut and style, framed a face of perfect symmetry. She watched as he greeted Julian, then turned to her. Edwyn raised her hand to his lips and kissed it, never once taking his eyes from hers. "I am delighted to meet you, Lady Montrose," he said. "I have heard so much about you, but neither my brother nor Anne prepared me to meet such a beauty." His brown eyes sparkled with mischief. Instead of releasing her hand he tucked it into his arm. He then turned about and reached out his other arm to Anne, "Come my loves. You must give me the opportunity to have a beauty on each arm."

Madelyn could not resist returning his smile. She glanced back at Julian, who, nodding at something Henry said, furrowed his brows at her. She ignored his dark look and led the way to the green parlor, where the party would have a glass of punch before going to the dining room.

"I had rather hoped we could gather in the library," Sir Henry said from behind her, when they reached the green parlor, "I have been reading the book Lady Madelyn was so kind to loan me, and there are a few things I would like to explore."

"The library it is then," Madelyn replied, thinking Henry's manners had not improved since their last meeting. She sighed. At least the library held the piano. Perhaps it would be the better choice for entertaining after all.

Edwyn led the ladies to the settee and pulled a chair up close to Madelyn. Once again Sir Henry declined a chair. He strutted immediately to the rear bookshelves. Julian hesitated, looking down at Madelyn before reluctantly following Sir Henry across the room.

"According to my architectural studies," Henry said, "the most common location for an entry to a hidden staircase to below would be above the old tower. And I believe the library's interior wall might be part of the old structure." He began running his hands along the heavy dark wood of the cabinets, while Julian stood a little to the side, his brows raised and an expression of amused disbelief on his face.

Anne objected in a soft voice, "Henry, do you really think now is the time to—"

"Leave him to his amusements Anne," Edwyn interrupted, then added in a quiet voice, "It will give us a little time to get to know our new neighbor without talk of livestock or heaven forbid, coal."

Madelyn caught Julian's gaze and smiled sympathetically. Sir Henry treated Montrose as though it was his own. Even the rules of etiquette and proper behavior could not curb his behavior.

Mrs. Waldron appeared in the open doorway with a carafe and several glasses. She walked into the room and set the tray on the side table next to the double doors. "I have brought punch," she announced, "I thought a little refreshment before dinner might be in order."

Edwyn immediately rose to his feet. "An excellent idea," he said, walking toward her, "let me help you serve the ladies."

Madelyn was momentarily struck dumb. First, it was uncommon to see Mrs. Waldron serve. She had thought the twins would be in service tonight. And second, the housekeeper had obviously dressed for the occasion. Instead of her usual black dress and white apron, she wore a dark navy skirt, with a matching snug jacket. A white blouse protruded around her neck and cuffs. Her head lacked the usual white cap, but instead was graced with a small navy hat pinned to hair rolled into a loose bun. She looked quite lovely, Madelyn decided. Even her cheeks had a rosy glow.

Madelyn assumed Mrs. Waldron was intent on making this evening a success and tried to catch her eye to smile her appreciation. But she was waylaid by the gracious Edwyn returning with their punch, while the housekeeper brought the men their drinks.

Edwyn handed them their glasses with a flourish, then seated himself and sipped his drink. "Ah, delicious," he said, "better than anything I have been served lately. Even Almack's famous punch does not compare."

Madelyn smiled. "I am sure that is not true, but kind of you to say—"

"You went to Almack's?" Anne interrupted and her eyes lit up. "You didn't tell me Edwyn. You must tell us all about it."

"I did indeed. And as luck would have it, I even managed to spy the Prince of Wales. One hears the man will soon be King."

"Really," Madelyn was surprised. Since the Prince's falling out with his usual cronies, Brummel for one, he had not been seen much in public. "Do not tell me you were introduced? Did you speak to him?"

"Oh no," Edwyn replied with a devilish grin. "I couldn't get too close. He had a bevy of gentlemen around him. Poor fellow had squeezed his arse into an armed chair, and it took a half a dozen of his cronies to pry him loose."

Madelyn had just taken a sip of punch. She had to use every ounce of willpower not to spit it across the room with a burst of laughter. The prince's bulging posterior and obesity had been whispered about, even in her less illustrious circles, but only whispered, not ridiculed in crude jokes.

"Edwyn no," Anne said in an attempt to admonish him, but even she could not resist a slight smile.

Edwyn continued to entertain them with stories from the city. He was able to describe in detail the current fashions, worn by the most popular women in town this season. His tales of the ridiculous antics of the upper classes had the ladies laughing. News from London was a rare treat, and Edwyn was certainly up to date with the latest gossip.

And he was an accomplished flirt. He managed to punctuate his conversations with outrageously forward compliments and sly innuendo. Somehow his boyish charm, and mischievous grin gave him license. Madelyn found herself laughing at his antics, when perhaps she should have quelled his forward behavior. But it was just the balm she craved to soothe her bruised ego.

When occasionally she stole a glance at Julian, she saw he was not amused. He stood a little removed from Sir Henry, who had even engaged Mrs. Waldron in his quest, and glowered at her. It was an odd series of events for a dinner party, with half their party browsing the bookshelves. Yet she could not help but be relieved to see Sir Henry happily entertained across the room.

Anne was smiling broadly. "And what of the debutantes. Might there be one who strikes your fancy this year brother?" she asked hopefully.

Edwyn chuckled. "This season the heiress, Faith Pembroke, has made her debut. She is the daughter of the Earl and his beautiful wife, Lady Arabella, you know." Anne leaned forward with a hopeful expression, eager to hear. He grinned at her. "And I did try to make her acquaintance, Anne. But I was so viciously tackled and elbowed away by her many suitors that I have had to take this sojourn in Yorkshire to recuperate."

"Oh Edwyn," Anne said, putting her hand over her mouth to smother a giggle.

Mrs. Waldron announced dinner was served. From the corner of her eye, she saw Julian come toward her, prepared to escort her, but Edwyn beat him to it. Once again, the young man had a lady on each arm as they walked into the dining room.

And Madelyn was pleased with the attention. If Edwyn's doting presence made her husband take note of her, then it could only be an improvement over the last couple of days. She could not resist answering Julian's scowl with a wide grin.

She was satisfied with Mrs. Waldron's choices for supper. There was the popular turtle soup for starting, then light vegetables: artichoke, cauliflower, and green beans, followed by a serving of venison and sweetbreads. There was even a curry, for those who had acquired a taste for the new dish from India.

Conversations at the table had been brief, restricted to compliments on the food until dessert was served. It was then Sir Henry leaned back in his chair, and resting his hands upon his rounded belly said, "I have been meaning to talk to you about the ridge, Julian. I rode by there the other day. The coal is just lying on the surface waiting to be scooped up."

Sir Henry was oblivious to the taut silence permeating the room with his announcement. Madelyn straightened abruptly and stole a look at Julian. His brow was furrowed. His gray blue eyes glittered a dangerous warning.

Sir Henry continued unfazed, "Now you may not know this young man, but there is plenty of money to be made in coal. To see it just lying there, like pennies in a fountain, is a bloody waste." He paused, stirred a spoonful of sugar into his tea, then took a long noisy sip. "Now if I were in charge here the profits would make this family one of the richest in the North. It is a pity I could not have gotten the business started, or at least cleared away the trees you love so much before you returned. Bloody Hamish wouldn't let me break ground."

Julian spoke quietly. "We have had this conversation, Henry. I suggest you leave it be."

Sir Henry sighed. "I think you are unaware of just what you are refusing lad, I—"

Edwyn interrupted. "Surely, we can leave this

conversation for another time. But speaking of the ridge," he turned to Madelyn, "have you rode out to see this rough land? Do you ride Lady Montrose?"

"I have and I do," Madelyn replied, smiling to encourage the change in topic. Then with a little pout she added, "But I have not been out lately. Julian has been too busy for me I'm afraid."

Edwyn grinned. "Well, you are in luck my Lady. It just so happens neglected wives are my forte." Sir Henry snorted from across the table. Edwyn ignored him, maintaining eye contact with Madelyn. "With your permission, I would be honored to take you out for a ride. Tomorrow afternoon? Two o'clock perhaps?"

Madelyn looked toward Julian, whose face was impassive but for an almost indiscernible twitching of his left cheek. She smiled, her eyes not leaving his as she answered Edwyn. "Why that would be lovely. Thank you Edwyn."

After the heavy meal, the party was much more subdued. They retired to the library where Lady Anne entertained the company with soft music from the piano. Thankfully even Sir Henry did not have the energy to debate the mining issue, and conversation was restricted to the more common subjects of politics and commodity prices. It was not long before they saw their guests out.

"Well, that went rather well," Madelyn said as the oaken doors were pulled closed. "I quite liked Edwyn. So entertaining."

Lord Montrose stood silently for a moment, his face a mask when he looked at her. "You do realize that young Edwyn is a bit of a rake. He did not take his eyes off you the entire night. I am not sure encouraging him by spending the afternoon riding is the best idea."

"Edwyn is harmless..." Madelyn answered. She moved past him to make her way up the staircase to her room. She could not resist pausing, then turning to look at him where he stood at the bottom of the stairs, and added, "Besides, it is such a pleasure to be with a man who wants my company."

Madelyn could feel his eyes boring into her back all the way up the stairs. It took an effort not to hike up her skirts and scramble to the safety of her room.

One of the twins waited in her dressing room to help her change. It had been a long day, and it was a relief to crawl into her comfortable bed. Despite her determination to stop focusing all her energies on her distant husband, she found herself straining to hear sounds from Julian's room. Just as she was about to drift off to sleep, her efforts were rewarded with the clank of his door closing. At least her husband would not be spending the night uncomfortably scrunched into a lounge chair to avoid her. She turned her back on the door to his room, attempting to block both the sounds of his movements, and the painful yearning of her heart.

Tomorrow she would ride with Edwyn. She was determined to enjoy the distraction while it lasted. And if Julian did not like it, so be it.

CHAPTER 18

EDWYN'S WARNING

It was almost two. Madelyn made her way down the stairs and turned down the hall toward the library. She had planned to meet Edwyn at the stables, and the library exit was the best route. As she approached the room, she paused. Voices were coming from within.

"Good grief, it sounds like the obnoxious Cousin Henry," she muttered to herself as she stepped through the open doors.

Sure enough. Sir Henry must have decided to continue his search from last night. Near the far interior wall, he and Mrs. Waldron were busy combing the shelves for a catch or device.

She cleared her throat to get their attention.

They looked toward her with identical expressions of surprise. "Ah, Lady Montrose," Sir Henry said straightening up, "I hope you don't mind me employing your housekeeper. We did not get time to do a thorough search last night. I am still convinced there must be a secret entrance here somewhere."

Despite her misgivings about conversing with the man, Madelyn could not contain her curiosity. "Why do you think an access to a priest hole would exist here? If there were one, a priest hole I mean, would it not more likely be in the cellars?"

Sir Henry puffed out his expansive chest, preparing to give her his best lecture. "Certainly, the priest hole would be below. But according to my research, it would not be where the priest would reside. He was more likely to enjoy the comforts of the house, when not conducting a service. Access would only be employed when necessary. If unexpected company arrived, instead of returning to the foyer, he would be able to make a quick escape to the rooms below. One could not have expected the clergy to actually live in the cellars."

"I suppose you are right. One does hear the priests enjoyed their comforts." Madelyn answered. "I will leave you to it," she said, nodding a farewell to Mrs. Waldron before exiting through the patio doors. It was odd to see the housekeeper engaged once more in a search for a passage. She was always such a stickler for keeping to assigned duties, for herself and all the staff. But then, of course, the house was a passion of hers.

A clear blue sky with only a gentle breeze made a perfect day for a ride. Madelyn had just reached the stables when the sound of hoofbeats announced the arrival of Edwyn. He looked dashing atop a white stallion. He wore a burgundy jacket, a black vest, with matching cloak and trousers, complete with a top hat trimmed in the same velvety shades.

She leaned against the open stable doors watching his approach. To her surprise when he was within ten feet of her, both horse and rider dipped into a perfectly executed bow. He doffed his hat with a flourish, and said, "My lady, your escort awaits you."

It was a neat trick; something she had only seen once before at a horse show in London. She laughed appreciatively. "Oh Edwyn, that was well done."

Edwyn grinned. "Anything to impress a lovely lady."

Julian's deep voice sounded from behind her. "Yes Edwyn, you are a regular horse trainer. You should apply to Astley's Amphitheatre. Sir Ducrow could use you for an upcoming show."

Madelyn flinched in surprise. She turned to see her husband behind her, holding the reins of both Queeny and a second horse.

It irritated her that even the soft tones of Julian's voice could have her heart pounding in her chest. "I thought you would be working far afield again today," she said.

Julian ignored her comment and looked up at Edwyn. "I am sending Ned as your footman today. It has been a while, Edwyn, since you were out on the moors. Ned will be sure the two of you do not stray into a bog." Julian gave him a hard look.

Edwyn grinned. "Well thank you cousin. How very thoughtful of you."

Julian silently helped her mount. His face was stoic, but his whole demeanor shouted his disapproval. Fine, she thought to herself. If the man wants to avoid me, he cannot expect me to mope about the manor waiting for an ounce of attention from him. She had done quite enough of that already.

After a gallop past the lane, they veered into the west pasture. Here the ground was firm, and the fields were dotted with cattle. They slowed up and walked the horses side by side, with Ned following discreetly behind.

"I wondered what kind of wife Julian would choose." Edwyn said, turning to her. "I am not sure what I expected, but it wasn't you."

Madelyn raised her brows. "Is that a compliment?' she laughed a little. "Just what did you expect?"

"Oh, but it is a compliment. You are like a breath of fresh air in this place. My worry is for you. Sometimes I feel as though Montrose smothers anything fresh or new. Everyone here is obsessed with the past."

Madelyn was distracted for a moment, carefully skirting Queeny around a badger hole before replying. "Perhaps it is because there is so much of the past here," she said, "It is not everyone who can claim to live in a manor house which served the Normans."

Edwyn waited until her horse was once more abreast of his, then kept pace with her at a walk. "I wasn't thinking about quite so distant a past." He shrugged. "Perhaps it is just my household."

Turning toward her, his face without its usual playful animation, he said, "I do not want to be too forward, but I did plan to warn you today."

"Warn me?" Madelyn asked.

"I am in this family as a second son—not of much use except as a kind of insurance. And that has been a good thing. At least I am left to my own devices, for the most part. For poor Anne and Henry's first wife, that was not the case." Edwyn grimaced, then glanced back at Ned before he continued in a soft voice. "My brother Henry will stop at nothing to secure Montrose. And now, with his coal mine operating, and obvious rich deposits on Montrose lands, his obsession has only become worse."

"Surely you are not suggesting Sir Henry might be a danger to me?"

Edwyn frowned. "I hope not. But I think of Anne, forced to wait a decade until Julian came of age. She was devastated when Julian rejected her. I still find it hard to forgive the man. My sister wanted children and a family of her own. But no. She was a pawn, pushed about by two men who cared only for Montrose."

Madelyn interrupted, "But Julian was just a boy. And even if he had been of age when Sir Henry made his plans, Julian was not obliged to adhere to them."

"I suppose you are right," he conceded with a sigh. "At any rate, Henry was furious when that scheme didn't work out. But not for Anne's sake, for his own.

With Henry it is always about control over Montrose." His voice had become tinged with bitterness. "He married Anne off to an old man incapable of producing children, and now it is too late for her. I am sure bitterness eats away at her happiness even now."

The vehemence of Edwyn's tone surprised her. That there was no love lost between the brothers was painfully apparent. "But Henry can have no effect on my life," she said.

"If Julian does not produce an heir, Sir Henry gets Montrose. It is all he has ever wanted. Don't underestimate him, is all I am saying. He will stop at nothing to secure what he believes is rightfully his. I shudder to think what the man is capable of—of what he may have already done." He looked at her intently, "I have my suspicions about the death of Lady Alice, your predecessor. And that is all I am going to say on the matter."

"But Edwyn—"

"No. I have done my duty and warned you, as I should." He grinned at her in the boyish way she had come to expect. It was as though the serious young man of moments ago had never existed. "And now let us just enjoy the day. I have a beautiful lady at my side, and do not intend to waste the afternoon on doom and gloom. Shall we canter?" He nudged his horse and the little party trotted forward.

Madelyn was left to consider his words. She had her own suspicions about the death of Lady Alice. Was Henry the culprit? He certainly had motive, and now Edwyn was suggesting exactly that.

As they cantered across the field, her thoughts strayed to Anne. Edwyn saw her as bitter and angry from the decisions made so long ago. Anne had claimed she and Lady Alice were friends. If Edwyn was correct about Anne's state of mind, it would have been difficult for his sister to befriend the woman who had taken what she must have considered rightfully hers. And when Lady Alice became pregnant, it could only have been a blow to her. Anne herself had admitted to finding Lady Alice on that fateful day.

Thankfully, she was not left to contemplate the dour possibilities for long. The next time they walked the horses, Edwyn was his usual self, an entertaining companion. As though determined to dispel the mood left by his earlier revelations, he regaled her with stories of growing up on the range. And always his tales ended with an amusing twist.

The afternoon passed quickly. It wasn't long before they returned to the stables. Madelyn noticed Julian stood like a sentinel at the stable doors, watching their approach. He did not look pleased.

Edwyn shot her a mischievous grin. "Shall we end this day the way it began? If nothing else, it irritates your serious husband."

Edwyn nudged his horse into a dressage maneuver, trotting diagonally in front of her, then behind, before coming up alongside her as they reached the barns. He then repeated his bow from earlier, his horse gracefully arching, this time in Julian's direction. "I have returned your Lady unscathed your Lordship," he said, his eyes dancing with merriment.

Glancing at Julian's dark scowl, Madelyn was forced to contain her nervous giggle. "Edwyn, you are a rascal," she said. Edwyn clearly relished the opportunity to annoy her husband.

"You are quite the performer Edwyn. Some things never change," Julian said reaching up to assist Madelyn from the saddle. "I would expect nothing less than a safe return. After all, you would be foolish to be careless with my wife."

It was a warning. As her feet touched the ground, Madelyn saw that Julian's ravaged face sported a cold glare. He looked dangerous indeed. Once again, she was reminded of the warriors of old.

But Edwyn was cheerfully unaffected. "Thank you my dear, for an entertaining afternoon. And now I must be off," Edwyn said, doffing his hat with a grin, before turning his horse about and trotting down the lane.

Julian led Queeny into the stable where Ned had already unsaddled his horse. Madelyn reluctantly followed.

Madelyn eyed Julian's stiff back with some trepidation. Flirting with Edwyn last night, and she admitted to herself she had encouraged the young man, then riding with him today may have pushed Julian too far. She considered turning about and retreating to the house. It was tempting to avoid what could be a painful scene. But Julian had said if she rode, she must also groom her own horse, and that she would do.

Besides, she thought, *I will not be intimidated by the man*. She raised her chin a notch; she had done nothing wrong. Still, there was the disconcerting feeling she was walking into a battle.

CHAPTER 19

THE SWEET SMELL OF HAY

"Would you like me to take care of Queeny?" Ned asked, as they entered the barn.

"No." Julian replied, "Lady Madelyn will handle the task on her own. And I will finish up with your horse. You may leave us."

Madelyn held back an objection. At least with Ned present, it was unlikely Julian would start an argument. But now she would be quite alone with her husband.

Julian said nothing as the two of them worked side by side to stable the horses. Once Queeny was secured in her stall, Madelyn turned to fetch her a reward for the day's ride. Julian followed her to the far stall, where they kept a variety of supplies. Beside a mound of sweet-smelling hay, was the barrel of oats. She could feel Julian's eyes boring into her back. Her skin tingled with awareness as she measured out a serving of oats into a bucket.

She wished he would say something. His silence

was unnerving. Finally, she could stand it no more. She set the bucket down next to the mound of hay and turned to him. "Surely you are not angry with me for riding with Edwyn this afternoon?"

Julian gave her a familiar scowl. With his ravaged face, and ice-blue stare, his looks were intimidating. Madelyn was sure he was aware of the impact he made, but she refused to be cowed, raising her eyebrows expectantly. "Well?" she persisted.

After a long minute she began to wonder if he would answer her at all. When he finally spoke, his voice was dangerously soft. "I told you Edwyn was a womanizer. And what is more the man takes particular pleasure in provoking me. He would like nothing so much as to make me a cuckold. Surely you realize that?"

Trying to contain her burst of anger, she glared back at him. "Are you implying I would participate in such a liaison, because for you to be a cuckold Julian I—"

He cut her off. "I don't know what game you are playing Madelyn. But it will end today."

Madelyn's face burned with indignation. "How dare you! You have no right to order me about!"

"I am your husband. It is my responsibility. No," he corrected, narrowing his eyes, "it is my duty to see to your safety."

She took a step toward him, put her hands upon her hips and glowered up at him. The humiliation she had endured over the past few days resurfaced. "That might be true Julian if you were indeed a husband. But given you take such pains to avoid my company and my bed, you can hardly claim the privileges of a husband now."

She immediately regretted her words. She had always been unable to control her blunt tongue, despite her mother's endless efforts. This was not how she had hoped to address the issues in their marriage. She stole a glance at him, to check his reaction. His face was still but for the ominous twitching of his damaged cheek.

Then Julian's face twisted into a half smile, contradicting the glitter of anger in his eyes. His voice was dangerously soft when he spoke. "Well, if that is what you are wanting, I can certainly oblige."

He put his hands on her shoulders and pulled her tight against his body. Julian angry, was a fearsome thing. She was made instantly aware of his powerful breadth and hard strength. She braced herself against the trickle of alarm coursing through her body, before reminding herself this was her kind and gentle man; the one she had come to love.

And then he just held her there, in complete stillness. Her head lay on his chest, where the scent of him invaded her consciousness. She was unable to resist turning her face into his body and breathing deeply of his scent. Her arms involuntarily found his shoulders, then his broad back.

Julian gave an agonized groan. His arms circled her as he leaned down to rest his head in the hollow between her neck and shoulder. His breath warmed her skin. She experienced the familiar headiness he inspired with just his nearness.

Tipping her head back, she willed him to meet her gaze. He did. And this time his face had a tender expression. She rose to her tiptoes to touch her lips to his, her eyes searching his surprised ones. That first touch sparked a storm of uncontrollable passion. What began as a tentative kiss, evolved into a passionate embrace. She gripped him to her, as a sizzle of lightning rippled through their bodies. The taste, smell, and feel of him was overwhelming.

A sudden need to have his skin against hers, had Madelyn pulling up his shirt. And then began a kind of madness. A flurry of hands sent shirts, jackets, and even her chemise flying to the floor, until at last there was nothing between them. There was only delicious nakedness and an uncontrollable urgency.

She was vaguely aware of Julian spreading out the skirt of her riding habit, his lips never leaving her body, while pulling them both down into the mound of hay. Their bodies came together, hands and lips touching and caressing, glorying in a flood of sensation. She was adrift in a haze of passion. There was only the sense of need—to have Julian on and inside her, to make them one.

Her legs and arms were wrapped around him; their bodies wet and yearning. A moan escaped her lips when at last she felt him ease into her body. She became lost in the ever-increasing tempo of Julian above her, until she could only arch her hips into his.

Just when she knew she could bear it no longer, when every nerve in her screamed for release, Julian thrust hard into her body with a hoarse shout. She tightened her grip. Her calves, thighs, and even her hands held him to her as his pulsing climax triggered her own release.

It was too much. An involuntary scream escaped her lips and was quickly smothered by Julian's lips on hers. And then the world blurred.

A tickling sensation along her jawline forced her to reluctantly open her eyes.

Julian tossed the bit of straw he had been teasing her with aside. "Ah, my lady lives," he said, leaning down to kiss her lightly upon the tip of her nose.

"Was I asleep?"

"I think you were," he said and smiled. He ran his hand lightly down the curve of her body finally cupping her hip. "Someday my dear, we will have to try this in an actual bed. I hear it can be quite comfortable." He brushed a bit of straw from her buttocks. "And not likely to give us the itch."

Madelyn smiled, reaching up and circling his neck. "I am all for it," she said, holding his gaze while arching toward him for a kiss. Her goal was interrupted by the rattle of a harness followed by someone whistling as they worked only a few meters away in the stable.

Their eyes widened simultaneously. For an instant they just stared at each other, realizing the reality of their circumstances. Madelyn knew a moment of sheer panic. It was unthinkable for the new Lady Montrose to be caught in such a ridiculous position—naked in a mound of hay. It would be on the tongue of every servant in the manor before she made it back to the house.

Julian leapt up, reached for her discarded chemise, and flung it at her. There was a frantic scramble to don their clothing. Somehow it was more difficult and awkward trying to get the clothing on than it had ever been taking it off.

Her blouse and jacket needed only a quick shake, to rid them of the dust from the floor, but her skirt was a disaster. Bits of hay clung to the finely woven wool, ground in by the weight of their bodies while it had protected them from the hay. She tried in vain to remove it, first by shaking it, then by brushing. But it was of no use. Giving up, she pulled the thing on.

To make matters worse, Julian looked impeccable. His tight trousers, tucked into tall leather boots were perfectly molded over his strong thighs. His shirt and riding jacket had not a single blade of hay on them to mark the occasion. There were only a few strands of dark hair escaping his leather tie, and these he nonchalantly tucked behind his ear.

She scowled at him. "How is it that I look exactly as if I were tumbled in the hay like a naughty milkmaid, and you look as though you could walk into Almack's? It is not fair."

He reached down and plucked a few pieces of straw from her hair. "There, you look presentable," he said, then glanced down at the skirt. "Turn around, it seems the back got the worst of it." He crouched down, attempting to pluck some of the hay from the skirt. "Oh dear," he muttered as he worked, "this is impossible. The stuff is ground into the fabric. It's like dealing with burrs."

After a series of grunts from her husband, with Madelyn twisting about in an attempt to check his progress, Julian said, "I have the perfect solution. Wait here." He patted her butt, grinning as he stepped past her into the stable aisle.

He returned in a moment holding up his prize. "The curry brush," he said, "works on all my mares." He chuckled.

Squatting behind her once more, he began combing out the material across her buttocks and down her thighs. "A fine set of hind quarters my dear," he said and laughed. "Who knew I could enjoy grooming so much?"

Madelyn did not appreciate being compared to his mares, but she was willing to ignore the insult if it meant she could walk into the house without a bale of hay clinging to her behind. Plus, Julian's obvious joy in his solution made the whole experience worth it.

Julian sat back on his heels to survey his progress. "Works like a charm," he said. "Just a bit more here on the sides." He pulled the material tight across her bum to continue combing it out. "Such a fine rounded arse."

"Arrr, hmm." sounded from the aisle.

They both looked up in alarm to see Hamish leaning against the beam at the stall's gate.

"I hesitate to ask," he said, grinning at them.

The picture they must have made had Madelyn's cheeks burning with embarrassment. She refused to meet Hamish's eyes, while she searched for a viable explanation.

Julian, however, was unaffected. He patted her behind once more, then rose to his feet and stepped around her to hang the brush on a hook. He too sported a wide grin. "I like to keep my girls well groomed," he said, which only added to her mortification.

Hamish laughed. "I don't suppose you're interested in riding out to check the east farms. The tenants there are wanting some cottage improvements—new roofs for starters. It won't take more than an hour." His eyes twinkled with amusement. "Or we could wait for another day if you are preoccupied."

Julian tilted his head in her direction, "Would you like to join us?"

"No—No thank you," Madelyn stuttered. She had ridden enough today. Besides her emotions, and indeed her body, felt tender and raw. She longed for the comfort of her room, where perhaps she would have a warm bath and contemplate the afternoon's experience. More than anything she wanted to escape the knowing eyes of Hamish, and even Julian, who looked at her now with a quizzical expression.

She turned around to hurry away, again feeling the flush of embarrassment on her cheeks.

"Wait," Julian said, stepping forward to catch her

arm. He pulled her close, his strong hands warm against her shoulders, and kissed her lightly on the mouth. Julian was not one to show affection in front of others. His gesture took her by surprise.

"I look forward to our evening together," he said. His eyes held hers for a moment. She was too flustered to read their depths and could only nod. Carefully avoiding what she was sure would be Hamish's amused gaze, she spun again and rushed out of the stable.

She was halfway across the back gardens before she could calm her scattered thoughts. Just ahead the freshly trimmed hedge marked the walls of the hidden garden. Hurrying along the path while skirting its perimeter, she found the gap in the foliage and peeked into the enclosure.

The workers had done the planting. Flower beds had been dug up, fresh new roses and perennials were beginning to leaf on the mulched earth. Against the gray walls directly ahead, the alcove sat, newly cleaned and inviting.

A few minutes to herself was just what she needed. A path of flat rock, recently unearthed, wound through the space, and she followed it to the bench. New rose bushes had been planted at its base; their stems cut clean and stark. Fresh green stalks, swollen pink with buds and only a few small green leaves promised a bounty to come.

Sitting back against the bench, she closed her eyes and contemplated the events of this afternoon. This intimacy with Julian was as confusing as it was wonderful. She had no idea her body could react as it did to her husband's touch. Surely this development in their relationship would lead to the love she so wanted in her marriage.

A breeze ruffled the top of the hedge, and as if to negate her happy daydreams, the familiar low moaning began. The hollow eerie sound produced a ripple of unease, tightening her stomach.

"Curses be damned," she said aloud, "I will have my happy marriage. There will be no wailing from this bride of Montrose!"

Rising from the bench, she strode purposely from the hidden garden, and down the path to the library doors. Lady Katherine, Lady Alice, and whoever else had lived out an unfortunate existence here on the moors, had played out their destinies. Madelyn was determined to design her own fate.

There was indeed a loneliness in Montrose's isolation, especially if one kept to the house, hoping to create a replica of city life as Lady Alice had done. She, on the other hand, had come to love her new home and the land, far from the niceties of London's society. Lady Abigal had been happy here, embracing the land and its people. Madelyn intended to follow her path. There was a beauty here. It suited her. As did the strong gentle man who was its master.

Pushing the library doors open, she was relieved to discover that Sir Henry and Mrs. Waldron had abandoned their search. If there were even a few strands of hay on her skirts, Mrs. Waldron was sure to notice. She hurried through the common rooms and up the grand staircase.

Her first order of business was to procure a bath. From there she would renew her strategy to win her husband's love.

CHAPTER 20

A HONEYMOON OF SORTS

Julian slowly opened his eyes. His wife lay on his arm, her warm body curled into his. He could smell her soft feminine scent, combined with the sweet odor of rose water from her auburn hair, strewn across his shoulders, and bunched up under his chin.

It was early. A crepuscular light crept in from the window to caress the pastel hues of the bedding and sketch the form of his sleeping wife. Using only the tips of his fingers, he carefully pushed the thick strands of hair from Madelyn's face, tucking it behind her ears. He could just discern the smattering of freckles across her nose and cheeks. She looked so very young.

The covers had been pulled back revealing the creamy white skin of her shoulder, and slender back. His mind wandered to their night of shared intimacy. It was a strange and wondrous gift—this passion. For the first few days after the incident in the stables they had not strayed from their suite. Day and night had blurred while they explored each other's bodies. It had been a month now since he had begun to share her bed, and still there was no respite from his constant need for her.

Julian frowned as he considered the degree to which he was attracted to his wife. Still, he hoped to steer the relationship in a different trajectory than the route he had taken with his first wife. Other than those first shared intimacies he had been careful to withdraw before spilling his seed. If Madelyn knew of his precautions, she did not comment on it.

That his lovely young wife would be an eager lover was a surprise to him. He had expected the reticent attitude of his previous wife, Lady Alice. The physical attraction between Madelyn and him was a rare and wondrous gift, one he would cherish.

He looked down to find the subject of his thoughts sleepy-eyed and watching him. He leaned in to kiss her softly on the lips, then arched back to gaze at her, a question on his lips. Madelyn gave him the gentle smile he had come to know so well and turned to him, her arms circling his back. It was the answer he wanted.

Pulling her slender body against his, he let his hands wander down the length of her back and over her slim hips. She felt so small against his hard body; warm and inviting. When she raised her hips to meet his, he slid slowly into her. He groaned and laid his head against her shoulder, tasting the salty tang of her flesh. He could not get enough of this woman.

Very gently he moved against her, taking care not to

disturb her from that dreamy state between wakefulness and sleep. She was warm, wet, and soft. He watched her face, her eyes were closed, her lips slightly parted as she moved rhythmically against him. Never had she been more beautiful. When she softly gasped her woman's pleasure, he held her close against his body until he was unable to contain himself and withdrew to allow his release.

"I love you Julian," she murmured.

It was not the first time he had heard those words from her. Several times this week, while in the throes of passion, she had given him her declaration of love. He knew she hoped for a matching response from him, but this he could not do. He would not fall again into the vulnerable position he had found himself in after the death of Alice. Never again.

Yet it delighted him to hear her speak the words—she pleased him. He refused to analyze his feelings beyond that. He looked down at her, asleep once more, and leaned in to kiss her lightly on the forehead. Taking care not to wake her, he eased his tangled body from hers.

It was time to start his day. Already the stable hands would be moving about. One of his mares had been brought into a pen last night expecting to have her foal. He was eager to check her progress this morning. Today, like every day since Madelyn had come into his life, he would try to leave the thoughts of his lovely wife behind and focus on his one true love—Montrose.

Julian found Hamish already in the stable checking the young mare.

"Ah, there you are. I wondered if you would come down this morning," Hamish said with a grin.

"And why would I not?" Julian answered.

Hamish chuckled. "Well, you've been a might distracted lately. Mayhap there is something up at the house that has you a bit fazed. You have the ragged look of a buck after the rut."

Julian shot him a dark look which prompted a burst of laughter from Hamish.

"Nothing has me, 'fazed' Hamish. And there is naught that can take me from my work," he said firmly.

"Aye, so you say," Hamish said, still smiling. He patted Julian's shoulder. "Not to worry lad, you'd be a strange man indeed if that pretty young wife of yours did not hold your thoughts."

Julian only grunted in response. It irritated him that Hamish assumed he was preoccupied with his wife. He furrowed his brow, resolving once more to banish Madelyn from his mind during the workday.

For the next two hours when he found himself distracted by the image of her soft sultry smile in his bed, the smattering of freckles which graced the bridge of her nose, or even her easy laughter, he squashed the thoughts. He was determined to keep a safe distance between them.

Yet when he and Hamish came in for breakfast at their usual time, he was displeased when Madelyn did not join them as usual. He found he could not concentrate on Hamish's words and instead focused on the entrance, waiting for her arrival. It was only Hamish's knowing grin that kept him from leaving the table to search her out.

It was unlike her to miss the morning ritual. Despite his best efforts he found himself wondering and worrying. It was going to be a long day.

CHAPTER 21

THE ARTIST'S INSPIRATION

Madelyn slowly awakened to the familiar sounds of one of the twins preparing her dressing room. She reached out across the cool sheets to where Julian had lain and smiled. The bedroom was the one place where she felt confident her marriage would be all she hoped for. Outside of this room, Julian was more distant than ever. The more intimate they became in this suite; the stiffer and more withdrawn Julian became. Sometimes she felt as though she was engaged in a battle, winning little victories only to lose ground, and be pushed back on another front.

The day promised to be an interesting one. Julian had commissioned an artist to do her portrait, which meant her mornings were taken up with sittings. Knowing her picture would soon join the other Ladies of Montrose left her with a queasy sense of misgiving. There was something unnerving in the idea of her image mounted in the gloomy hallway alongside her long dead predecessors.

Today her afternoon plans included a ride with Lady Anne. She was pleased with the relationship she had begun to develop with her neighbor. Though Anne was not an extroverted conversationist, the two of them shared a love of riding, and the moors.

There was no time to lounge about this morning and contemplate her battle plans in the ongoing war to win her husband's love. The bedroom was already filled with light, which meant she must hurry to catch Julian and Hamish at breakfast. But the moment her feet touched the floor a wave of nausea overwhelmed her. Snatching up her dressing gown, she scrambled to the dressing room to vomit over the basin.

Annmarie hurried forward. "Oh dear," the maid exclaimed.

The episode left her shaken. "I think this morning I will have breakfast in my room," she said. Though she felt no further queasiness she thought it might be best to move at a slower pace.

She had just settled down to eat in her sitting room when an abrupt knock sounded at the hall door and Mrs. Waldron entered. She stepped into the room and stood rigidly by the door, her usual stern expression on her face.

"Annmarie informs me that you were feeling sick this morning. Is this the case?" she asked. Her expression was almost accusatory.

Madelyn felt her cheeks redden. "Y-yes," she stuttered, "but I am feeling much better now."

The housekeeper ran her eyes over her person as though assessing the truth of her statement. There was a long pause. Madelyn felt the need to fill the silence. "I am sure it was just something I ate."

"Harumph!" Mrs. Waldron grunted. "And you have not had your courses since your arrival."

It was not a question but a statement of fact. Madelyn's first reaction was one of indignation. How dare the woman monitor her privacy. Her second thoughts created a shockwave. The implication was that she was increasing!

But how could this be, she thought, I have been a wife for less than three short months? Surely that is not the case, not so soon. It simply could not be true. Mrs. Waldron must be mistaken. She took a deep breath and attempted to calm her racing thoughts.

Mrs. Waldron stood by the door waiting for a response.

"It is simply that I—I am a little nauseous, nothing else," Madelyn stuttered. She refused to consider any other possibility.

"Harumph," the woman grunted once more. Her brows furrowed and her lips compressed with firm disapproval. Madelyn had to bite her lip to avoid apologizing for her audacity in becoming so quickly pregnant.

"Well, we shall see, it is early days," the housekeeper

said, giving Madelyn an abrupt nod before turning and leaving the room. Madelyn heard her mutter something as she closed the door. Mrs. Waldron behaved as though her becoming pregnant so quickly was a gross indecency. And perhaps it was, she thought with a grimace —not indecent, she corrected, but certainly shocking.

Madelyn was left with a whirlwind of thoughts. The idea of a pregnancy so early in her marriage was not something she had foreseen. She shook her head at her naivety. It was the natural order of things. "I don't know why I had not considered it," she whispered aloud. Somehow in her daydreams of the perfect and loving relationship with Julian she had not foreseen the idea of a child.

Not for the first time, she wished her mother were here. If only she was within visiting distance. Railway lines were being constructed all over England. Indeed, rails were even now being laid on routes North. But that was for the future. As things stood now, it would take several days to travel to London by coach. She decided to write to her mother this afternoon. If she was indeed pregnant, her mother would surely calm her misgivings and help her accept this startling development with the grace expected of her. Mama always knew the proper behavior for a lady.

Her mind wandered to the birch cradle so lovingly crafted and waiting under its sheet in the nursery. The image left her with a feeling of dread. Lady Alice too had quickly become pregnant. Perhaps history was repeating itself. She pushed the awful thought out of her mind.

"Don't be ridiculous," she muttered, rising from her little table, and tossing her napkin on her plate, "I am just a bit nauseous."

There was no time to consider the possibility now. She was due downstairs in the green room for her sitting. Besides, she reassured herself, I feel perfectly fit —the whole thing is just speculation. There is simply no cause to become agitated by the notion. If I skipped my courses, it is likely the result of all the recent changes in my life.

The artist, an elderly Italian man named Mr. Caldonus, was working at his easel when she walked in. He was short in stature with long greasy hair which curled at his shoulders. He wore a brocade paisley vest over a faded linen shirt and the old-fashioned short pants and leggings of previous decades—an outfit which had remained unchanged since his arrival over a week ago.

They had decided to paint her on horseback, and thus a side saddle had been mounted on the back of a stuffed couch. She was required to balance awkwardly on this homemade contraption.

After sitting in a strained position for what felt like a lifetime, she began to regret agreeing to this unusual pose for a lady. She had readily consented in part since it was so different from the perfect portrait of Lady Alice in quiet repose. She did not want to compete with that.

"Raise your chin just a little," Mr. Caldonus instructed, "Ah good, good. And shoulders back. Good, good."

She sighed, and he scowled at her, gesturing with his brush that she should resume her stiff posture. She ignored her instinct to return his scowl, obediently straightening her shoulders.

"How much longer sir?" she asked.

"A little, a little." he replied, not looking away from his work. It was the same response she had received an hour ago.

Little indeed, she thought, odious 'little' man.

This morning's sitting was even more difficult than usual. Her mind kept returning to the possibility of a pregnancy. The idea left her with a confusing mix of emotions—the most predominant of which was a panicked dread. Each time the unsettling topic came to mind, she tried to banish the thought, but she was unsuccessful.

Again, she thought longingly of her mother far away in London. Images of home brought such a wave of homesickness that Mr. Caldonus made a tut-tutting sound. "Enough, enough. You are frowning madam." He rapped his brush on his palette. "Pleasant thoughts please." Madelyn suppressed the urge to stick her tongue out at him and obediently smoothed her brow.

After what felt like hours, Mr. Caldonus leaned back in his chair and announced. "We are done here this morning. A little work on the background and the portrait will be complete." He took his brush and made a few quick strokes. "I will not need you tomorrow," he said without looking up from the painting.

Relieved, Madelyn slid awkwardly from her perch, and rotated her cramped shoulders. She walked to the easel. "May I see it please?" Thus far the artist had not allowed her to view his progress, saying she would have the opportunity only when it was complete.

Today Mr. Caldonus leaned back and gestured to the painting. Madelyn hesitantly stepped forward to examine the work.

The portrait had her seated on a horse at the end of the lane with the outline of Montrose in the background. She wore her green habit with a small bonnet set back on her head, and a braid of auburn hair was pulled forward to lay across her breast. Her chin was raised in an almost arrogant expression, and her eyes looked out of the painting as if daring anyone to question her right to be there.

It was not the sedate portrait of the Lady of the manor, not that she had wanted that image. Instead, it appeared to convey the blunt, stubborn personality her mother had worked so hard to quell. There was a quality of strength in the rendition. This woman looked invulnerable. And she wondered if she truly emitted the confidence this painting had captured. It was certainly not how she felt this morning.

Mr. Caldonus cleared his throat. "Does it please you?" He did not wait for her reply. Instead, leaning back and puffing out his chest, he answered his own question. "It is one of my best works. Yes, yes...I am quite satisfied. The portrait in your gallery was an excellent inspiration. Similar pose, different ladies."

Madelyn complimented the painting, but the man had already picked up his brush and was back at work. He only grunted in response and waved her away.

On her way to her room Madelyn glanced up at the ancestors. Soon her portrait would be among them. It was strange to think she was now the Lady of Montrose. Her likeness, hung here with the others, would be a final farewell to the young woman of London she had been. It was her tangible admittance to the clan of Montrose. Whatever her fate, she was forever a member of this exclusive group.

Curious about the portrait which had inspired Mr. Caldonus, Madelyn walked the length of the hall, scanning the faces of the ancestors. Pausing before the warrior with the brandished sword near the entry to her suite, she grinned up at him. "It seems you are my kinsman now. No need to fend me off with that fierce stance." But the soldier glared down at her, unrelenting.

As she progressed slowly down the hall, she examined the images of past wives of Montrose. They were sedate and lady-like, posed in sitting rooms, or as busts only, with faded nondescript backgrounds. One was set in a garden, but the picture was so browned with age and in need of cleaning, the details were lost. She decided to speak to Julian about the business of restoring them. Perhaps Mr. Caldonus would be up to the task.

Finally, near the back stairs she found a portrait of the mounted Lady Montrose. Yes, this one must have inspired Mr. Caldonus. This painting too was badly in need of cleaning. Madelyn rose onto her toes to examine it. The setting was familiar, with the woman posed in almost the exact position she had been. Montrose hall sat alone and desolate in the distance, its central tower jutting out into a dark sky. The house was unchanged, but for a wall which circled it, with its arched gate—the one still remaining today—closed and unwelcoming. The existence of the ancient walls informed Madelyn that the painting must date back at least two hundred years.

She leaned in close to examine the darkened image of the woman. The lady was wearing a full-length cape over a bronze riding habit, the folds of which cascaded elegantly across the flank of a black horse. A patterned headdress sat atop her golden hair with attached scarves discreetly wrapped around her face. The artist had allowed one thick strand of blonde curling hair to escape and trail scandalously down to her waist. The Lady was young with the hint of a smile on her perfect features, as though she was privy to some secret knowledge. *A beauty to be sure,* Madelyn thought.

Resting back on her heels, Madelyn looked at the name plate embedded in the portrait's heavy frame. The little plaque was dusted over and illegible. Her fingers hesitated over the grimy nameplate. The awful certainty that she knew what name would emerge had her frozen in place. And she was right. After a few quick swipes of the bronze plate, the inscription was revealed: Lady Katherine Stallridge 1630-1649.

So young, she thought to herself, *and if legend is correct, newly pregnant*. She looked up once more at the painting. There was no evidence that the woman was increasing in the image. But of course, there would not be. Even the portrait of Lady Alice had no such hints.

The thought gave her pause. It was another strange coincidence. Three new wives, three pregnancies, all cursed.

She turned abruptly from the image and marched back to her room, scolding herself as she went. She had allowed her thoughts to go wild this morning. The whole scene with Mrs. Waldron's insinuations had her nerves on edge. She was not increasing, and there was no curse on the brides of Montrose.

But in the back of her mind, a lingering uncertainty remained.

CHAPTER 22

A PICNIC GONE AWRY

Julian had spent a long week at his desk. Without a secretary, all rental agreements had to be handwritten by him personally. It was a monotonous and time-consuming business, one that left him exhausted and irritated.

In London, Hamish had suggested a clerk, or a young lawyer be hired, at least for the spring, to help with the lease renewals on his properties in the village, whose ten-year contracts were due this year. The documents would all reflect the same terms, only the dates would be changed, extending the agreements. Unfortunately, this time a simple alteration would not do, and the bloody papers had to be rewritten, signed, and dated. But the wages of such an employee would make a hearty contribution toward the price of a thoroughbred stud he had his eye on, and he had chosen the stallion.

Badly in need of a break, he put his pen in its

holder, stood, and stretched his stiff shoulders. He walked the length of the library to look out at the stables and the land beyond. All but two of the pregnant mares he had purchased in London had already dropped their foals and were now grazing in the small pasture behind the stables. Though it would be some time before the horses could be sold for a profit, their purchase was a wise decision. He was convinced the new thoroughbreds would be the next popular choice of the equestrian community.

Montrose could not rely on wool alone to secure its future. Even the rent of his tenants came indirectly from the wool markets. And since the war with Napoleon was over, the prices of wool had dropped. Furthermore, much of the estate was beautiful, but boggy moorland was unfit for grazing or the production of wheat. The estate needed a secure income.

What the holding did have was coal; scores of it, near enough to the surface to tempt the likes of his cousin Henry. All his decisions upon returning home were aimed at saving this beautiful land. Even procuring his young wife—an extravagant expense, would be well worth it if it meant keeping his beloved Montrose intact. Should Henry ever become the Lord of Montrose, the land as it was would be forever altered.

He was distracted from his thoughts by the sight of Ned leading a saddled Queeny from the stables. He smiled. Madelyn and Anne had planned another ride, complete with a picnic today. Ned was bringing the horse to the front of the house for his Lady.

He was pleased with the friendship between the women. More than anything, he wanted Madelyn to be happy. But the week had been a long one, with Madelyn twice missing breakfast, and arriving late when she did appear. He was uncertain whether it was contentment or some anxiety which altered her usual schedule. He had even considered the possibility of pregnancy, but the usual wave of unease tightened his belly, and he closed his eyes to banish the thought. It was too soon, and surely the fates would not issue him the same awful scenario. Hamish was right, he assured himself, Madelyn was not Lady Alice. There would be no repeat of the past.

He was distracted from his musings sometime later by the chatter of feminine voices from the hall. He stepped into the hallway just as Madelyn and Anne emerged from the green room. His wife looked pretty in her chocolate brown riding habit with a small hat perched saucily atop her auburn hair.

"Julian," she said, coming toward him, "I have just shown Lady Anne the portrait. She thinks it's marvelous."

He glanced at Anne. As usual she cowered uncomfortably in his presence, her cheeks stained pink. "It is beautiful; a remarkable likeness," she said.

"Well then," he replied, taking his wife's hands, to walk her to the door, "you are in agreement with me."

"Won't you change your mind and join us on our

picnic? I am sure the kitchen has packed enough for all of us," Madelyn said.

She smiled up at him, and he could not resist returning her grin. "Would that I could," he answered, "but alas my paperwork awaits me."

He walked them through the doors to where the horses stood ready, picnic baskets attached to their sidesaddles. He released his wife to assist Lady Anne into the saddle and was handing her the reins when Queeny gave a snort of alarm.

Madelyn had not waited for his help, but instead held the reins and saddle horn with one hand while she put her foot in the stirrups to hoist herself up. Queeny's ears were back, and she snorted nervously, sidestepping away from her.

"Madelyn—" he warned. But it was too late. Before she was even able to hook her leg behind the pommel, the horse let loose a frenzied bray and began to buck.

Julian lunged in their direction, but the horse was already in a frantic mode, leaping and twisting to throw its rider. Queeny leapt forward, kicking out her heels then arching into the air. Julian's attempts to reach her were in vain. He could only flay about in a mad effort to secure the dangling reins. The horse reared high, then plunged into a bucking gallop, circling the courtyard. Madelyn was flipped from Queeny's side to the cobble stones below, landing squarely on her behind.

He rushed to her. "Are you hurt? Have you been injured?" he asked. Without waiting for an answer, he scooped her up into his arms. He was vaguely aware of the little crowd that had gathered in the courtyard.

"Julian, I am fine. Please. A little shook up is all. Just put me down," she said, pushing against his firm grip.

He looked down at her disgruntled face, a grimace of pain evident in her expression. "There will be no riding today," he announced. "Ned, send someone from the stables to fetch Old Bess. And have Hamish see to Queeny. Something is wrong with the mare."

He carried his wife through the entry, ignoring her protests. "Bring my lady her lunch, the picnic is cancelled. And get her something to settle her nerves," he ordered to the little gathering of bystanders hovering at the door. "And you, Annmarie, may help her out of this gear. As I said, there will be no riding today."

"Julian, really. Set me down," Madelyn protested, "We cannot abandon Miss Anne in the yard. She is my guest. I am fine."

"I am sure Anne can find her way back to the dower house without our help," he replied, then ignoring her further protests, continued on to her suite, with one of her maids following in their wake.

"Julian, for heaven's sake," she admonished as he set her carefully on her bed. "This is entirely unnecessary. I am perfectly fine."

"Humor me my love," he replied. "Now then, let's get this riding gear off and check the damage, shall we." He nudged her to her feet. Once satisfied she could stand on her own, he helped her remove the jacket and began fumbling at the ties on her skirt.

He turned to a rosy-cheeked Annmarie, "You may give us a minute or two. In the meantime, find my lady something more comfortable to wear." The girl rushed out.

"Julian, I—"

"Let's take this skirt off and have a look," he insisted, "I'll not leave here until I see for myself that no damage has been done."

She sighed. "Fine. But you may quit scowling. All is well with me."

He helped her remove the skirt and tossed it aside. Hiking up her chemise he squatted down and ran his hands along her legs, much as he would have had she been one of his prized mares. He made her bend her knees to check for injuries, then lift each leg to check her hips. To his relief all was well. He could feel the nervous tension leave his body. She would be stiff and sore, but she had come through the incident relatively unscathed.

He gently turned her to look at her backside. When he examined her derriere, he could not contain a low whistle. "You have some nasty bruising here my dear." The damage was extensive but looked to be limited to bruising which thankfully would heal without permanent injury. But the sight of her purple backside left him shaken. Being thrown onto the hard cobbles in the courtyard could have meant her death.

She winced when he applied pressure to her hips, "It is a little sore Julian."

"I can see that it is. You are turning a ghastly shade of blue." Madelyn tried to twist around to see the injury. Realizing he was scaring her unnecessarily he added, "But I think, my love, that you have been most fortunate." Wanting to relieve her worries he gave a little chuckle. "Lucky that you have such a fine round arse to protect you at times like these." He patted her bum, then leaned in and planted a kiss on each rounded cheek.

"Julian," Madelyn gasped, just as the young maid came into the room holding a nightgown draped across her arms. The poor girl's cheeks could not be redder as she stood frozen in the entry.

He laughed, letting Madelyn's chemise fall back in place as he rose to his feet. "I will leave you ladies to it. But only if you promise, my love, not to leave your rooms until Old Bess has seen you and assured me that all is well."

"Julian is that necessary? I thought to—" His glare made her pause. He crossed his arms, raised his brows, and waited for her compliance.

For a moment she glowered at him. Finally, with a sigh of resignation she said, "Fine. I will sit here and wait for Old Bess. But after that I will go about as I please."

She did not take orders well. He was accustomed to having his commands followed without question, both as a captain in the king's troops and here at the estate.

If his position did not intimidate, then the fearsome sight of his scarred face was enough to have men jump to do his bidding. It was a wonder to him that his wife was the only person, besides perhaps Hamish, unaffected by even his most intimidating scowls.

Back in the stables, he found Hamish returning Queeny to her stall. He waited while the man secured the gate.

"Well, I think I determined Queeny's trouble," Hamish said, reaching into his jacket pocket, "I found this tangled in her saddle blanket, directly under the seat."

Hamish pulled out a metal object and handed it to him. Julian examined the piece. It was a jagged shard of metal with a flat-backed plug. The kind used by tinners to connect handles to a tub or a bucket.

Hamish continued. "Stuck as it was under the saddle, it would have bothered the mare. Then, when Lady Madelyn mounted, it cut Queeny's skin. Can't say I blame the horse for acting out the way she did."

"What the hell was this doing in the gear?"

Hamish grimaced. "Yes, well, that is the question. It seems the horse blankets were fresh back from laundering. Ned collected them only this morning. The bit of metal must have become tangled in the wool while being cleaned. Ned says he did not notice it when he saddled Queeny. It must have been completely embedded in the wool."

Julian was not appeased. "It is a mistake that could have cost her Ladyship dearly. Luckily, she hasn't broken any bones, and will heal." He could feel his anger rising as he contemplated again what could have happened. "I cannot have this kind of incompetence, not when it concerns my wife."

Hamish nodded. "Glad to hear Lady Madelyn was not seriously injured. Young Ned is packing as we speak. The poor lad is devastated. Keeps saying he noticed nothing when he saddled the mare. The thing could have been impossible for him to see, wound up in the material most likely." Hamish waited a moment for Julian to process the information.

Julian sighed. It would have been satisfying to boot the boy from the premises. It might even have helped calm the nervous tension still churning his stomach, but it would hardly be fair. It seemed to have been an honest mistake; an anomaly not likely to reoccur.

"Tell Ned he will be staying on. But inform him that I expect him to personally examine every piece of tack to ensure it is safe. Anything, and I mean anything, that is to be used by Lady Madelyn will be checked and double checked, each and every time she rides. There will be no such accident in the future. Is that clear?"

Hamish nodded again, with a hint of a smile. "A good decision my Lord." He touched Julian lightly on the shoulder. "I will go now and relieve the boy of his worries. It's glad I am to hear your Lady is unhurt. Lady Madelyn is not as delicate as she looks. I am sure she will recover from this incident without a lot of fuss."

Watching Hamish's back as he left the stables, Julian

had to admit the man was right. Any pain or anxiety his wife had experienced from this ordeal was more likely the result of his demands that she remain in her suite until Old Bess arrived, rather than from being thrown from her horse. He recalled her disgruntled expression when she begrudgingly gave her promise to stay put and smiled.

Still the knot in his stomach remained. He knew what it meant. It had taken him ten long years to accept his inability to protect his first wife. He had failed her. But more than that, his feelings for Alice had left him vulnerable, with the terrible pain of loss. This time, he had vowed to keep Madelyn at a distance, their marriage designed as a partnership to ensure the future of his estate. Somehow, the woman had wriggled her way into his heart.

"Damn!" he muttered, his scarred cheek twitching in an attempt to match the scowl on the right side of his face. He pushed all thoughts of Madelyn and his feelings aside. He would deal with it later.

On his way back to the house, he realized he was still holding the bit of metal in his hand. He examined it once more as he walked. It was certainly a nasty shard of metal. Strange how it had ended up entwined in her horse blanket. For a moment, a niggling suspicion nibbled at the edge of his consciousness, but he dismissed it. This was his home. Surely, there could not be such a threat to her safety here.

CHAPTER 23

A DIAGNOSIS AND A PRESCRIPTION

Old Bess was not as interested in her bruised backside as she was in the possibility her Ladyship may be carrying. After a brief examination, Madelyn invited Old Bess to join her for a little luncheon. Annmarie brought a light soup, fresh scones, and gooseberry jelly. After eating, the ladies sat comfortably at her little table in her sitting room, enjoying a bit of tea.

"And your breasts my dear, have they been tender?" Bess asked.

"They have," Madelyn answered. "The last two weeks they have been noticeably sore."

"I think we can be quite certain you are with child, m'lady. My, that was quick. Your symptoms say you're at least eight weeks along."

Madelyn thought back to the early days of her marriage. She must have become pregnant that very first time amongst the crocuses near the pond. She smiled to herself, resting her hand on her still slim waist. It was an auspicious start to this new life.

Old Bess interrupted her thoughts. "Have you told the Lord?"

"Not yet. I only just realized." Madelyn's mind turned to Julian's extreme reaction after her fall this morning. She frowned. "I am not sure I want to tell him just yet. He will only fuss."

Old Bess chuckled; her startling blue eyes shining in her nut-brown face. "I heard he was a little overwrought this morning. Ah, but it's early yet, deary. The wait is much longer for men. Always wise to shorten it a little by holding off telling them for a week or two."

Eyeing her Old Bess became serious once more. She reached across the table and patted her hand. "Thus far there are no signs your little one is disturbed after your accident, but I think it wise to stay quiet for a time. Move slowly, keep to your rooms, and rest as much as possible. If there is even the slightest trace of blood, you must take to your bed and send for me."

Madelyn sighed. "If you think it is for the best, I should be able to manage to rest for a few days. But I do plan to keep this news to myself for a while. After this morning, I don't trust his Lordship to not confine me to my quarters for the duration." Madelyn paused for a moment, "If there are no further complications, will I be able to carry on like usual? Will I be able to ride?"

"Do what you always do, I say," Old Bess responded. "Though you should probably not exert yourself over much, and getting lots of rest helps…it's always best to remain active. Riding shouldn't be an issue—until later in the pregnancy of course. Lady Abigal rode until her sixth month." Old Bess chuckled. "I can't think you'll be wanting to ride much just now anyway, what with that bruised backside of yours. It'll be a week at least before you can sit a horse."

The old woman grinned and shook her head. "As to keeping this pregnancy to yourself, there's little hope of that. If the servants of Montrose know then those in the dower house will soon know too. Servants talk and a new heir will be powerful news. The twins have a sister who cooks up at the dower house. Mildred is her name. That woman lives to talk. By the week's end the whole village will have heard. Gossip is dear in this county—especially when it involves the folks up here on the rise."

Annmarie entered with a tray. "Cook sent up Old Bess' favorite lemon cake for a spot of dessert," she said, arranging the cake on the table. "And Mrs. Waldron asks how you're faring. She gave me this tincture to settle your nerves." She held out a small glass of a vile-looking opaque substance. "She told me to be sure you drank it all," she added, handing Madelyn the glass.

Before she could bring the glass to her mouth, Old Bess stopped her hand. Smiling at Madelyn she said, "We'll have the cake first," then turning to Annmarie she added, "Give cook my thanks. And assure Mrs. Waldron her medicine is much appreciated."

Old Bess waited until Annmarie left the room before taking the glass and sniffing the concoction suspiciously. "Hmm," she grunted, wrinkling up her weathered face, "even I'm unsure of what this is." She set the glass down with a thump. "My advice to you my dear, and you may heed it or not, is to avoid any potions or elixirs. It's always tempting to relieve your symptoms, especially nausea, with a tonic." She made a tut-tutting sound and shook her head. "Never works well. A spot of lavender tea is the only thing I recommend."

"I would not want to hurt Mrs. Waldron's feelings. I am sure she means well," Madelyn said.

"Oh aye, well, I'm sure too. But sometimes having only a little knowledge is not such a good thing, eh? And I do recall that Florence's potions did little to help Sir Henry's wife, poor woman." Old Bess picked up the glass again and winked at her. Her eyes sparkled with mischief. "There are always ways to avoid displeasing others," she said, raising the glass in a mock toast, then in one quick movement tossed its contents into the potted plant near the window. "Done, and none's the wiser." She cackled happily.

Madelyn could not resist smiling with her friend.

After Old Bess left, Madelyn thought again of Julian and his reaction to her injury. It was not his extreme concern that held her interest, but the fact that he had twice called her 'my love.' She was sure he was unconscious of the phrase, but whether he was aware or not, he had used the endearment.

She persistently told him she loved him, and each time he either pretended he hadn't heard her or kissed her to avoid a response. But stubbornly refusing to say the words did not mean it was not so. She wrapped her arms around her body and smiled to herself. Julian cared for her; of that she was certain. And now, there would be the heir Julian needed. She would have all she wanted in this marriage.

To her surprise, Madelyn had no trouble keeping to her room for the day. Though her entire body ached, her thoughts were on the heady realization that her distant husband might truly love her at last. So elated was she by this notion, she was not even tempted to drink a dose of Mrs. Waldron's tincture, which the housekeeper delivered to her personally again in the afternoon, to relieve her pain. Mrs. Waldron, the twins, and Julian had been diligent in seeing to her care. Though her hips, back, and even her arms were stiff and sore, she was feeling rather pampered.

She forgave Queeny once she had been told of the metal shard beneath the saddle. How the twisted metal had come to be under her saddle she did not know. Certainly, it was an accident of some sort. However it came about, she realized how lucky she had been. Thankfully, it was her buttocks and not her head which had hit the cobblestones. Certainly, she could have been killed.

The blasted curse flitted across her consciousness, threatening to ruin her newfound joy. Lady Katherine had vowed that no Lord of Montrose would ever find happiness and love in a marriage until she was released from her tomb. The same curse promised an early death to any woman who dared to love a Montrose man. And Madelyn loved Julian; of that she was certain. Envisioning the poor woman's bones lying encased in the stone cellars below had her shivering with a kind of horror.

Was it coincidence that just as her husband was finally able to release his demons and build the happy, loving home she always envisioned, it was almost all taken away? Could the fateful words of Lady Katherine destroy their happiness? Perhaps she too was doomed to die young like her predecessors, leaving the Lord of Montrose to a life of misery.

She banished the thoughts, once again remembering Lady Abigale's happy life here on the moors. Not all the wives of Montrose were cursed. She put her hands to her stomach and closed her eyes, determined to dream of the loving family destined to be her future. But still, the awful thoughts persisted, ruining her vision of the happy future she so craved.

CHAPTER 24

AN INCIDENT IN THE DARK

Resting most of the day made sleeping that night difficult. She wished she had a glass of warm milk to help her relax. Ringing one of the twins was out of the question so late at night. After tossing and turning for what felt like hours, she decided a slow and careful trip to the kitchen would not be harmful and might be just what she needed to find her sleep. She wrapped her dressing gown around her and even remembered to don her slippers this time before venturing forth.

Outside her door, Madelyn stood for a moment, bracing herself to confront the dreaded hallway with its forbidding faces leering down at her. An overpowering foreboding clenched her stomach. It almost felt as though the ancestors were whispering a warning, their black eyes boring into her, denying her passage. She shook off the absurd notion and forced herself to step forward, fighting the powerful urge to return to the comfort of her bed.

Reminding herself she would soon join the ancestors when her portrait was mounted in this dark corridor, did little to relieve her tension. Keeping her eyes lowered, she hurried through the shadowed hallway to the staircase. She paused for a moment and grasped the heavy oaken handrail at the landing, taking deep breaths to ease her beating heart. Her childhood fear of the dark threatened to have her scurrying back to the safety of her room.

"Get a hold of yourself. This is ridiculous," she muttered aloud. Still, the dark cavern of the entry loomed before her, lit only by a feeble light at the bottom of the stairs. To the right an amber glow leaked into the gloom from the kitchen beyond, promising a haven. She concentrated on that, tiptoeing as quickly as her body would allow down the ancient stairs.

So focused was she on reaching the safety of the kitchen, that she bumped into the little table at the base of the stairs. It screeched across the stone tile, rocking the lantern on its surface, which clattered onto its side. She reached out and snatched it up before the light was extinguished. Carefully setting it back on its table. She paused, listening, hoping the racket had not awoken any of the staff. Nothing stirred.

Thankfully, the kitchen was indeed well lit. Rather than facing the gauntlet to her room, she perched on a stool at the wooden worktable to enjoy her milk with a slice of lemon cake, left over from her visit with Old Bess.

Feeling sated and drowsy at last, she was able to smile at her earlier misgivings as she slipped from the stool, ready to return to her suite. How silly and childish of her to be so frightened by a dark house. *It is my jangled nerves,* she thought, *I am overwrought from the day's events.*

But when she pushed through the swinging doors, the entry was completely black. Despite her bravado in the cozy kitchen, she froze for a moment and her stomach clenched. The lantern at the base of the stairs had gone out. It must have been damaged earlier when I knocked it about, she sighed.

She was determined not to be intimidated this time. Being scared of the dark was a childhood fear; one she had long since conquered.

"I am a grown woman now," she muttered aloud. "Besides," she assured herself, "I have travelled this route hundreds of times. I have even done it the dark without all this silliness."

Still, her unease persisted, and she turned back to scan the kitchen looking for a lantern to light her way. There were wall sconces, but that was all. Finally, she wedged her stool between the swinging doors to allow the kitchen light to bleed into the foyer and marched forward, comforting herself with the knowledge that once she reached the upper landing there would be the feeble light from the sconces in the hallway. Madelyn could not resist grinning about her perception of the dreaded hallway as a sanctuary.

She hesitated at the base of the stairs, waving her hands about in search of the heavy oak post. It was pitch black. Taking a deep breath, she peered upward, but could see nothing except a faint glow from the hall above. Just as she was about to begin her trek, she heard a strange scraping sound from above. "Is someone there?" she asked, her voice echoing in the cavernous room.

But there was only silence.

The first few steps were taken tentatively, with one hand gripping the rail. But her heart began to pound in her chest, and a surge of panic brought with it the urge to run. Despite her stiff body, she found herself scurrying up the stairs ever faster, her eyes trained on the glow above.

When Madelyn had almost reached the top, her shin slammed into some sort of obstruction. Her momentum sent her plummeting forward. She landed with a painful thump onto the oak stairs, her arms and shoulders taking the brunt of the impact.

Finding herself awkwardly imbalanced, and unable to get a proper grip, her body began to tumble backward. She rolled down several steps before instinctively reaching out for the railing. It was sheer luck that her hand connected immediately with one of the oak posts and she clutched it with all her strength, twisting to bring her other arm in position to get a secure hold. A slam to her shoulder almost had her losing her grip.

She hung on with both hands to the railing, until her body stilled.

It was several minutes before her labored breathing calmed enough for her to take stock of her situation. Her hands still gripped the oaken post, and she lay sprawled across several stairs, but the danger of falling had passed. There was only her ragged breathing in the inky darkness. She forced herself to sit up carefully, bracing herself on the heavy oak steps. Only then was she able to pry her fingers from the post.

Her arms and shoulder hurt where she had landed, and her shin ached from the impact. Other than that, she could discern no further injuries. She exhaled a cleansing breath and allowed relief to flood her senses. There was no fear of the dark now, only a self-recriminating irritation. How ridiculous that she had allowed her distress to overwhelm her. Her hand instinctively went to her belly as she thought of the possible consequences of tumbling all the way down this massive staircase.

I have been lucky indeed, she thought with a grimace, but there will be more bruising. It serves me right for running like a mad woman up the stairs in the dark.

Slowly and carefully, she crawled a few steps toward the landing. Her hands encountered the obstruction that must have caused her fall. She paused and ran her fingers along what felt like a pole of some sort, until she reached its bristled end. It was a broom. Unconcerned now about awakening the household, she tossed the thing over the railing. It hit the floor below with a satisfying clatter.

Only after reaching the upper landing and the faintly lit hall did she rise to her feet.

Once in her room, and safely tucked into her bed she reviewed the incident. How was it that a broom had been so dangerously braced across the stairs, and why was it that she had not noticed it on the way down? She remembered concentrating on the kitchen light and thought it entirely possible she could have unknowingly stepped over the thing.

And then there was the sound she had heard before negotiating the stairs. Again, this could be explained. The house was ancient. All old houses had their creaks and groans, and Montrose Manor was older than most.

Finally, her mind settled on the awful perception of a force slamming into her back when she was clamoring for a hold on the railing. Could it be possible she had not been alone on the stairs? Had someone attempted to send her careening down the staircase? No, she thought, it was not possible. She had been rotating downward—it must have been her body hitting against the hard oak. To believe otherwise was to believe someone was deliberately out to hurt her, and that was too horrible to contemplate.

But then there was the accident with Queeny.

Over and over, her mind replayed the scenarios of the day. Could someone here at Montrose truly be out to hurt her? The idea seemed preposterous. Again, her mind wandered to the dreaded curse of Montrose, and she forcefully pushed it aside.

She had more than herself to worry about. There was this new child inside her. Her pregnancy brought another series of worries. Once more, she thought longingly of home. If only her mother were here to help her through this confusing time. If she wrote to her, might she come to visit?

A gentle light was already filtering through the drapes before she finally drifted off to sleep, leaving her unanswered questions to be sorted out in her fitful dreams.

CHAPTER 25

A VISIT FROM ANNE

Madelyn did not awaken early after the night's escapades. Indeed, it was lunchtime when the sound of the drapes being pulled back had her slowly opening her eyes to face the day.

"I've brought you a little luncheon ma'am. I'm thinking you'd be up half the night if I let you sleep much longer," she said.

Madelyn frowned. After last night's wanderings it was not a prospect she looked forward to. She yawned and moved awkwardly to sit up in bed. Madelyn rotated her stiff shoulders. Every part of her body ached this morning.

"We cannot have that," she said, "thank you Annmarie."

"It's Annmargaret ma'am," the girl replied. "Would you like this served in bed? I've a little stand here and can prop it up nicely."

Of course, it is Annmargaret, she thought. She was

the more serious of the girls. Before she could answer a wave of nausea overwhelmed her. Despite her aches, she found herself rushing to the dressing room and the basin waiting there. Annmargaret attended her with a bemused expression.

By the time her stomach settled, and she had completed her morning ablutions there was no point in going back to bed. Fortunately, her morning sickness was temporary. She found she was quite hungry, eating everything on the tray.

Remembering Old Bess' warning, she regretfully tossed the accompanying tonic into the potted plant. It might have been a comfort this morning. Instead, she requested a bath to ease her aches and pains, while she once again went over yesterday's events. Madelyn considered confiding in Julian her suspicions about the incident on the stairs but decided against it. In the light of day, the whole business felt unreal—a product of her fear of the dark and an overactive imagination.

It is the bloody curse that has me spooked, she thought with a scowl. Not for the first time, she wished she had never heard the tale. On an intellectual level, Madelyn knew the old story was nonsense, kept alive by superstitious villagers who relished a good legend—the gorier the better. Still the idea that as a bride of Montrose she was doomed to unhappiness and an early death, lingered in her consciousness. And Lady Katherine had existed; her portrait in the gallery proved it.

She spent the next two days resting obediently in

her rooms. Her only visitors were Mrs. Waldron and Julian, who both fussed over her until she was tempted to shout her frustration. Mrs. Waldron was adamant about the benefits of her special tonic, and Madelyn was loath to tell her the mixture was watering the potted plant. The poor plant was suffering from the damp; its leaves turning an unwholesome bile green.

By the third day most of her stiffness was gone and to her relief there had been no dreaded spots of blood to indicate a problem with the pregnancy. Sheer boredom had her itching to be out and about. Clear blue skies promised a lovely morning and it would be a shame to waste it indoors. Since riding was completely off the table, she decided to visit the hidden garden. It had been a while since she had checked its progress. Since the library doors provided the shortest route, she headed there.

She was surprised to find Sir Henry once again perusing the bookshelves when she entered. She could not contain her frown. It felt as though the man was constantly underfoot, if not here in the house, then in the yard. Many times, in the last few weeks, she had seen him wandering around the stables. He had brought several mares to be covered by the new thoroughbred stallion and was hanging about to check their progress.

Loitering at the stables was understandable, as it was only a short walk from his home, and a bother to present himself at the door first. But for him to be in the house unannounced was disconcerting. And after her series of accidents, the idea that the entire Stall-ridge clan had unlimited access to their home was unnerving. She decided to have a talk with Mrs. Waldron at their next meeting.

"Ah, there you are my dear," Sir Henry said, "I see you have quite recovered from your little tumble. One must learn to manage a mount. Keep a firm grip on the reins, I always say."

"Yes," she replied, attempting to hide her irritation. The last thing she wanted this morning was instructions from Sir Henry on how to manage her horse.

"Especially in your condition," he added.

Madelyn felt her cheeks burn. "In my condition?" she asked. How was it possible this man knew her secret? "There is no condition."

Sir Henry winked at her. "Ah, just idle gossip then. Knew it couldn't be true. Far too soon."

Madelyn struggled to keep her anger in check. Old Bess had warned her about local gossip, but she was surprised all the same. She wondered if she should have a talk with the twins but dismissed the idea. It was likely to cause even more gossip.

She turned her attention back to Sir Henry. His insinuation was an unforgivable breach of etiquette. It was simply not done—especially by a man. The fellow was beyond rude. "Can I help you with something?" she asked, her question purposely designed to indicate to Henry that his unannounced presence was an intrusion, but as usual, the man was oblivious.

"I have brought back your book on architecture. I

put it there for you on the desk. Quite enlightening, I must say. A fellow named Nicholas Owen designed many of the priest holes in the houses here about. He was a Jesuit, apparently, and quite adept at the business. Just checking to see if there are any records of his work here. There are a few journals, but Julian must see to having them bound. They will soon be lost otherwise. Such a waste."

"You really should bring it up with him," Madelyn said. She could not resist a quick grin, picturing Julian's dark scowl, his scarred cheek twitching with annoyance, should Henry be brave enough to give him direction once again on his management of Montrose.

"Hmmmph!" he grunted. "I will do that," he said, turning away from her to continue his search.

Madelyn picked up the returned book and left him, eager to see the growth in her secluded garden. She was not disappointed. The new plantings had begun to branch out. Around the perimeter tucked up against the hedge the irises and daises had begun to bloom. The buds of a yellow shrub rose had just begun to open, and the foliage near the arbor had climbed all the way up the trellis. An abundance of new buds were sprouting on their vines, swollen with the promise of a grand display. In a matter of days, the arbor would be in full bloom.

She settled on the bench, her ears perked for the usual wailing of the Montrose wives. But the wind was nonexistent today, and her predecessors were silent.

Setting the book on her lap, she took a moment to

mull over the last few days once more. This morning she had written to her mother. In the letter she revealed her pregnancy, her thwarted efforts to win her husband's love, a rambling account of Lady Katherine's curse, and even the tragic death of Lady Alice. She had described the incidents of the last few days, including her fears that she too would be a victim of the curse. Finally, she ended the missive with a plea for her mother to come. The whole thing sounded like the rantings of a mad woman. She ripped it up.

Yet the act of putting to paper her worries had not been in vain. She could imagine her practical mother reading her letter and tut-tutting over her absurd claims. Pregnant women were known for lapsing into periods of nervous apprehension. Surely that was the cause of her anxiety.

What she needed was a distraction. Opening the heavy text on 16th century architecture, she scanned the table of contents for the segments on hidden rooms and priest holes. She skimmed the sections in question. An entire chapter was dedicated to the constructions of Nicholas Owen, the priest and craftsman who helped Catholics design their secret hideaways. There were several illustrations of the Jesuit's work taken from country houses here in the North. She examined them with interest. The drawings showed stairways which could be pulled forward and bookshelves which acted as hidden doors. Each secret entrance led to a hidden enclosure. One of the sketches showed an entire wall which could be rolled back to reveal a chapel.

She was amazed at the lengths to which people had gone to disguise their participation in the Catholic faith. But given the consequences of a powerful family acknowledging their adherence to the old religion, it was only rational for them to take every precaution. Had their secret been revealed in the Elizabethan era, they would have been labelled traitors. To adhere to the Catholic faith meant not accepting Elizabeth as England's true monarch. To a Roman Catholic, Anne Boleyn's marriage was a ruse, making Elizabeth a bastard and ineligible to take the throne. Furthermore, the pope himself had called upon all Catholics to attempt Elizabeth's assassination.

As a result, Catholics were enemies of Queen Elizabeth. If a citizen were openly Catholic their land would be forfeited to the crown, they would be arrested, tortured, and possibly sentenced to death. Thus, hidden passageways, secret rooms, tunnels, and chapels tucked away in dungeons or squeezed into concealed rooms were the order of the day for closeted Catholics.

Slowly closing the book, she leaned back and envisioned the library in the manor. It sat over the old portion of the cellar next to the ancient tower. Sir Henry and Mrs. Waldron were correct in that it was the most practical portion of the house to possibly contain a hidden escape route—if one existed. But if such a device had been constructed, there would be over two hundred intervening years. Many renovations could have occurred over time.

Mrs. Waldron and Sir Henry had spent days poring over the shelves, finding nothing. It seemed to her that a better method might be to begin in the cellars of Montrose. If a secluded priest hole, or even a chapel existed, it was likely to be tucked away below the public rooms of the house. With the escape route no longer necessary, its access would likely have long since disappeared. But the room itself might still exist somewhere below. She shivered when she considered what that search might entail. She replayed the scene from the armory. A dark cavern loaded with decaying artifacts, and entangled spider webs. Even more frightening were the two doors leading off into the black recesses of the dungeon.

"Ah, there you are. Mrs. Waldron said I might find you here," Anne interrupted her thoughts from the hedge opening, "It is almost like old times with L—" she cut herself off, blushing a little before continuing. "I came by to see for myself how you fared. I have been so worried." As usual she wore her widow's weeds. Her tall frame was slightly humped, and she appeared to hide in the folds of her heavy cloak. But she smiled a greeting as she walked toward her. "I am so glad to see you are moving about once more."

Madelyn set her book aside. "I am feeling much better," she said. She watched Anne's eyes appraise her, noticing that she stared for a moment at her midsection. So, Anne too must have heard the rumors.

Moving her arm to shield her still flat belly she rose from the bench.

"I was about to go in for tea. Won't you join me?" Madelyn asked, then reached down to gather up the heavy tome.

"I would love a cup of tea, if you are feeling up to it," Anne said, reaching for the heavy book. "Let me."

Did Anne think to pamper her because of her pregnancy? She felt her cheeks burn.

As though reading her thoughts Anne added, "I am sure you are stiff from your fall."

The ladies were quiet as they walked to the house. Madelyn found herself wishing she could confide in Lady Anne the news about her pregnancy. After their numerous visits over the past month, she counted Anne as her friend. But she remembered Edwyn's description of his sister as a woman bitter and angry with her fate as a childless widow. Hearing that Madelyn was to have a child with the man she had been destined to marry could only be painful for her. She held her tongue, maintaining the awkward silence between them.

Once settled in the library, having already taken Anne's cloak and rang for tea, Madelyn searched for a safe topic of conversation. It was always difficult to converse with Anne, who was quiet by nature, and today with her mind focused on her pregnancy she found the effort grueling.

Thankfully, it was Anne who broke the silence. "I would have come to see you yesterday, but Edwyn is home. It is just a short visit; he will be gone this afternoon. He came for his quarterly allowance." Anne said.

"How nice for you. I know how you love his company." Madelyn replied.

"Yes." Anne frowned, "But allowance time is never comfortable. It stresses poor Henry so." Anne shifted restlessly on the sofa. Today, the topic of her beloved Edwyn appeared to fill her with nervous tension.

Anne's hands fluttered to the book she had placed on the tea table. Abruptly changing the subject, she said, "Have you too become obsessed with architecture? It is a passion of Henry's you know. It is more his love of Montrose Manor than anything else." Anne fidgeted with the black bows on her skirt, her hands nervously flitting over the gown. Madelyn got the impression the woman was desperate to steer the conversation away from any personal confidences Madelyn may be inclined to share, a circumstance which suited her entirely.

There was a pause while one of the twins served tea. Madelyn noticed her friend's hand trembled slightly as she raised her cup for a sip. Anne looked more uncomfortable than usual, huddled on the sofa, and not making eye contact. She continued, "When we were young, Henry and I spent a good deal of time combing the cellars. We were convinced we would find the tomb of Lady Katherine," she said, her head down and her eyes focused on stirring her tea. "We once found what we thought might be a hidden door, inside a huge old cabinet. I remember hauling everything out of that cupboard," she looked up and smiled. "Hard work for two children."

"And was there a hidden door?" Madelyn asked, her curiosity piqued. Anything to do with Lady Katherine was of interest to her.

"We never found out. The old Lord caught us down there. He said it was too dangerous a place for children to play. He shut the old cupboard and locked the entrance to the dungeons. We were forbidden to go below and that was that."

Madelyn felt her heart rapidly beating in her chest. A door to a secret room could be a priest hole, but it could also be the fabled entrance to Lady Katherine's tomb. An image of the beautiful blonde woman, mounted at the end of the lane with Montrose Manor in the background flashed across her mind.

"Do you think you could find it again?" Madelyn asked.

Anne sighed. "It was all so long ago. I would not have thought of it now except for all this latest talk of priest holes and such…" Anne paused and thought for a moment. "I remember we said it was hidden in plain sight and laughed about the idea. It was just off the armory, a huge cupboard stowed in a widened enclosure."

"I wonder..." Madelyn said, pausing as a burst of excitement set her heart fluttering in her chest. "I wonder if the two of you actually found it. The tomb I mean."

Anne shrugged. "I suppose it is possible. Although

one would have thought Lady Katherine's husband buried her somewhere deep within the dungeons or barricaded her in one of the existing cells. It seems to me that would have been easier."

"Easier perhaps, but it would have been an obvious choice and long since found. You said the cupboard was just off the armory?" That would be beneath the old tower—where Sir Henry is convinced a priest hole must exist. "What if..." Madelyn had to pause to gather her thoughts. "What if the old man locked her in an abandoned priest hole?"

"Again, I suppose it is possible," Anne said, "And you are right, it might explain why the tomb was never found. For generations, the curious have been scouring the dungeons, searching for a hidden cell in the old prison section below. The dungeon was indeed the obvious choice for Katherine's confinement."

Madelyn rose to her feet. The very thought of dispelling the ancient curse had her enthralled. It seemed to her that all her worries were wrapped around the final words of the doomed Katherine as she was sealed inside her tomb.

To her, irrational as it may be, finding the tomb meant the end of the bloody curse. And that in turn meant there was a chance her dreams could come true.

Surely solving the mystery of Katherine's tomb would end her anxious misgivings.

CHAPTER 26

THE MONTROSE DUNGEONS

"Oh, let's go down to find the cupboard. We could go now. Do you have time Anne? I would so love to explore the cupboard you found!"

"Are you up to it? Might it be too much for you?" Anne blushed a little, her eyes darting to Madelyn's midsection once again.

"Oh posh, I am fit as ever."

Rather than journey all the way upstairs to get the oval ring of keys, Madelyn found Mrs. Waldron near the servants' wing. The housekeeper was not pleased with their plan to go below. "It is not a fit place for ladies. You will be covered in dust, the both of you," she said, her brows furrowed in her usual scowl. "You'll not find anything of interest. The place has been thoroughly searched over the years." But she unlocked the double doors to the east wing. "You best take a lantern," she added, "wait here."

Moments later, Madelyn pushed the heavy door to

the dungeons open, stepping aside to allow Anne to lead the way. She glanced back at Mrs. Waldron who stood back, next to the old fireplace, her scowl still firmly in place. "I wouldn't wander too far into the dungeons. It is easy to get turned around," the housekeeper said, her voice echoing in the high-ceiled room, lending an ominous quality to her warning.

"We won't." Madelyn assured her, hesitating before she turned to follow Anne. Rather than pull the door closed behind her, she purposely pushed it further ajar. There was some comfort in knowing the exit was here, open and waiting for their return. Madelyn followed Anne down the stone stairs. As before a filtered light shone through the high narrow windows of the spacious entry.

Anne walked around the first room with its tidy crates and boxes. She glanced down the long hallway to the left at the end of the room, before turning to the right. "It has been so long," she said, "if I remember correctly the armory is this way."

She led them through the hall. As before there were only a few paces of narrow corridor before it opened to the dusty armory. At the entry to the armory Anne paused. Her black gown blended into the inky darkness, and only her pale face glowed in the feeble light. "Best we turn up our lanterns," she said.

The extra light did little to brighten the scene. Next to Madelyn, braced against the wall, the familiar suit of armor stood like a sentinel at the entry. The silken threads of a spider web, trailing from its rusted helmet caught the light and danced toward the stone wall above. It was here that warriors of times past would have stored their weapons. The walls still housed their numerous hooks, sometimes with scraps of rotted leather or rusted chains dangling above heaps of long forgotten weaponry, slowly decomposing amid the layers of debris.

Ahead of her Anne moved forward, her dress stirring a layer of dust, and her long slender shadow flitting across the many piles of rubble in the chamber's recesses.

Madelyn followed close behind her, swallowing the urge to turn back, and race up the stairs to the open doors at the main level. It was more than just her usual fear of the dark that plagued her. It was the closed stone walls, and the suffocating weight of the manor pressing down upon them.

The thought of Lady Katherine forever trapped in this ghastly prison left her nauseous. Whether from fear, or the itching irritation from the dust, her mouth dried, and she found she had to gasp for breath.

To be locked in these dusty caverns was a horror beyond comprehension. She stayed close to Anne, so close that when she stopped abruptly, Madelyn only just managed to stop herself from bumping into her back.

Anne held her lantern high. "Are you quite all right? Do you wish to go on?"

Madelyn swallowed then cleared her throat before attempting to speak. "I am fine. A little fazed is all."

Anne nodded. "The cellars can be a little disconcerting," she said, "especially so when one is not accustomed to them." Madelyn was struck by Anne's composure. Where most times Anne was reticent and shy, today in the cellars she appeared to relish taking charge. Instead of her usual shrinking posture, she stood straight, with her shoulders back. The nervous fidgeting creature she had been upstairs had disappeared. Now it was Madelyn who trailed behind her skittishly.

"I recall these entries," Anne said, gesturing toward the two gaping doorways Mrs. Waldron had pointed out before, "and I think it is the one near the back."

Madelyn swallowed then cleared her throat before attempting to speak. "Yes." Her voice sounded high pitched and quavering to her. She cleared her throat once more. "You said it was next to the armory. It cannot be far."

Anne nodded once more. Madelyn hesitated in the armory while Anne moved toward the furthest entry. "I distinctly remember the hallway opening onto a raised platform of sorts, like a stage. We could see a rather large room before us, the dungeons, I think. And the cupboard faced the room." Anne's voice faded away as she disappeared through the dark entry.

Not wanting to be left alone, Madelyn hurried after her. Hesitating at the gaping doorway, she eyed the dark stone passage dubiously. Its high ceilings emphasized its narrowness and the heavy stone walls threatened to crush intruders. About twenty feet ahead, Anne stood still, her lantern beckoning. Madelyn took a deep breath, straightening her hunched shoulders before she pressed on. She fought through a maze of cloying spider webs, waving her free hand before her to part their sticky mass while she clutched her lantern.

It was a relief to step out of the gloomy hall and up onto a sheltered dais, much as Anne had predicted. Here the light from their lanterns was trapped in an enclosure. Compared to the dark passages, this room was almost bright. Madelyn felt the tension leave her body.

Anne stood before her, her eyes glittering with a strange passion. "It is truly magnificent, is it not?" She gestured to the wall behind her. It was covered from floor to ceiling in deep oak shelving, with a pair of heavy wooden doors at its center. "The cupboard is there, just as I remembered it, and still as solid as ever."

Anne turned and walked to the edge of the platform, where several steps lined the entire structure, leading down to a cavernous dark room. There at the edge of the stage, cloaked in black, with the lanterns casting the long finger of her shadow into the gloom of the dungeons below, she looked almost like an ancient druid, preparing to address the creatures of the underworld. Madelyn repressed a shiver and banished the thought, determined this time to control her fears.

There would be no blind scramble back to the safety of the stairs—not with the possibility of finding Lady Katherine so close at hand. She breathed deeply of the stale air and straightened her shoulders.

Holding her lantern high, Anne announced, "This massive hall has passages leading to a series of cells." Her voice echoed ominously. "The chains and brackets still remain, used to torture prisoners—even an iron cage winched high above the ground if I remember correctly. We could explore it if you like."

Not on your life, Madelyn thought, swallowing to relieve the tension in her throat. Once again, she marveled at the fortitude of her friend.

She focused on the back wall covered from floor to ceiling with dark wooden cabinetry. There were deep shelves on each side and a set of tall double doors at its center. To the left of the doors was a pile of rubble, iron tools of some sort amidst a snarl of rotting leather, attesting to Anne's depiction of her and Henry clearing it out years ago.

The wall unit was certainly large enough to act as a doorway to a hidden room, she thought, ignoring Anne who still stood at the edge of the platform peering into the dark, and striding purposely toward the cabinet. "Let's search the cupboard first," she said.

She grabbed the handles of the double doors at its center and gave a tug, but the cabinet had a little hatch holding it closed. She flipped it back before trying again. She expected the doors to be jammed, but this time they opened easily. Anne joined her as she held her lantern up to examine the cupboard's wooden interior. It was at least two feet deep. She stepped inside, held her lantern with one hand and pressed the other against the cupboard's back wall. Her heart leapt with excitement when it gave way a little. It was on a runner of some kind.

Anne squeezed in close beside her. "Look here," she said, her fingers running along the right-hand corner. "There are ridges." Anne began gripping the wood to pull it back, but it would not budge.

"Wait a moment," Madelyn said, "if this is indeed a priest hole, there should be a catch of some kind." She remembered the illustrations of the Jesuit's handiwork from her book of architecture. "It is likely to be inside the cupboard somewhere."

She handed her lantern to Anne who stepped back out of the cabinet to allow Madelyn room to investigate. Running her hand along the edge of the side panel, where a brace of wood served as a frame, she was immediately rewarded with the discovery of an iron lever. "I found it!" she gasped. An old lock dangled from the solid iron circle meant as a finger grip. It was rusted out and open. She removed it and set it carefully on the floor.

She hesitated before pulling the device and looked out toward Anne. "We have at the very least found a secret entry Anne! Imagine!"

Anne peered back at her. The light and shadow played tricks on the woman's face, hi-lighting the bony contours of her gaunt features. Black eyes glowed at Madelyn from the dark.

"Pull it," Anne said, in a raspy voice.

The latch came forward with a grinding screech. Madelyn then braced her fingers into the ridges on the cupboard's back to slide the heavy panel aside. To her surprise it moved easily.

Anne held up the lanterns, and the two women stared at their discovery.

A brick wall.

Madelyn shared an exasperated look with Anne.

"How odd," Anne said dryly, but her eyes still glittered with excitement.

Madelyn's first reaction was disappointment. How could it be possible? Why would someone bother to hide a secret door which led to nowhere? She turned away from Anne to stare at the faded brick with disgust.

Crouched inside the cabinet, she looked more closely at what was in front of her. Along the edges of the wall were the straight cut stones found in the rest of the dungeons. The central part, a doorway of sorts, was filled with reddish brick; chunks at least twice the size of the standard pieces used now in construction. This was different than anything she had seen thus far in the cellars.

She let her hands trail across the brickwork, the putty between the bricks was dry, and crumbled away easily with her touch. She noted that the brick work ran all the way to the floor.

So engrossed was she in their discovery, she was taken by surprise when it suddenly became dark in the cabinet.

Madelyn's heart lurched, and in an immediate rush of panic, she twisted around, pushing against the heavy cabinet doors. They flipped open, banging hard against the cupboard exterior.

"Anne!" she gasped, scrambling out into the room.

But Anne was near the entry to the passage. "Someone is coming," she said. Sure enough, a lantern glowed from its depths.

Moments later Mrs. Waldron stepped onto the open dais. "There you are," she said, "I am pleased to find you here. I had visions of searching the dungeons for the pair of you." Her eyes rested on Madelyn who stood with an arm still holding open the cupboard door. "Nothing but dust and rubble here. And I did warn you."

"Actually, we did find something," Madelyn said, unable to resist the opportunity to preen just a little. She pulled back the cupboard door. "There is a secret door at the back of this cabinet."

Mrs. Waldron strode across the room, holding her lantern up to peer into the cabinet. "Huh," she said reaching into the cupboard and rattling the sliding panel. There was a long pause while Mrs. Waldron leaned into the enclosure examining their find. "Interesting. But bricked in I see." She stepped back, shut the door panels, and turned to the ladies.

If Madelyn expected the woman to share their enthusiasm, she was to be disappointed. "Probably nothing," Mrs. Waldron said, "It is likely this wall of cabinets was moved here from above." She waved her arm as though brushing aside their find as irrelevant. "But there is no time at the present to putter around below. His Lordship is asking for you upstairs. He sent me to fetch you." Mrs. Waldron walked briskly back to the passage, then turned to the ladies. "Shall we?"

Madelyn gave Anne a sympathetic glance. "I am afraid we will have to explore it some other time."

"Yes," Anne replied, "And I must return to Stallridge house. Edwyn will be leaving soon. I do not wish to miss him."

Anne handed back her lantern, and the two of them turned to follow the housekeeper.

Before stepping into the dark passage Madelyn took a final look at the wall cabinets. She did not for a moment believe the cupboard had been moved into place. It was too large, too perfectly fitted within its niche and covering the entire back wall. It could only have been custom-made for its location.

This time on her trek through the narrow stone hall and gloomy armory with its decaying relics from the past, it was not fear that occupied her mind. She hardly noticed the streams of cobwebs in her path, or the rusted helmets lurking in the rubble like forgotten skulls. Instead, her heart fluttered with excitement.

Could it be they had found the fabled tomb of Lady Katherine? It was possible. Something was behind the bricked-up entry, she was sure of it. At the very least it was a priest hole.

She would deal with whatever it was that Julian needed her for, and then make her way back to the dais and its secret entry. The old brick with its crumbling plaster would not be a barrier to her quest. Certainly, there was enough metal lying about to use as a tool to pry the rotted brick free.

She decided the fortuitous discovery of the brick wall was a boon, as it certainly corresponded with the ancient myth of the immured bride. *If you are there, Lady Katherine, I will soon set you free, and you will then return the favor.* Madelyn smiled at the thought. Surely when the walls holding the Lady captive crumbled, there would be an end to the superstition, and her growing obsession with this perceived barrier to her happiness.

CHAPTER 27

A PASSING FANCY?

Hadley had just finished packing a few necessities into his saddle bags when Julian heard the door to Madelyn's door open at last. The old servant hoisted up the packs and quietly withdrew.

He strode into her room. "Ah, there you are. I was afraid I might miss you entirely. I am off to the high country with Hamish."

"Right now?"

He could not help but be pleased by the instant disappointment on his wife's face. "Right now," he said, "The steward sent word of a fire. My people have it under control, but two of the cottages burned over the night. If we go now, we can assess the damage before nightfall."

He walked to his wife and took her in his arms. "I wanted to tell you personally. I am afraid that is all I have time for. Hamish will already be mounted and waiting at the door."

"Oh dear. How long will you be away?"

"A day or two, at most." He leaned in to kiss her but was distracted by a smudge of dust on her cheek. He wiped it away with his thumb, then pulled a sticky mass from her braid. "I hesitate to ask what you have been up to. Gardening again, my love?"

"No, no. It's—well, there isn't time to tell you now," she leaned in for his kiss and he obliged.

He forced himself to step back from her before his plans lay in ruins. "I must be off. Just promise I will recognize the place when I return," he said and kissed her lightly once more. "And no riding, not yet" he warned.

"No riding," she answered, then grabbed him once more. "Oh Julian, do hurry back. I have so much to tell you."

He could not resist one last sweet kiss, then forced himself out the door and strode quickly down the hall before he changed his mind.

When he and Hamish reached the end of the drive, he paused for a moment to look back at Montrose. He had the strangest urge to send Hamish on his way without him. Something did not feel right. He shook off the feeling, wheeled his horse around, and continued.

It is just that I am loath to leave my wife, he admonished himself. *I am behaving like a lovesick boy.* He forcibly pushed all thoughts of Madelyn from his mind.

He and Hamish kept a steady pace, riding silently over the rise, and keeping to the main trails over the moors. Though he tried to block all thoughts of home from his mind, he could not stop the growing suspicion that something was amiss. His mind was on Madelyn and Montrose.

As he rode, he went over their last meeting again and again. She had looked excited to tell him something, but there hadn't been time. She was not upset or unhappy. The images swirled around his mind. There was nothing that warranted this aching burn in his stomach—this feeling of panic.

It was almost two hours since he'd left Montrose, and still the urge to turn back had not left him. They had begun the trek through the darkest bog of the journey, with thick brambles cloaking pools of brackish water amid mossy knolls disguising their treacherous bottomless pits. Pagan fidgeted and fussed with each step forward. A deep foreboding settled in his gut, then crept up to his throat, making it difficult to swallow. The more he tried to fight the sensation the stronger it became.

A cold sweat dampened his tunic, and beads of perspiration began to trickle down his forehead. He pulled up his horse and removed his glove to wipe his brow. Madelyn needed him, he was certain of it.

Hamish stopped a few feet ahead of him. "What is it that has you so fazed Jules?" he asked, "You look like death."

"I need to go back. Something is wrong." There was an immediate relief in making the decision. *It could be nothing,* he thought, *and if it is just a passing fancy, then all the better.*

Hamish looked at him curiously but did not question his decision. "Do you want me to return with you?"

"No. You go on. Do what needs to be done. I trust your judgement."

Hamish nodded. "And I yours. Good luck to you."

Julian whirled his horse about and immediately began the trek back to Montrose. Without slowing, he reached behind him, pulled off the heavy packs and flung them to the ground, keeping only a canteen of water. He would make better time without them.

He nudged Pagan into a gallop. Julian's black cloak billowed behind him, as he leaned forward to whisper encouragement to his mighty steed. His determined face was set in stone as he negotiated the winding trail through the moors. Around him the shadowed landscape blurred and only the vision of Montrose Manor with its auburn-haired Mistress dominated his thoughts.

"I am coming for you, Madelyn." he said aloud. "Please God keep her safe until I arrive."

CHAPTER 28

A RETURN TO THE DUNGEONS

It was hard to maintain her enthusiasm for the hidden door after Julian left. She could not help but feel deflated. Montrose presented a lonely place without him.

Annmarie entered her suite with a tray. "Mrs. Waldron suggested I bring you a little luncheon," she said. "She also ordered a bath."

Madelyn sighed. She could almost hear Mrs. Waldron's instructions for the afternoon. And as usual, the woman was right. There was no rush to return below. The secret door had sat for centuries and could wait a few hours. Besides, she was hungry. She glanced at her reflection in the mirror— dusty. A bath might be just the thing.

After soaking in the warm water, and sated from her midday meal, she decided to further pamper herself with a nap. Her body was still sore from the incidents of the past few days, and it felt good to climb into bed.

As a result, almost three hours had gone by, before she prepared to face the journey through the cellars to explore the cupboard. First, she donned her new boots —slippers were of no use amongst the rubble below. She did up her hair in a tight braid, then covered it with her oldest hat and secured it with a hatpin. Last, she found an old, bibbed pinafore to protect her dress, and a pair of sturdy gray gloves. She was about to depart when Mrs. Waldron burst into the room.

Her eyes scanned Madelyn, dressed as she was, in her work clothes. "Ah, I see you are about to go below," she said with a wide smile, her eyes glittering with some unspoken excitement.

How odd, Madelyn thought, I believe this is the first time I have seen the woman truly smile. Clearly something was afoot.

"I have a surprise for you. I took the liberty of clearing away the brick from your cupboard below. You will be quite pleased with what I have discovered."

"Did you?" Madelyn could not contain her excitement. "What was it? What was there?"

Mrs. Waldron emitted a strange rasping sound, and it took a moment for Madelyn to realize it was a laugh. "All good things come to those who wait," she said. "Come my dear, let's not ruin the surprise. I will show you."

The housekeeper opened the door to the hall and began striding toward the stairs. Madelyn had to scurry to keep up with her. She could not stop herself from asking one more time. "Is it Lady Katherine? Have you found her?"

"All in good time my dear. You shall see."

Madelyn bit her lip to keep herself from questioning further. Obviously, Mrs. Waldron had no intention of revealing her prize. She busied herself pulling on her gloves as she scrambled after her.

At the top of the stairs Mrs. Waldron paused briefly. Madelyn had time to look over the woman's shoulder to below and saw Gertrude leave the foyer for the kitchen. As soon as the swinging doors closed, they carried on, negotiating the stairs at the same brisk pace.

They did not pause again until they reached the ancient fireplace in the east wing. Mrs. Waldron handed her a lantern and took a second one for herself. Her enthusiasm was palpable, the very air around her crackled with excitement. "You will be so pleased with what I have for you. It is perfect! An ending suitable for my beautiful Montrose," she said, flashing Madelyn her rare smile once more.

Madelyn had no chance to reply. Mrs. Waldron had already swung the wide doors open to the cellars and was hurrying down the stairs. She followed.

It must be the Lady Katherine, she thought. How wonderful it would be to find the ancient bride and release her at last. The prospect of freeing the doomed Lady from her suffocating tomb, forever ending the curse of Montrose, had her brimming with enthusiasm.

In front of her Mrs. Waldron moved at the same vigorous pace through the ruins. Her skirts picked up the layers of dust in the armory, and it caught the light billowing around her in a choking swirl. Madelyn hardly noticed. She held her gloved hand to her mouth to filter the air, her mind repeating the mantra, "We are coming for you, Katherine. Soon you will be free."

Through the narrow hallway with its crushing stone walls, she scrambled behind the housekeeper. The spider webs clawed at her face; a sticky clump catching her full across the eyes. She stopped to swipe frantically at the cloying mass, her fingers pushing the crisp carcasses of insects against her cheek. She shook with revulsion, forcing herself to press onward, this time moving slowly with one hand stretched out before her.

When she stepped up onto the familiar dais, she had to pause to catch her breath. Mrs. Waldron stood at the cupboard; one hand holding open its dark oak doors and the other holding up the lantern, illuminating her face. There was something ominous in the housekeeper's stance. Her eyes glittered with an unholy light. Her lips were pulled back unnaturally, displaying a row of teeth, white and stark next to the lantern's glow. From Madelyn's perspective it looked to be more of a snarl than a smile.

She hesitated.

"Come my dear," Mrs. Waldron said, pushing the cabinet door wider, "you must see. It is all you hoped for, a hidden room."

"Oh, Mrs. Waldron, could we possibly have found her? It must be the Lady Katherine!" Madelyn hurried forward. "I wish Anne were here to see. It is really her find after all."

Mrs. Waldron stepped aside, still holding the doors while Madelyn peered inside. The old brick had indeed been pulled away, cleanly along the base. Pieces and bits of brick jutting from the sides created a narrow gap about five feet high and a foot or two across, but large enough to squeeze through. The bottom of the closet was littered with debris. Poking out from the rubble was a hefty iron ring and at the top of the gaping hole was an iron brace with bars extending upward. It looked like the base of a gate.

"But what is this? It looks like the door to a cage." Madelyn said.

Mrs. Waldron gave another rasping laugh. "It is just that. Designed to be pulled up or down. I had a time prying it open, let me tell you." She laughed again. "If it is Lady Katherine's tomb, the old Lord wanted to be sure the woman could not escape. Of course, it makes sense…adding the bars. Fresh brick work would not have held her."

Madelyn lifted her lantern trying to discern something through the jagged hole. But there was only an inky blackness. "Is she inside then? Have we found her?"

"I have not checked. I thought to leave the discovery for you. It was you and Miss Anne that found the secret room, after all. It is only fair that you be the one to find her. I could not help but imagine the fine ending to our ancient story; the new Lady of Montrose and the illusive Lady Katherine."

Mrs. Waldron held wide the cupboard door while Madelyn took a step inside, holding out the lantern. But again, she could make out nothing.

"I think you must slip through the hole to see below. I did notice there were steps down into the cell when I was clearing away the brick."

Madelyn moved further into the cupboard, her boots crunching on the dry plaster. She put a hand on the ancient brick. "I don't like the dark," she said, unable to keep her voice from quavering. "Perhaps we should wait until Julian is home."

"Oh, but you really must see if you've found her at last. Just three steps, you need not go farther than that. And I will be here to hold the other lantern."

Madelyn leaned into the gap, thrusting her lantern ahead. She was able to see three stone steps, leading down into a cavity below. Beyond that she could only discern the vague outline of furnishings of some sort. "It does look like an apartment of some sort. It may just be the priest hole Henry was searching for." Despite her desire to find Lady Katherine and release her at last, she was almost relieved that the secret door was probably not the entry to a tomb.

She looked back at Mrs. Waldron, but could not make out her face in the lantern's glare. "Go," the woman said, nudging her forward. "We cannot possibly leave here without discovering the truth."

Just three steps down, Madelyn silently chanted. She could manage that. So, she braced her shoulders, took a deep breath, and squeezed through the jagged bricks, keeping her head low to avoid the iron bar. Once through the entry, she carefully traversed the narrow steps.

Holding her lantern high she peered into the gloom. The outlines of furnishings became clearer. There was a chair, a desk perhaps, and in the far corner what looked like a bed, with a heap of rumpled bedding still piled atop.

She turned back to the entry. "Mrs. Waldron, I think—"

The terrible screeching sound of metal grinding against metal followed by an ominous clang interrupted her. Her mouth dropped.

Illuminated above her, bars now covered the entry. Mrs. Waldron was crouched low, her hands working frantically. The sound of a metal chain being pulled through the bars echoed in the stone chamber.

Madelyn stood frozen in place. This scene was incomprehensible to her. "Whatever are you doing? Mrs. Waldron?"

A dry rasping laugh sounded from above. "Everything is working perfectly, my dear." There was a final rattle of chain and the crisp clink of a lock snapping into place. "All right. It's locked tight." Mrs. Waldron laughed again, an eerie humorless sound. "I promised you a fine ending, fit for a bride of Montrose. And there could be no better one than this—the two of you, bound together in a shared crypt."

Madelyn tried to speak, but it was as though a bony hand gripped her throat, choking back the words. "No," she finally managed to squeak out, "you cannot think to leave me here."

"Oh, but I can. It is perfect, don't you see? Another Lady of Montrose doomed, immured beneath the manor."

"Immured," Madelyn repeated in a whisper. "No. You cannot be serious." The room began to blur. Madelyn shook her head, both to deny this scene being played out before her, and to clear her murky thoughts. She tried to take a few steps forward, back up the stone steps, but her legs failed her, and she sank to the stone floor.

She heard the woman's boots grate on the cupboard floor above her. The housekeeper was leaving. Once the cupboard's panel was slid shut and the cabinet doors closed, she would be trapped here forever. Think Madelyn, she silently urged. Her only hope was to delay the woman and pray for a miracle —discovery.

"But why Mrs. Waldron? You must tell me why," she blurted, finding her voice at last.

"Tell you why?" the housekeeper implored. Madelyn could hear the smirk in the words. "I can tell you why. I am the true Lady of Montrose, that is why. And my son, my darling Charles, is the rightful heir to this manor and all its lands."

"Your son?" Madelyn asked, desperate to keep her talking, "how can that be?"

"Charles is a Stallridge. I was so young, only sixteen, when I met Henry in London. I loved him. He promised me the world, but when I fell pregnant the offer changed. I was to be his mistress, not his wife. I was not good enough, not the lady he wanted for his bride." Her words were bitter, her anger evident despite the intervening years.

"He tried to set me up in town, but I followed him here to Montrose. And still he denied me. He took a wife. A proper genteel woman to give him children. I was only a vicar's daughter, not true quality, so he said." She snorted. "I fixed that problem. Each time his woman conceived; I gave her my special tonic—not sure why the potion failed in your case. Worked like a charm before." Mrs. Waldron gave her dry laugh. "It was Henry's lust for a child that finally killed his woman. And my Charles is his sole heir. It is only a matter of time before Henry acknowledges him, and me," she added, "as his true wife."

Madelyn remembered the opaque tonic delivered to her room several times a day. Her hand crept to her stomach and rested there. "But what does all of that have to do with me? Sir Henry can marry where he chooses."

"Don't you see? If the Lord dies without an heir, it is Henry who inherits everything." Mrs. Waldron grasped the iron bars and glowered at her. Her eyes glittering in the amber light. "Montrose is mine—mine and my precious son's," she growled, her voice rasping now—threatening, and filled with hate. Madelyn shuddered. The woman was mad.

Mrs. Waldron shook the iron bars with both hands, the sound of the metal clanging in its tracks echoing through the chamber. "I have cared for this place all these years; tended it and loved it. Montrose is not yours—and certainly never belonged to that sniveling Lady Alice. I made short work of the chit. Took her to the tower, knocked her on the head, and chucked her out." She laughed, the low grating sound sending shivers down Madelyn's spine. "She thought to provide an heir...wanted to take everything away from me. But I took care of her, ended it."

There was a pause, and a sigh. "...And you," the housekeeper said, her voice now soft and menacing. "You come along just as I am about to claim what is mine. The Lord was missing, perhaps dead, and Henry was about to acknowledge my Charles. And just like the other lewd chits you are quick to breed. How disgusting. Shameful really." She made a face, crinkling her nose and shaking her head. "But I think I have quite out done myself with the solution this time." She chuckled, sounding pleased. "It was fortuitous, finding the tomb at last. You will be trapped with Lady Katherine, sealed together forever. A fitting end, and one that suits the house. I am almost glad you came to Montrose. Only it's too bad I cannot share the tale with anyone. Or perhaps I will," she added, "I will leave a little note in my last will and testament. That way you shall become a part of the legend. A pleasant gift for you, don't you think my lady?"

"Please Mrs. Waldron," was all she could think to say.

Madelyn could hear the woman shifting from foot to foot. Afraid the housekeeper was about to leave, she rose to her feet, but her movements had Mrs. Waldron flinching back from the bars. She quickly sank back to the floor. Somehow, she must continue to delay her; to keep her talking. She frantically searched for something to engage the woman.

"But how will you explain my absence?" she asked, trying to keep the desperation from her voice.

"Do not worry my dear, I have it all worked out. I sent Ned and Jimmy into the village with the twins. There is no one about. I will simply lead your horse Queeny to the bogs and watch her sink. I shall toss in a satchel of yours for good measure. With Edwyn leaving today, I need only hint that you packed a bag, and must have run off to be with him. Heaven knows the two of you were getting cozy when he was last home, and with the lad's reputation it will be easy to believe."

Madelyn gasped. "It will not work. Julian will never believe you. And Anne knows about the secret room."

"Oh, but the Lord will believe me, my dear. And even if he does not, it will be days before he returns, and then a couple more shall pass should he decide to chase after you to London. By then, it will be all quiet here…if you know what I mean. And as to Anne, she will be the first to believe you ran off with Edwyn. She more than anyone relishes his escapades after all." She laughed again. "Of course, by the time the Lord returns, I will have miraculously found Queeny. It will be assumed you are lost to the moors... poor unfortunate Lady. You strayed off the trails in your eagerness to follow your lover and got swallowed by the bog." She gave a hoarse laugh. "Another bride of Montrose comes to a tragic end."

There was a moment's silence, then the terrible words, "Farewell my dear," followed by the dreaded sound of the panel closing.

"No!" Madelyn scrambled up the steps. "No, Mrs. Waldron!" she screamed as her hands grasped at the iron bars. She shook them, yelling, "Mrs. Waldron, please. Come back! Please don't leave me here." She screamed again, shrieking until her throat ached and her words deteriorated into nonsensical gibberish punctuated with sobs. Finally exhausted, she slid down the steps onto the cool stone floor.

CHAPTER 29

A SILKEN TOMB

Madelyn was not sure how long she lay on the stone floor and may have even slept a little. She sat up, rubbed the salty remnants of tears from her eyes and took stock of her surroundings. Her lantern sat on the floor next to her, still giving soft amber light, and for that she was thankful. She reached out and picked it up, assessing its weight. It was full and for that too she was thankful. She estimated she would enjoy light for at least six hours, perhaps more if she dimmed the flame. She carefully turned it down. She had no way to light it should she carelessly douse it.

It was good to focus on practical matters. She knew if she allowed herself the luxury of panicking, she would be lost. There was still a chance she could be found. Anne could well come for her. Her friend knew how enthused she had been to discover the secret door. Surely, she would check the dungeons.

And Julian would never believe she betrayed him.

He knew she loved him. Julian was not the jealous old Lord of legend. He would know she'd never leave him; that she was still here in Montrose. Her strong warrior husband would rip the house apart in search of her. He would find her.

But it might be days before Julian came home, she reminded herself, choking back a sob. It was tempting to capitulate to the oblivion of insanity, to remain on the stone floor, pound her head hysterically against the cold stone, and withdraw into a peaceful unconscious.

"No," she said aloud, the single word sounding hollow against the stone walls. Her first order of business was to hold on to her sanity, and that meant crushing thoughts of grim prospects. She forced her shoulders back, fighting the terrible suffocating weight of her stone prison, and took a deep breath. The air was surprisingly fresh.

She still sat facing the steps, as if denying the reality behind her. Pulling herself to her feet, she picked up her lantern and adjusted the flame until the room was filled with soft amber light. It was time to acknowledge her surroundings.

Like the tower room, she was in a square cubicle of solid stone, but this time without windows. It was small, perhaps twelve feet square. The ceilings were high and draped with spider webs, stretching across to the walls and softening its stark corners. She took a few tentative steps forward. An old desk, with a broken chair lying before it sat braced against the side wall. At the back of the room a bed took up most of the space.

Piles of grayed bed linens were shrouded by thick silken spider webs, forming a canopy which angled from its corners to the ceiling. The amber light playing off the webs gave an illusion of sheer draping silks—like the sleeping quarters of a fabled princess.

The bed drew Madelyn, her boots shuffling steadily forward as if on their own volition. She knew what she would find.

Poised over the bed, she peered through the gossamer threads to what lay below. What she had taken to be crumpled linen was indeed the remains of a gown. It had faded to a dark hue and spread in perfect folds across the surface as though posed. It could only be the Lady Katherine.

She forced her eyes to travel up to the headboard. Tresses of blonde hair, grayed by years of accumulated dust, were partially covered by a headdress of some sort. Only a portion of white skull could be seen from beneath the remnants of a tattered scarf, attached to the headdress and draped elegantly across the face.

Madelyn was not certain how long she stood next to Katherine, but her face was wet with tears before she reluctantly turned away. It was strange that she felt no sensation of fear or horror. Instead, there was a deep sadness and a feeling of comradery. Katherine had succumbed to the horrific sentence forced upon her by the old Lord, but she had done so with uncommon courage and grace. She had laid herself out in spectacular fashion. This was not the actions of a woman crazed or hysterical; insane and cowering in her final hours. It was as though Katherine had defied her captor, accepting her death, but refusing the torture of her confinement.

"Share your courage with me Katherine," she said. And immediately it felt as if her prayer had been answered; her request granted. Madelyn felt a weight lift from her shoulders. The comfort of insanity was not for her. If she kept her wits about her, she might find a way to free herself from this prison.

Taking her lantern, she returned to the barred entry. She grasped an iron bar and shook it. There was play in the iron gate, and it clanged against its iron tracks, rattling the chains at its base. "Excellent," she muttered aloud, "If someone searches the dungeons I will be heard. There is no brick wall now to smother the sound."

If there had been a clasp to hold down the barred gate, it would have long since deteriorated. Mrs. Waldron had linked a sturdy chain through the bars and the iron loop embedded in the floor, then attached a heavy padlock. Madelyn set her lantern beside her and began to work the chain. After several minutes, she managed to pull the lock around to her side of the enclosure.

She had never picked a lock before, but if it could be done, she was sure she would accomplish it. She twisted about on the top step and surveyed the room. There must be something here she could use to pick the lock.

The only possibility was the old desk, braced

against the wall under a haze of spider webs. *Ghastly spiders,* she thought, *however did the beasts manage to invade even this sealed prison?* She shuddered, running her hand across her cheek to her hairline as she considered the task of sweeping aside the sticky masses to search the desk drawers.

Her fingers encountered her hat, still securely anchored. "The hatpin!" she gasped, pulling the long needle from her hair. It was perfect.

"It won't be long now Katherine," she said, "We will both be freed." The sheer elation combined with an overwhelming relief had her laughing aloud. The absurdity of finding joy in such a place struck her as funny, and she laughed again. But this time there was an edge of hysteria in her outburst. She forced herself to calm enough to begin to work the lock.

Her elation did not last long. Picking the lock was not an easy task. In novels, the hero was always able to open these gadgets with a few deft twists. She had no idea what she was doing. Her hatpin encountered the mechanisms inside, but whether to push them, hook them, or attempt to turn them, she did not know.

Her frustration grew. Beads of sweat formed at the back of her neck, then trickled slowly down her back.

A breeze stirred the air. She twisted her neck in appreciation, lifting her heavy braid off her neck to take advantage of the coolness. It took a moment for the oddity of the scenario to register. A breeze? Twisting around on the step, she looked up to find the source. The haze of cobwebs at the ceiling was indeed swaying.

A vent! There had to be one along the roof line. It made sense, given the fact this cell had originally been a priest hole. It certainly explained the presence of spiders. Madelyn left the padlock. Taking the leg of the broken chair, she climbed atop the desk. After a few swipes to clear away the myriad of webs, a grated panel came into view. It was too small to squeeze through, a square with dimensions of less than a foot. She hooked her fingers into the tightly woven iron grill and pulled. To her surprise it gave way easily; so easily that she had to steady herself to keep from falling with the momentum. Shards of crumbling rotted plaster fell to the desk with a satisfying rattle.

Still holding the grate in one hand she stood on tiptoe to peer through the gap. A square tunnel of perhaps five feet ended in stripes of white light. Extending her reach with the piece of the chair, she hammered away at the external grate, until it too fell from its frame, leaving a clear small window into the world outside. Another gust of fresh air tickled the hair at her forehead, cooling her sweating brow. This time she was sure she could hear the wind rippling through the hedges outside. It was the secret garden.

Though the vent was too small for an escape route, it provided Madelyn with two benefits. The first was light. Even at the depth of five feet the glorious sun seeped into the room. More importantly it connected Madelyn to the outside. It was as though the suffocating weight of the ancient house had been lifted from her shoulders. Yes, she was still imprisoned, but she was not immured.

She hopped down from the desk, and in a flurry of movement swung her stick about, gathering the cloying masses of webbing from the walls and ceiling, leaving only the hazy sheets shrouding the tomb of Lady Katherine. Removing the billowing clouds of eerie sludge made the cell more livable, if such a thing was possible. Out of breath, she stood for a minute and glared at the offending bars holding her captive. She would defeat that lock.

And if she did not, Julian would find her. He would move every brick and stone in this manor until he did. She made her way up the stone steps and began to work at the lock once more.

"One way or another, Katherine, we will be freed," she said aloud.

CHAPTER 30

THE WAILING WALL

The scene as he approached Montrose was quietly pastoral, with the horses grazing nonchalantly in the pastures, their foals romping in the warm afternoon sun. *Perhaps I have overreacted,* he thought, *all is as it should be.*

Julian dismounted and led Pagan into the stable. It was his intention to leave the horse with the stable hands and go immediately to the house to see Madelyn. "Ned! Jimmy!" he called, but no one answered. The place was deserted. Pagan was wet with sweat after the long ride, and there was no help for it; he would have to tend to his horse himself.

He led Pagan down the aisle to his stall. Queeny leaned out of her enclosure and gave a soft whinny of welcome. He patted her nose as he passed.

He had just closed the gate to Pagan's stall when he heard a rustling behind him. He spun about. "Mrs. Waldron?" he asked, curious to find the woman in the stable. She stood twisting her hands nervously, wide-eyed.

"M-my Lord," the housekeeper stuttered in response, "You are home. We hadn't expected you."

"Yes," he replied. "Is something amiss? And where are the lads?" The full force of his anxiety returned with a gut-clenching furor.

"I sent them to the village with the twins. I...It was a nice day," she said, her hands still busy clutching at her pinafore. "They were entitled to a bit of time my Lord."

"And my Lady Madelyn? Is she up at the house?"

"She, uh...That is just the thing my Lord. I cannot find her. I came out here to the stables thinking she must have—"

"What do you mean you cannot find her?" Julian asked, trying to keep the panic from his voice.

"I searched the house, my lord. She—"

Julian did not wait for her response. He strode purposely down the aisle and hurried toward the house with Mrs. Waldron scurrying in his wake. All the way to the manor his mind was awhirl. Madelyn was in some sort of trouble, but he had no idea what.

On the edge of his consciousness, he could hear the ramblings of Mrs. Waldron jogging beside him.

"She must have left...Edwyn..."

His eyes settled on the pair of gardeners carving out new flower beds. Perhaps she had gone for a walk. "Stop your work and search the grounds for Lady Madelyn," he hollered. They stood still, looking at him stupidly. "Now!" he added. The two men dropped their tools, each heading in a different direction. "I want every employee I have on the task," he said to their retreating backs.

And still Mrs. Waldron chattered beside him. "Edwyn was leaving...she packed...ran away...Edwyn." He caught snatches of her rambling in his rush to reach the house.

At the library doors, he stopped and gave the housekeeper his full attention. "Just what are you trying to say?"

"I...I think Lady Madelyn may have left." The woman gasped; her face flushed from her exertions. Her eyes darted about nervously, refusing to meet his gaze. "Edwyn was here. He left this afternoon. I believe she must have gone with him."

"Nonsense," he said pushing open the library door. Gertrude stood at the entry to the library and he addressed her. "My Lady is missing. Go across to the dower house, Lady Madelyn may be there. And if she's not, have Henry send everyone he has to search the grounds." Gertrude stood dumbly for a second. "Go now!"

He turned to Mrs. Waldron. "Have the house searched. Damn," he said remembering that half his staff had gone to the village. "Everyone we have. Even cook must help," he ordered.

"Yes, my Lord," Mrs. Waldron answered. "And I will search the dungeons. I know them best. But I still think Edwyn—"

"Go," he said, unable to listen to her prattle about

Edwyn. He stood for a moment to take stock of the situation. His instincts told him something dire had happened to Madelyn. He knew not what. Her horse was here, he thought with a sense of relief, at least she could not be floundering about on the moors or sunk in a bog. She must be in the house. He would find her.

He made short work of the common rooms, looking into every nook and cranny, before going up the staircase. In the hall upstairs every door was open. A noise from the nursery had his heart leaping. "Madelyn," he called.

Old Hadley stepped from the room into the hall. "I have searched this floor my Lord. She is not here,"

"Look again, every closet," he said. His eyes rested on the narrow staircase at the end of the hall. The tower, he thought, feeling his stomach twist.

He took the stone steps two at a time. When he reached the top, he was relieved to see the shutters still firmly closed. She had not been there.

He wasted no time, taking the back stairs all the way to the ground floor. Once in the foyer, he stood for a moment, unsure where to next look. The doors to the east wing were open wide, with the clanging sounds of doors evidence of the ongoing search.

"The secret garden," he said aloud.

He ran through the library, out its double doors, and across the grounds. But the rose garden too was deserted. For the first time he allowed the awful spears of panic to invade his consciousness. He knew with a sickening dread that something had happened to his wife, but for the life of him, he could not determine what. Would he fail again? Had he once more lost his precious love?

He walked to the alcove and rested his hand on the iron trellis. A fresh red rose bloomed at eye level. He reached out and touched its soft petals.

"Madelyn," he called, "my God, where are you?" He gripped the trellis and took a deep breath. Control yourself, he admonished, there are still the dungeons left to search, but heaven forbid she be down there.

"Julian," the faint sound of his name, wispy and echoed, came to him as though being called from a great distance. His head snapped up. Behind the trellis the gray stone wall loomed above him. He knew well the legend of the wailing wall—the long dead wives of Montrose moaning their fate, cursing the inhabitants of the manor. He did not believe in fairy tales. *I am losing my reason,* he thought, *hearing voices.*

But again, he heard his name. "Julian," It sounded, long and drawn out. This time it was followed by a louder clanking of metal.

He did not stop to consider how or why Madelyn called to him from afar. Instead, he frantically followed the sound to the place where the tower and the main hall met. "Keep talking! I hear you," he shouted, "Keep making noise!" He scoured the back wall to the sound of his wife's cries interspersed with the jarring clangs of metal.

Half covered by a mound of shrubbery, and low to the ground, he found the vent with its grate lying before it. He had to lay down to peer into its depths. "Madelyn, I am here Madelyn." The face of his wife appeared at the end of the stone shaft, bathed in amber light. She was crying.

"I knew you would come. I knew you would come," she repeated. "Oh, Julian, you found me. Julian—"

"I am here now my love. All is well," he said, using all his willpower to give her his calmest voice. "Tell me where you are, love, and I will come for you."

"The dais in the dungeon, Julian. There is a cupboard. It has a secret back. Mrs. Waldron, she locked me in the room behind it. Oh, Julian, I am so glad you found me. Katherine is here, Julian. Lady Katherine. Oh Julian..."

"Madelyn I am coming for you. I will be there in just a minute or two."

He tried to rise, but she called him back. "No Julian, please don't leave. I am afraid you are an illusion—that you'll disappear. Don't leave me here alone." she said.

"Madelyn, I will never leave you. I promise I will be there in just a moment." He waited for a response, but only her frightened eyes stared back at him. "Tell me that you understand Madelyn. Tell me you believe me."

"All right Julian," she nodded, her face awash with tears, "I—I will wait here."

Julian ran back to the foyer. A little crowd had gathered; the servants having returned from the village. His years as a commander served him well now. "I have found her. She is trapped below," he announced. "Ned, find Mrs. Waldron and detain her, it's her that's done this monstrous thing. She is not to leave." He turned to the twins, "Prepare a warm bath, and send for Old Bess." The orders brought a sharp twang of déjà vu, and he realized this was not the first time Madelyn's life had been at risk. Though there was no time to sort it all out now. "Jimmy come with me."

As they took the cellar stairs two at a time, he instructed Jimmy. "You'll need to watch my back. The woman may still be hovering about. She volunteered to search the dungeons." But the gloomy depths were deserted, with no sign of the housekeeper.

The cupboard was easy enough to find. The sight of his beautiful wife trapped inside the dreadful tomb shook him. His eyes burned with indignation. How could such a thing happen? Though his body trembled with anger, he kept his voice calm, careful to give his love only his reassurance.

Julian forced himself to concentrate solely on the task at hand. With a piece of iron, he and Jimmy were able to pry loose the iron ring holding the chains. In seconds, he had the grate up. In one fluid motion he grabbed Madelyn by the shoulders, yanked her out of the gloomy prison and into his arms. With her firmly in his grip, he immediately turned to carry her from the dungeons. His mind was entirely focused on taking his wife to safety.

He was on the steps leading out of the dungeons before he realized Madelyn was desperately trying to communicate something to him. Her hand rested on his damaged cheek urging his face toward her.

"Julian," she said, her voice quietly insistent, "...Lady Katherine. She was there with me. You must save her too."

He paused only long enough to nod. Once in the foyer, he turned to Jimmy. "Get Sir Henry. Take him to find Lady Katherine in that godforsaken cell. He will know what to do."

He carried his bride up the wide staircase, down the hall, and into her suite.

Once in the safety of her room, he found he could not release her. He stood with his long legs braced, his arms holding her tight against him, and a fierce expression on his face. The twins were bustling about, preparing her bed and bath. They scurried around him wordlessly, not meeting his gaze. Gertrude arrived with a tea service and set it on her table. He could only stare at her as she awkwardly backed out of the room, bobbing her head.

And still he stood, gripping Madelyn against his massive shoulders, his scarred cheek twitching ominously.

Madelyn sighed. He looked down at her at last, afraid of the terror he was sure to see on her face. What he saw surprised him. Her head was nestled into his shoulder. She wore a bemused expression on her face.

He watched, fascinated, as she gave him a slow smile. "You are scaring the staff, my warrior husband," she said, reaching up to touch his ravaged cheek. "I believe my bath is ready. You may carry me there."

It was difficult to release her, but he managed it. He

knew he must go below; see to Mrs. Waldron and check on the arrangements for Lady Katherine. There would be time to speak to his wife later. He had something to say to her—words she had waited a long time to hear.

CHAPTER 31

AN END AND A BEGINNING

Madelyn pulled her black shawl more tightly across her chest and leaned against the warmth of Julian's chest as a cool wind swirled around the handful of mourners gathered at the graveside. The minister gave his final blessing gesturing the sign of the cross over the polished ebony coffin.

The last few days had been emotional ones. Mrs. Waldron was given over to the magistrate. The woman was charged with the murder of Lady Alice, but it appeared her sentence was to be carried out at Bedlam, in a wing reserved for the criminally insane. Her son Charles had arrived to sort out her affairs the best he could. It was interesting to note that Sir Henry put him up at Stallridge House.

The truth behind the death of Lady Alice had been both a relief and a sadness. Julian had at last been relieved of the burden of guilt he had carried for ten long years.

The burial ritual today served as an ending to all the tragedies of the past. Madelyn watched as the coffin was slowly lowered into the ground. Lady Katherine was in her proper place at last. Around her final resting place were the stones marking the lives of the Montrose ancestors.

Madelyn looked up at her fine husband and smiled, pleased that he had arranged this ceremony for Lady Katherine. It was odd, but she considered the woman her friend. It was Katherine who had comforted her when she was locked beneath the manor and had given her the courage to hold on to her sanity. She would be forever grateful to her.

Julian put his arm around his wife, pulling her close. The two of them walked silently across the grassy yard toward the manor.

At the break in the hedge Julian said, "I have a surprise for you." He led her into the secret garden and along the rock path to the alcove where the two of them sat closely together upon its ancient bench.

She expected him to give her a gift of some sort. Instead, he sat as though waiting for something. When the wind ruffled the hedges and the garden filled with the familiar hollow sound, he said, "Do you hear it? I had to replace the grates. It seems the whistling could not occur without them." He grinned his crooked smile, thoroughly pleased with himself. "Do you like it? After all, what is a secret garden without the wailing wall?"

"Oh Julian, it is perfect. I do love you."

There was a pause before Julian answered. "And I

love you, Madelyn. I love you with all my heart," he said, emphasizing every word. He pulled her close and kissed her, then held her gently in his arms.

For once Madelyn was speechless. She could only hang on to his broad shoulders. She felt tears of joy fill her eyes. It was everything she had ever wanted in this marriage. Julian's love was a precious gift.

Julian arched back to look into her damp eyes. "Are you happy Madelyn?" he asked.

"I am gloriously happy," she replied, smiling up at the ravaged face she loved so well. "I could not be happier."

He grinned. "I would have told you sooner, but there were too many shocking revelations. I thought one more might overwhelm you."

Madelyn took his hand in hers and rested it on her flat corseted stomach. "I am afraid you will have to deal with one more shocking revelation," she said.

The wide-eyed expression of distress on Julian's face made her giggle. "It is wonderful my love. Don't fret. There is no worry," she said to reassure him, then turned and leaned back against his broad chest. Julian would need time to process it, she thought with a smile, there was still work to be done to help him overcome his lingering fears. But he would soon realize this pregnancy was one to celebrate.

Around them the alcove bloomed in abundance. The roses had crawled up the trellis, winding in and out of its ironwork designs. Deep red blossoms graced every juncture. Among the blooms the darker vines of a white clematis were interwoven. Huge swollen buds promised an even greater beauty to come.

A gust of wind set the hedges swaying, and the wall began to moan once more. This time she imagined the wives of Montrose had chosen to share her happiness, sighing with joy at her happy beginning as the new Lady of Montrose.

The End

YOU CAN FIND four other novels by Cynthia Keyes on Amazon. The Meadows, The Smuggler, The Spy and The Heiress. All are set in the 19th century and though they are part of a series they are only loosely related and can be enjoyed in any order. Enjoy----Cynthia Keyes

Printed in Great Britain
by Amazon

32816937R00199